THROUGH KINGDOM COME

A Matt Striker Novel

L. ALLEN VEACH

DENVER, COLORADO

Through Kingdom Come
A Matt Striker Novel
All Rights Reserved.
Copyright © 2013 L. Allen Veach
v5.0

Outskirts Press, Inc.
http://www.outskirtspress.com

ISBN: 978-1-4787-2025-6

Outskirts Press and the "OP" logo are trademarks belonging to Outskirts Press, Inc.

PRINTED IN THE UNITED STATES OF AMERICA

So was I once myself a swinger of birches.
And so I dream of going back to be.
Robert Frost

Chapter 1

The blue Chevy Blazer pulled up to the curb on the grimy west side of Newark, New Jersey. The two men who got out couldn't have looked more different even though they were dressed identically. Dark blue wind breakers, blue jeans and black ankle height Rocky duty boots. The tall one looked over the target building while the fire plug looking guy glanced around the empty street looking for anything that seemed out of place. Both satisfied, they made their way swiftly to the ratty building and disappeared into the entrance.

The men did not speak to one another. They had been over and over the plan and knew exactly how it would go down. Almost.

Ali Dahab was getting complacent. It had been nearly six years since the glorious 9/11 attack and still it had not come back on him. He was even getting used to his new name. He had been Kalid al Hazmi when he had conducted his research for Kalid Shaikh Mohammed. Maybe it had been that his role was rather minor by comparison. All he had done was parlay the ideas of jailed jihadist Ramzi

Yousef into an actionable plan. He was particularly proud of the idea of using flight schools in the U.S. to train the attackers. He loved the irony.

Ali looked around the dingy apartment and his eyes came to rest on the girl. She had been a gift to him. She was very lucky. In the villages of Egypt her sins of the flesh would have put her under the lash before being made into a concubine.

He watched her at the computer. She had a knack for it, constantly searching through blogs looking for the things that he had instructed her to locate. Life was relatively easy now; she was doing his work for him and keeping him satisfied in carnal ways as well. She would never look at him nor show any emotion at all, not that it mattered in the least to Ali. He looked at the curve of her neck and the swell of her breasts; he would have her off the computer soon.

That's when the door crashed open.

Vito DeBenadetto -- or Detto -- the stocky one, gave Matt Striker, the big guy, an affirmative nod outside the apartment door, stepped back and in a smooth swift action kicked the door with shattering effect.

Striker was first through the door, Detto fast behind.

"Down," Matt shouted as his suppressor Glock fanned the room. He saw the man first, on the right but kept moving his weapon to the left. He knew Detto would take the man as they had practiced many times over. As he swung left the suppressor came to rest on the girl. Even in this situation he was struck by her beauty and her youth. What the hell was she doing here?

The girl's right hand came off the desk and swung around toward DeBenadetto. It held a small pistol.

"No," Matt shouted.

The Glock coughed.

The bullet hit her temple and exited the other side of her head with a red gray mist.

After the backup team had shoved Kalid al Hazmi into the big black Suburban and whisked him away, Detto looked at his partner and didn't like what he saw.

"You okay?"

Matt didn't answer. He just started walking toward the blue Blazer.

"You had to!"

Matt spun on his buddy. "Suicide. Death by cop. I'm sick of this shit." He turned back toward the truck.

Chapter 2

"**K**eep your damn hands off of me, Buck!" a female voice shrieked.

Matt jerked his head around to look across the street. The building across from Gidding's store was a big old restored Victorian covered with gingerbread trim. The main part of the building, including the wrap-around porch, had been converted into a comfortably upscale restaurant with a trendy name —Blueberries in Thyme. Exactly what the name meant Matt hadn't a clue. Like many old Vermont buildings, the old Victorian extended back on the lot with a section that was at one time a sort of garage-woodshed-barn combination. It was now turned into an attractive ice cream shop, "The Cream Dream." An old driveway between the building and the next building over formed an alley leading back to the ice cream shop. This was Monday, the only day the shop was closed.

Matt looked down the narrow alley and could see a man and woman struggling. "Buck, I mean it!" The woman was swatting at the man as he moved toward her with groping hands. The man was saying something that Matt could not hear.

Matt Striker had ridden his ten-year-old Vulcan 1500

motorcycle the four miles from his cabin up in the woods down to the town of Big Larch Pond, Vermont. When he rolled to a stop in front of Wendell Gidding's general store, flipped the side stand down with his size 12 foot, he threw his leg over the big bike to dismount. He unbuckled his helmet, hung it on the mirror and stepped back from the motorcycle into the sun and warm breeze of the early afternoon. He indulged himself an admiring look at the motorcycle. The big Vulcan was a massive ride, one of the biggest motorcycles made when it was new, and now ten years later, even though it was no longer king of the hill, he loved the bike no less. Keeping it in mint condition was one of his rare mindless joys.

Matt was now alternately looking quickly up and down the street and back toward the alley. *Surely someone around here can get involved in this besides me.*

This was his first week in town and only his second trip in to the store. "Hell, I didn't come here to get involved in this kind of crap," he grumbled as he continued to look for someone to intervene. No one was on the street. Except for the fracas in the alley, all was quiet.

Now the guy in the alley had the woman up against the building across from The Cream Dream. His hand was up under her chin holding her head against the siding. The woman was now struggling wildly. "Buck, you get your fucking hands off me!" she hissed.

Big Larch Pond had no police department. Like many

small townships in Vermont, there was an elected constable, but he was not a trained law enforcement officer, just a citizen with some ticketing and arrest powers that were seldom called for. The State Police and county sheriff were really the law here and both their barracks were miles away, out by the interstate highway. A patrol car in town was a hit or miss occurrence at best.

Matt's long legs covered the distance to the alley in less than ten seconds. He spent the time complaining and cursing to himself. *This is just the kind of bullshit I'm trying to get away from*, he selfishly reasoned. He was three feet from the struggling couple before they knew he was there.

"Hey, asshole!" Matt shouted at the man.

The man jerked sideways facing Matt and released the woman. She brought her hands up, instinctively protecting her neck and chin, and slowly slid along the building away from the two men.

"What did you call me?" The man's face was twisted with rage.

"How about you keep your hands off of the lady there?" Matt said.

"How about you mind your business before I whip your ass."

Matt looked him over. He was a head shorter than himself but he had wide, powerful looking shoulders. His hands were balled into fists.

Matt brought the tone down a notch. "Look, I don't

want to get involved here, but you got to leave this lady alone."

The other man took it for weakness. He started for Matt yelling, "Get out of my face. You don't know who you're talking to here!"

Matt tried once more throwing up his left hand. He said, "Stop right there or...."

The other man slapped at Matt's left hand with his left as he threw an overhand right. Matt's training kicked in as he deftly turned to his right away from the punch. As he did so, he was moving forward past the other man grabbing the thumb of the man's left hand. As if by magic he was holding the other man's arm up in the air, the thumb bent at an odd angle. The man was instantly bent over double, writhing in pain. Matt was now using the arm in the air like a rudder guiding the man out of the alley and into the street. He pushed the man and simultaneously tripped him spilling him onto the pavement. The man went down like a sack of potatoes. Matt looked at him moving slowly on the ground. He was disoriented and at least for now, out of the game, Matt concluded. Matt turned back toward the alley.

The woman was walking toward him, her fists clenched, her face beat red. *Uh, oh*, Matt thought, *tell me this isn't going to get worse*, he begged silently.

"Look lady, I didn't want to have to hurt your boyfriend. He gave me no choice."

The lady's big blue eyes narrowed as they locked onto

Matt's. "My boyfriend?" she sputtered. "What are you, an idiot?"

Matt had had about enough of being a Good Samaritan. "Look, I don't care what your relationship is...."

"I don't have a relationship with that buffoon!"

"Okay." Matt looked over his shoulder. "It looks like he's going to leave you alone now."

The lady looked past him doubtfully as she watched the man struggle to his feet, slowly dusting himself off. His face had a good case of road rash where it hit the pavement as he went down.

"Who <u>are</u> you?" the woman demanded of Matt.

Matt shook his head and took a step to walk away saying, "I'm nobody, just someone who happened along."

The lady jumped forward as Matt was turning away and touched his arm. Surprised, he turned back toward her.

Softly now, she said, "I'm sorry, this really scared me. I'm Kate Halliard." She stuck out her right hand. "I'm pleased to meet you."

"Matt Striker — call me Matt."

"Okay, Matt, call me Kate." She smiled.

Great smile, Matt was thinking. He looked over his shoulder, the other man was gone. "And who was that idiot?"

Kate looked worried again. "That was Buck LaDue. And Buck LaDue is trouble around here."

"I can see that."

"Say, would you like to go to Blueberries and Thyme for a cold drink?"

"Actually, I was just on my way into Gidding's for a few things I need up at the cabin," Matt returned clumsily.

"Oh, well. It was a pleasure meeting you, Matt. Maybe I'll see you around town? And by the way, thanks!"

Matt took her hand in his. *That smile is back*, he thought. "I'll look forward to it. Stay away from Buck LaDue," he advised.

Matt started across toward the store browbeating himself with every step. *A good-looking lady asked you to go have a drink and you say, "No, I gotta go to the store." What kind of jerk are you?*

As Kate walked toward the restaurant, she watched Matt's tall, lanky, muscular form start across the street. *Cowboy.* She had no idea that "Cowboy" was one of Matt's nicknames in his Special Forces Unit. She liked the little she did know and all of what she saw. *God, Kate, did you have to come on so strong and ask this big guy to go to a foo-foo restaurant for a drink?* she chided herself. *Why didn't I just ask him to go purse shopping?*

She watched as Matt started up the beadboard steps to the old store. She could see three alarmed faces staring out the window at him.

"That was Buck LaDue!" Wendell blurted.

Matt had walked into Giddings store and looked around. Three men turned toward him staring. Matt recognized Wendell Gidding from his previous visit. The other two were hangers on — old guys that Matt had seen playing cards or checkers the last time he was in the store.

Matt tipped his head as if to say, "hello" to Wendell.

"So I've heard," Matt said levelly.

"That was Buck LaDue," one of the old coots offered as if Matt hadn't heard the first time.

Matt just looked at him as if to say "And?"

Not to disappoint, the old guy added, "He's trouble!"

"Well, he sure was to that lady over there," Matt allowed.

Wendell picked up the conversation now. "He's been pestering her like a hound dog for months now."

"Well, it appears that he took it to a new level today," Matt said.

"Well, friend, just so ya know, that won't be the end of it with LaDue if I know him. What did you say your name was?" Wendell Gidding had seen Matt in the store on numerous occasions, but never heard him say his name. Generally, a respectable native New Englander kept to himself. Wendell was of that ilk, but any enemy of LaDue couldn't be all bad in his book.

"Didn't say," Matt returned, playing the New England

game. Then he smiled and said, "I'm Matt, Matt Striker. Got that cabin on the meadow up on Burke Hill." He stepped toward Wendell holding out his big right hand and thinking it was looking like he could use a friend around town, especially one in the town's "command central" general store.

"Name's Wendell Gidding," the store owner returned.

"I figured," said Matt. Now looking at the two old fellows with Gidding, Wendell caught the look saying, "Forgot my manners. This here is Cecil Bouchard and Howard Lafleur." The men each exchanged greetings. Matt then chanced a glance out the front window across to the Blueberries in Thyme restaurant. He could see the outline of a woman sitting at a table near the front window. Wendell followed Matt's glance and smiled. "That Kate Halliard is a fine woman."

Matt snapped back, embarrassed by getting caught red handed.

Brusquely he said, "Mr. Gidding, what have you got for .280 ammo here?" He was looking now at the rifles and shotguns racked behind the counter.

Wendell moved quickly away from the front window and behind his cluttered counter. He walked past his sixty-year-old black and gold cash register that didn't have a wire or chip in it anywhere and over to the guns. Clucking his tongue, he was saying, "Lemme see here, we got the Remington core-lock 140s and the Federal Premium 150s, that's about it."

"How many Federals you got?" Matt asked, all business now.

"Got three boxes of the Federals. We'll get more closer to deer season, I reckon."

"Let me have all three."

Wendell Gidding scooped up the three boxes and slapped them down heavily on the old varnished oak counter, then double-bagged the heavy shells.

"Appreciate it," Matt responded handing the portly storekeeper four twenties.

Matt pulled one of the cartridge boxes out of the bag, opened it and pulled out one of the big 150 grain .280 rifle cartridges and held it up inspecting it.

Wendell tried to read the man's mind venturing forth with, "got the Nosler partition bullet in it. I reckon it would stop about anything you'd likely find in these parts, bear and moose included. Course it ain't season for a good while yet."

Matt looked at the store owner squarely now and responded, "No, it's not season for a good while, but I like to stay sharp." He popped the cartridge back into the box and dropped it on top of the other two boxes. Wendell automatically picked up the ammo and placed them in the reinforced bag, handed it to Matt saying, "Be anything else?"

Matt looked back at him blankly. There was something

else, but damn if he could remember it now. He mildly cursed himself for getting older and losing his edge, but he knew the real problem was trying to shake his mind away from Kate Halliard. Other people might also be preoccupied with Buck LaDue after the experience twenty minutes ago, but not Matt. That was a mistake.

Matt stood a moment longer looking at Wendell Gidding blankly and finally said, "Guess I forgot."

Relieved that he said anything after the pause, Wendell cheerfully replied, "Well, when you think of it, we'll still be here for you."

Matt nodded his thanks and turning, noticed the two old coots staring at him. He gave them a nod also which they returned in exact unison. Matt smiled thinking this must be a big exciting day to them. They hadn't sat down to checkers for a full twenty minutes.

He headed to the door. Looking at the glass in the storefront, he noticed two things. First he saw the reflection of Cecil Bouchard and Howard Lefleur heading over to the counter where Gidding stood. No doubt they wanted to spare not a moment in getting some juicy gossip going with Wendell. Secondly, he looked through the glass to see the woman, Kate Halliard, still sitting at the window in the restaurant across the street. *Good.*

He went through the doorway to the steps on the porch. He looked across again. She was looking directly at him. He smiled awkwardly and gave a wave as he turned toward his motorcycle.

Kate Halliard felt like a teenager sneaking a cigarette. She was sitting at a small table by the window glancing periodically across at Gidding's store, silently hoping to steal another glance at the cowboy. She had been sitting there sipping bad ice tea, no reflection on the establishment; no one in New England knew how to make respectable ice tea. They seemed creatively inclined to lace it with mango, or kiwi, or who knows what, the result being a cold foo-foo liquid that locals passed off for ice tea. Kate focused on the store across the street. In a couple of moments, she was rewarded when Matt Striker came gliding out the front door onto the porch. He caught her look and smiled at her. She was in the process of smiling back when he turned away toward his motorcycle. *Huh.*

It was then that she saw Buck LaDue. She jumped up from her table, lifting the table as she did. Her ice tea flew off and shattered on the floor. She was screaming "Noooo!" The few other patrons jerked their heads toward her.

Why do I feel so clumsy around this woman? I'm hardly a schoolboy, Matt was thinking as he moved toward his bike. He was about to steal another glance back toward Kate when his peripheral vision caught movement to his left.

He instinctively ducked his head to the right, raising his left shoulder. The next thing he knew, a freight train blow had connected with his shoulder and side of his head. He was in the air briefly before his right side plowed into the pavement. He was down.

Buck LaDue had a demonic look on his face and a two-fisted grip on the piece of cord wood he had taken off the stack along the side of Gidding's store. He had swung the two and a half foot length of hickory like a short, fat baseball bat. He had come from the side of the building with all the momentum his stout body could muster, winding up for the strike. The blow glanced from Matt's shoulder to his head. He had the big man down.

Matt looked up and had a blurry vision of Buck LaDue standing over him. Buck was yelling at him — something about flatlanders minding their own business. Matt could see Buck cranking for another blow. Most people without Matt's training would have held up a hand in a feeble attempt to ward off the attack. But as Buck was measuring for his coup de gras, Matt, still down, was spider hopping on the ground, swinging his right hand in a big arc. The hand was still laced through the handle of the double bag with three boxes of heavy ammunition. It was like swinging a giant blackjack.

Before Buck could get off his second strike, Matt

connected with the bag of ammo on the back of his attacker's knee. The sledgehammer-like impact lifted LaDue up off the ground and for a split second, he was suspended horizontally in the air. The cord wood was falling from his hands behind him and fell to the street just before the back of his head sandwiched the hickory club to the pavement.

In a flash, LaDue was down and Matt was back up. Striker had his left foot on Buck's neck and was holding the attacker's left arm out straight, twisting the hand around clockwise. Buck's eyes were glazed and he was moaning in pain. Striker cranked his hand around further. Now Buck was bug-eyed and making a gagging noise.

Matt was in full warrior mode. His brown eyes looked menacingly black and he was growling at LaDue. "You dumb bastard, I'm trying to cut you some slack." Crank the hand. "I'm trying to be civil to you." Crank the hand some more. "But you just don't get it, do you?" Crank the hand. By now, Buck had been reduced to a primal gurgling sound.

Suddenly, Matt was aware of his audience. He looked up at the shocked expressions on Wendell and the two old men on the store porch, then to his left at the pained expression of Kate Halliard. Behind her, over close to the restaurant, some other people were standing in the street. On up the street on the next block, a man was standing at the open door of his dark green pickup truck. He had a hat with a shield of some sort on it. Matt thought it might be a uniform but it was clear he was not intending to render any assistance.

Great, thought Matt. *Here I am looking like a crazed killer and I'm the new boy in town. I'm supposed to be relaxing. I'm supposed to be changing my ways.* He threw Buck's arm down in frustration. *So much for getting plugged into real life.*

He gave Buck an agitated kick to the rump and ordered the man, "Stay away from me, stay away from Kate and mind your manners!"

Matt threw his hands out, looked up to the porch and asked bewildered, "Isn't there any law in this town?" He followed their gaze up the street. The green pickup was gone.

Wendell Gidding shrugged sheepishly. "Constable is all, but he never could do much with Buck. Don't know where he is today. Sheriff Drew and the State Police are the real law but they're both located out by the highway." He looked back and forth as if a lawman would magically appear.

Buck clawed to his feet and was staggering toward an old blue Chevy pickup truck parked across the street. He was clearly dazed but alert enough to extract himself from this humiliation.

Kate was returning an intense serious look toward Matt. *Now she thinks I'm a mad dog,* Matt lamented. But, to his surprise, she turned toward Wendell Gidding and started barking orders.

"Soap and warm water. I'll also need some antiseptic cream, gauze pads and first-aid tape." Kate now had Matt by the arm and was guiding him toward the store.

"Hey, really, I think I'm…."

"Mr. Striker, I'm a nurse and a damn good one. I'll be the judge of whether you're okay or need further care!"

Matt smiled. "Whatever you say."

Kate maneuvered Matt toward an old bow-backed chair at the checkers table sitting by a cold wood stove. Wendell Gidding was hustling around the store gathering up the things Kate had ordered. The two old boys, Cecil and Howard, were standing shoulder to shoulder, wide-eyed.

"Thank you, Mr. Gidding," Kate addressed the storekeeper as he delivered the necessary goods.

She had Matt's chin in one hand and the back of his head in the other, tilting his head to examine it. "Ear is where all the blood is from; more of a nasty scrape than a cut," she was muttering. Then she took her fingers and parted Matt's short hair above his ear. "Hmmm." The area was red and oozing blood, bruising was starting around the perimeter. Kate took a long look at the area, then she turned Matt's head toward her and held the sides of his face in her hands. She got her face very close to Matt's and was looking deeply into his eyes, one at a time. "Mr. Gidding, have you got some of those reading glasses around here?"

"Will these do?" Wendell was saying as he reached into his own pocket.

"Perfect," Kate answered. She donned the little wire rim glasses. She looked intensely at the pupils of Matt's eyes. They looked normal and they matched perfectly. "I don't think you got your bell rung too badly," she murmured as she turned her attention back to the wound above the ear. She began cleaning and dressing the side of his head and very top of his ear.

Kate noticed that during the parts of the well practiced procedure where she expected her patient to wince or jerk, he did neither, just sat calmly and quietly. *Bonafide tough-guy*, she was thinking.

She barely had that thought processed when she noticed a scar that ran parallel with his sideburn about two inches long.

As she finished with the side of Matt's head, she looked down at the top of the shoulder. Matt's shirt was torn open and the hide on his shoulder had been peeled back several inches.

"This is a bit of a mess," she announced. "We're going to need you to take your shirt off so we can get this cleaned up." Matt gave her a reluctant look which she easily picked up on. "Has to come off," she said empathically now.

"Okay," he said and shucked the shirt.

The reason for the hesitation was now evident to Kate. The front of Matt's left shoulder was a mass of ragged scar tissue. She recognized the work of military triage when she saw it. The nasty wound had been closed up with utility and expedience in mind — nothing pretty here. In spite of the wound, Matt's shoulders and biceps were big and well tuned. *This guy works out — a lot.* She glanced up at Matt's face for a split second. He was looking forward away from her with a veiled faraway look. Before she started on the shoulder, she found one more surprise.

A smallpox vaccination mark on Matt's biceps, about the size of a nickel. The problem was, it looked far too fresh to be any kind of childhood vaccination. It was in the wrong place and there was a matching "vaccination" mark on the inside of his biceps. This one was about the size of a quarter -- a bullet wound, entrance and exit. *Very lucky.* She had seen these before, usually not nearly this clean. *Who is this guy?* She shuddered slightly, then went to work.

Suddenly, Kate looked up into the staring faces of the old coots, Cecil and Howard. "Well, Mr. Striker, you certainly made their day," Kate whispered as she finished patching up the skinned shoulder.

"I'm glad I could be here for them," Matt mumbled.

"This town will have the skinny on this little episode before the sun goes down," Kate warned.

"That bad, huh?"

"Probably worse," she smiled. "I'm really sorry I got

you into all this."

"Well, in any event, Kate, you're going to want to steer clear of LaDue. He may be around again."

"Oh, he'll be around, you can bet on that, and he'll be keeping an eye on <u>you</u>, Mr. Striker."

"I'm sort of hoping he might want to avoid me," Matt said.

Kate pursed her lips thoughtfully and shook her head no.

"Slow learner, huh?"

Chapter 3

Abu bin Seidu cursed his worthless brother-in-law. His resentment grew with each inch that was gained in this godless North American swamp. By Allah, how could Rashid be so inept? But bin Seidu cursed himself as well for it was not even twenty-four hours previously that he actually allowed himself to believe that Rashid could complete the small tasks that were required of him. Would this great jihad be doomed by the ineptitude of his obsequious relative? *Allah is too great for that to happen,* he thought to himself.

Bin Seidu allowed himself a quick glance over the ATV at his companion, Kahrim Raziq Khan. Like bin Seidu, Khan was a battle hardened veteran of the tribal areas of the Pakistani mountains north and west of Peshawar where the Khyber Pass led to eastern Afghanistan. They were trained, experienced, stone-cold killers.

Bin Seidu did not show his frustration to his companion for in the mountains above Peshawar, devout Muslims and secular tribesmen gave away nothing in their countenance. Revealing thoughts and feelings on the face was left to little girls and spoiled boys. The men, the warriors, shared their innermost thoughts with Allah alone. Their faces bore no testimony.

But Khan knew. He was slogging through the same cold, muddy, strange swamp with their precious cargo, their message to the infidels. He knew the mission was in jeopardy.

They had gotten the ATV stuck in the swamp once again. Covered with mud, they extended the winch line out to a stout tree and bin Seidu was at the front of the vehicle working the winch controls while Khan put his considerable heft at work, pushing from the rear. The ATV inched forward up onto slightly frozen ground. As it did so, Khan lost his footing once more and went down full face in the black mud. He came up hissing a string of epithets.

The two men spoke in Pashto, the language of the tribal areas. Stifling a laugh at the mud-caked face of Khan, bin Seidu wisely mustered a serious look and sternly chided Kahn, "Keep your voice down. We cannot afford to attract attention!"

"What other fools would be in this godless swamp?" sputtered Kahn.

Abu bin Seidu and Kahrim Raziq Khan had arrived in Montreal a week earlier under false passports. Two businessmen from Karachi, Pakistan with briefcases full of samples of Pakistani leather and brochures depicting finished goods; jackets, gloves, vests made of inexpensive

Pakistani leather. They said they were calling on shoe, boot, glove and purse manufacturers in Drummondville, Quebec City and Sherbrooke.

The cover was plausible enough. The leatherware manufacturing industry, once robust in the area, had fallen on hard times as the cheap labor and raw materials of China had encroached on the industry. Stubborn manufacturers were grasping at any string of hope to remain viable. Lower cost in the leather itself would at least delay the demise if not thwart it.

Background on the Canadian leather industry had been the work of a three-man cell out of Sherbrooke, Quebec. The men posed as brothers, two of them operating a small convenience store while one of them went to work at a shoe manufacturer in town. They had been in place, dormant, since a year prior to the 9/11 attack on the United States. They had lived in paranoid fear for a year after the attack and had suspended communications with Peshawar during that time. Then they gradually progressed from inane test messages for a couple of years to a full scale plan of attack. The convenience store was the perfect stereotypical cover. They were fulfilling a role that did not seem out of place to Canadians, dealt in a significant amount of cash, and had abundant comings and goings related to restocking of goods for sale and the general supplies needed to do business.

When Omar, one of the "Ramzi brothers," took their

white Ford van to the little St. Lawrence seaway port of
Three Rivers to meet Seidu and Khan, it drew no attention
whatsoever in Sherbrooke.

Bin Seidu watched the white van approach the entrance
of the self-storage area. He picked up the cell phone
they had rented along with their silver Nissan sedan and
punched in a number. When the driver of the van picked
up the phone, he told him in Pashto to describe back to
him the scene around him. When the driver answered in
perfect Pashto, describing the entrance of the self-storage,
bin Seidu stepped out of the Nissan, walked across the
street to the passenger side of the van and tapped on the
glass. The door unlocked and he got in with Omar Ramzi.
"Allah akbar," he said softly.

"Yes, Allah is great," came the only reply.

Ramzi punched a code into the door by the gate and
pulled the van into gear as the gate opened. The van slowly
proceeded back toward the rear of the storage area. They
stopped in front of one of the many identical doors and
Ramzi unlocked two silver round padlocks. Bin Seidu
smiled as he contemplated the simple ingenuity of the
locks. He had never seen such locks before but he knew
immediately of the utility of the shape. It would be nearly
impossible to get the jaws of a bolt cutter into the bolt to
cut the lock.

As bin Seidu finished his thought of padlocks, Ramzi
was opening the flimsy overhead door. There was but

one item in the small storage area. A wooden crate about two feet by two feet and six feet long sat on the floor. The crate was stamped with references to leather samples from Pakistan. Bin Seidu's heart quickened at the thought of opening the crate, grabbing the different cuts and colors of leather and tossing them aside and reaching for the instruments of death and terror under the false floor. He was on the North American continent, the weapons were here, and by the will of Allah, the plan would work. The Satan America would be cowed once more.

Bin Seidu and Ramzi hauled the crate into the back of the van and as they drove back through the gate, bin Seidu gave Khan, now behind the wheel of the Nissan, a slight wave. The Nissan fell in behind the white van for the two-hour drive from Three Rivers to Sherbrooke. The two-vehicle caravan proceeded at exactly the speed limit, drawing no attention on the trip.

It was afternoon when they pulled into Sherbrooke. They proceeded directly to the hillside two-story with garage under, leased by the Ramzi brothers. The van backed into the garage. Khan backed the rental car into the driveway, went into the garage and closed the door. The garage was two car lengths deep under the house leaving ample room to swing open the rear doors of the van and slide the crate out onto the gray, dusty floor. With the help of Khan, bin Seidu pried the crate open. Omar Ramzi stood back a few feet against the garage wall; he looked frozen in place.

Bin Seidu and Kahn peered into the crate at dozens of binders holding leather samples. Red leather, black leather, tan leather, brown leather. Some thick, some thin, some smooth, some with heavy grain or a pebble look.

Who would have thought there were so many kinds of leather? thought Khan as he eagerly began to grab the samples and throw them askew on the garage floor. Bin Seidu smiled thinly at Kahn's zealotry thinking, *Yes, in all endeavors, Khan attacks.* He bent over and likewise began throwing samples out of the crate. In minutes, they came to their prizes. Both bin Seidu and Khan reached into the box and softly touched the black PVC tubes that were as long as the box itself.

The tubes had been carefully packed one beside the next with eggcrate padding. Each tube was capped on the ends with standard threaded "sewer tube" caps and each tube was about eight inches in diameter. There were no markings on them. Khan hefted one of the tubes out and held it on his shoulder, mockingly "aiming" it at points in the garage. *Death to the infidels.* Bin Seidu looked on with his arms crossed, satisfyingly nodding his head.

Omar pressed back against the garage wall fidgeting. He stared at Khan with wide eyes.

Khan deftly set the two missile tubes on the floor and lifted a false bottom out of the crate. Bin Seidu and Kahn gazed at the final item in the box with awe, reverence even.

The two men looked at each other with grim satisfaction and together reached into the crate and pulled out the lead-lined aluminum case. Only the weight of the thing would give this oversized briefcase away as the first nuclear dirty bomb to touch North American soil.

Omar Ramzi looked on with bewilderment.

"I must relieve myself," Ramzi suddenly announced as he disappeared up the steps from the garage into the house.

Now the two terrorists looked first at each other and then to the doorway through which Ramzi had just exited. Bin Seidu realized that Omar Ramzi could be a dangerous loose end. Bin Seidu cursed as he instructed Khan, "The problem with sleeper cells is that their members begin to get soft and forget the taste of the Jihad."

"I don't trust him," Khan said.

"He will give his life for Allah," bin Seidu assured.

"For now, leave the leather and the crate, put the missiles and case back into the truck," Seidu commanded. "It is time to go to the border."

A pale Omar Ramzi returned to the garage. He was alternately cajoled by Bin Seidu and Khan and given orders and instructions.

"You have served Allah well, Omar," Bin Seidu commended. "Now we need you to leave instructions for your brothers as we prepare to go to the border. First, you must leave a message for them indicating that you will need to assist us for a few days. We will need you to help with the equipment for this trip to the home of the American pigs. Also tell them to place the leather samples in the rental car and drive it to the Black Bear shoe factory in Quebec City where they are to leave the car in the parking lot."

Bin Seidu smiled and continued. "The Canadian police will eventually find the car and be looking for the two missing salesmen. Meanwhile, we will be deep into America."

The security of the border between Canada and the United States along the state of Vermont was a joke. Obvious crossings like I-93 were manned and protected. The back roads had guard shacks at the crossings. But there was much wooded frontier covered with only electronic devices and some of the recreational areas were hit and miss at best in terms of surveillance.

Hearty French Canadians lived to the north. On the Vermont side, it is the Scots Irish and the long-ago immigrated French Canadians that make up the "real Vermonters" population. Vermonter wannabees are of every color or cloth. Ex-hippies are well represented in the populous and are downright disproportionate in Vermont politics. Power to the people.

The actual borders are deeply wooded with balsam and fir mixed with ever-present maple, hickory and birch. It is a quintessential north woods. Moose, bears, bobcats and snowshoe hare abound.

In the midst of this wild border is one incongruous remnant of glaciers long retreated. Directly astride the US-Canadian border for a distance of some five miles lies the silver shimmery cold water of Wallace Pond.

By contrast to the wilds of the border, Wallace Pond is a modest playground for simple hearty souls of both countries. Their little lake homes and fishing camps line the pristine shores. The place is bustling both summer and winter. In winter, veritable cities are constructed of ice shanties and the ice abounds with people, dogs, snowmobiles and old cars with the doors removed.

The weekends, both summer and winter, are communal-like. However, in the late Fall, prior to hunting season, it is something else altogether. Most of the people are gone, the buildings shuttered and the boats put away under tarps, in garages and boat houses. Docks have been drug up onto the shore so as not to be crushed by the coming ice. The skies turn gray and the winter takes on a cold black hue.

This place where for five miles the border seems not to exist becomes quiet and abandoned in late October. The leaves this far north are mostly down and the leaf-peepers, what few venture to this extreme, are long gone, back to Boston, Hartford and New York.

Wallace Pond. The weak link.

"Ramzi is gone for the boat. It is time to unload," Khan said.

It was fully dark when bin Seidu, Khan and their escort Omar Ramzi pulled up to the deserted rental camp. The Ramzi "brothers" had scouted and selected the Wallace Pond cottage after many trips to the border area. During the summer months they had leased the property from a spinster from Drummondville. The state of repair reflected her inability to attend to the wood structure in her older age. But, for the Ramzis' purposes, it was ideal: quiet, secluded and lacking in any characteristic that would call attention to it. What's more, it was a straight shot across the lake to a quiet public boat launch and stream that led to a small bridge under U.S. Route 114 in Vermont, U.S.A.

The white van, heavy with its deadly payload, pulled up the long pebble and grass drive to the old gray camp. The three men got out in the faint light of the quarter moon which provided a dim silver stripe across the black water.

Bin Seidu stood cross-armed as he gazed across at the U.S. shore. It had been eight years since he had been in the country attending an engineering school in Massachusetts. He attended the school for two years, learning of the United States: the language, the geography, the people and their decadent culture. He even grew somewhat fond of some of the other students and faculty. Compared to the broad spectrum of Americans he became acquainted with through short travels and through the American media, he found the people on campus to be sufferable -- for a godless lot.

At the two-year mark, he transferred to an engineering school in Wales where he learned something of British culture. Along the way he added some knowledge of metals, chemicals and physics to stimulate his natural mechanical inclinations.

Even as a small boy, bin Seidu liked to know how things worked. Whether it was a mill, a well pump, or his father's beloved Kalashnikof, he could take it apart, put it together and fix it when necessary. But the opportunities to use his skills and sate his curiosity were severely limited in tribal Pakistan.

The tribal chiefs and local mullahs turned their attention away during the wind-down of the Mujahideen. The "freedom fighters" had sent the Soviets packing. The only Afghan battles left were between ever-bickering, ever-competing warlords in the wilds north and west of Peshawar. Bin Seidu's father, a chief himself, knew that his son must be sent abroad to learn of the world. Like fathers everywhere, he knew that bin Seidu could be more than he.

In the months prior to his worldly travels and education, bin Seidu was embraced by the local mullahs and the mysterious Arabs who held places of stature in the tribal areas. In fact, these foreigners were the only outsiders bin

Seidu had ever witnessed that could glide freely among the warlords and their tribes. They were largely unchallenged.

During this time the Arabs went through the subtle metamorphosis from Mujahideen to al Queida. Also, bin Seidu learned his Wahhabist doctrine from these people with zeal, thus becoming part of a grand crusade.

All these memories washed through bin Seidu's mind as he gazed across Wallace Pond at the target. Khan had no such philosophical inclinations and so fidgeted as he waited for bin Seidu to rejoin the present.

"Yes, it is time to go to America," bin Seidu answered Khan as he stared malevolently.

Meanwhile, Omar Ramzi was dragging a small black inflatable boat from under the raised porch of the old camp. "I will take this down to the shore," he whispered.

"Do you have the things we asked for?" asked bin Seidu.

"Yes, they are here on the side pouch of the boat," Ramzi whispered.

Khan came around the van with one of the tubes holding the rockets and quietly headed for the shore. He deposited them softly and headed back to the van for the other rocket passing bin Seidu carrying the aluminum case.

"Open the pouch," bin Seidu commanded Ramzi when they were all on the shore.

Omar Ramzi reached into the pouch as he opened it and brought his hand up with an object. Bin Seidu and Kahn heard a small click sound and the inside of the boat illuminated with a deep blue hue coming from the machined aluminum flashlight in Ramzi's hand. The blue lens on the torch provided just enough light to see inside the boat. The packet contained a second metal flashlight, two box cutter razor knives, a roll of nylon cord, and a compass.

"What will the heading be?" asked bin Seidu.

"Two degrees west of due south," Ramzi said.

Bin Seidu held the compass in the blue light and looked across its face, across the black water to slightly west of due south. All he saw was blackness. *Will Rashid be there? Allah be with us.*

"Load the boat," bin Seidu commanded.

As Khan and Ramzi turned to the darkness to gather the deadly payload, bin Seidu reached into the boat's open pocket and grabbed one of the razor knives. He held it in the darkness, blade open.

Kneeling next to the small rubber boat, he waited. While Khan loaded the rockets, Omar Ramzi was loading a car battery which was connected to the small black electric trolling motor on the wooden transom of the little boat.

"Test the motor," he told Ramzi.

Twisting the handgrip first clockwise then counter-clockwise, the small motor hummed with life, the propeller turning first one direction then the other. "It works, just as it should," returned Ramzi.

"Get the food and water and your gear from the truck," bin Seidu instructed.

Omar Ramzi was off in the darkness. Had it not been dark, the terrorists would have seen that the color had drained from his face.

Khan stood in the darkness looking toward the truck, the keys he pulled from the ignition in his pocket.

When Ramzi got back to the boat, bin Seidu was still kneeling next to it, his right hand dropped down to his side.

Suddenly, bin Seidu had Ramzi by his hair, jerking his head down toward the razor knife. Bin Seidu's right hand shot up, deftly slicing Omar Ramzi's neck from one side to the other. The left hand still holding his hair pushed Ramzi's face down to the ground already covered in Ramzi's gushing blood.

As the body twitched and thrashed, Khan assisted by holding his foot on the struggling man's back. The thrashing, gurgling sounds were over almost immediately. The maneuver went just as it had in the training camp, back in the tribal areas when it was practiced on unsuspecting prisoners from rural tribes or captured spies working for the Pakistanis.

"Find something heavy we can sink him with," bin Seidu told Khan.

Without a word, Khan grabbed the flashlight and was off toward the cottage. In the brief time he was gone, bin

Seidu slid the limp body of Omar Ramzi down partway into the lake. Khan returned with a concrete block from under the porch.

Handing Khan the roll of nylon cord, bin Seidu whispered, "Tie him by the leg and send his bag with him."

In a few moments, the two men were in the boat with their deadly payload and the concrete block. A small line went over the side and the floating body of Ramzi drifted alongside the boat, leg first.

When they were perhaps fifty meters from the shore, bin Seidu took a compass reading in the blue light and then with the other flashlight blinked the bright white light four times as he pointed it just west of due south. For a moment he held his breath. Suddenly the blackness on the enemy shore was broken by the return of four long flashes of white light.

"Rashid, you worthless little pig, you *are* there," bin Seidu muttered through a thin smile. He turned to Khan. "Let us say goodbye to our friend Omar Ramzi." Khan grabbed the concrete block and lowered it into the water.

Ramzi's body was immediately pulled under the dark clear waters, down leg first into the depths.

The little boat purred through the darkness, bin Seidu holding the compass in the blue light and giving silent hand signals to Khan to hold the course of just west of south. Within an hour, the dark shoreline began to be silhouetted in the slight light of the moon.

The American Hiroshima was becoming real.

Rashid had a revelation as he stood on the shore of the junction of the lake and the little river flowing into it. He wanted to run away. *What if this was all a set up?* He knew by the news accounts that many messages were being interrupted. *What of the border agents? Were they watching him now with their night vision technology? Was he standing in the cross hairs of a thermal rifle scope even now? What was that?* Rashid strained to hear a low humming noise and the faint sound of lapping water. Then as if by magic, a little black boat with two men appeared out of the darkness merely ten meters in front of him.

Chapter 4

Matt Striker was in dangerous territory. One minute he saw himself as a regular member of the human race and in the blink of an eye he was a cold-stone killer. How did he get in this mess? Murder for hire or the good fight?

After several years of "dark ops" work in Special Forces including stints in Gulf War I and then some strategic work on the African continent, he left the Army in a post-war downsizing. He alternately welcomed the move for himself but wondered about the wisdom of the downsizing generally. But it was for those far up the chain of command to deal with. It was above his pay grade.

He was immediately a man in demand. First the CIA, with whom he had worked on certain clandestine operations, recruited him strongly but he rebuffed the approach. He had never been comfortable with the ambiguities and manipulations of their world. Word of Matt's experience filtered over to the FBI and they took a run at him as well but the rigidity of the organization felt unnatural to him. In his Special Forces outfit, the structure of chain of command and procedure were set aside in place of creative, extemporaneous problem solving. Delta

Force was a world apart from the "regular army." Even during their training at a remote base within Fort Bragg, they were expected to be independent, think on their feet and solve immediate problems with quick decisive action.

Finally, it was a top secret deal with the U.S. Marshall's operation that attracted him. He found the agency at the same time serious yet less uptight than the other feds. With the urgent blessing of his former C.O. in the secret unit, he settled into his work of tracking down fugitives and protecting a cadre of characters of "the system" from federal judges to witnesses testifying against terrorists.

This was his home for the next dozen years. And Matt soon understood the push from the Colonel. The National Security Agency wanted people with the skills of the special unit from which Matt had come, to be cross-pollinated into other security branches in the federal system; and they made special accommodations to see that it happened. This arrangement skirted the Posse Comitatus Act which prevented the military from having domestic arrest powers while at the same time taking advantage of the highest caliber of counterterrorism capabilities in the world. Matt was on the payroll of the U.S Marshall's service and at the same time designated as a "contractor" to his old military unit. The setup had been the brainchild of the President at the time and was honored through administration changes. Only the head of the Marshall's service, the N.S.A, the Delta unit, and the President knew of the arrangement.

Now, by a turn of events, Matt was on administrative leave. The period was indefinite. His brain was scrambled. The years of squeezing the trigger had caught up with him. Matt himself was as surprised as anyone by the meltdown. He had gone for years seemingly oblivious to the pressure, able to spring back from horrific circumstances with a boundless energy and cool proficiency.

Then, the day he shot the beautiful young girl it all came rushing to the surface. Enough. How could he destroy such a thing of beauty and have a shred of good in him? he wondered. There had to be more. More to life, more inside himself, and other people ready to step forward to do the dirty work. He was an efficient predator but there were empty places, dead places in his spirit.

His superiors saw it too. They couldn't believe he had gone *this* long. "Take a break, Matt! Sort things out. We'll wait for you."

So here he was at his childhood getaway at Big Larch Pond. Maybe being in the Kingdom would provide a few dreams to go with the nightmares.

When Matt first arrived at Big Larch, he was self-conscious. At some level he questioned whether he had a right to even be in such a peaceful setting

The cabin was a hillside two-story affair with most

of the living area on the second floor. All across the front were south-facing windows offering a commanding view of a ten acre meadow that extended downhill to the edge of a woods filled with white pine on the edge, then spruce, balsam and larch with a sprinkling of sugar maples, different hickories, and paper-white birch. The woods and meadow combination created a perfect habitat for an abundance of wildlife. On down past the tree line was the pristine, blinding sparkle of Big Larch Pond. The town of the same name stood two miles to his left along the shore. The white buildings were punctuated by the tall white steeple of the Congregational church. God, he loved it here.

Why did it take a personal meltdown to come here? Maybe if he had allowed himself to be human enough to seek refuge here on occasion, the meltdown could have been avoided.

Now here he was away from the shadows, threats and abject evil, in this wonderland of beauty, serenity. And people he cared for. He felt like an interloper.

Chapter 5

I*might as well be a goddamn neon sign.*
Matt was a trained professional of the clandestine and in a matter of a few short days he had made himself a spectacle. Was this going to be the respite he desperately needed? It wasn't looking good.

"Okay, Cowboy, you're patched up and ready to go." Kate looked immediately self-conscious.

Matt jerked his head around and gave Kate a wary look. It was a chosen few who referred to him as "Cowboy." She couldn't possibly know that or anything about those people. *Where did she get that?* He studied her face. Kate flushed and dropped her eyes.

"I don't think you have a concussion. You might want to take it easy for a few hours and stay awake and alert at the same time."

"Yeah, I'm familiar with the drill on that."

"That doesn't surprise me, Mr. Striker," Kate said.

"Still Matt."

"Matt it is then."

There was an awkward pause. They both gazed around the store. They were being stared at by Wendell Gidding and the handful of customers who had drifted in during the past few minutes. They turned back toward each other and smiled mischievously. Matt hiked his shirt back on and buttoned it up. He got up and nodded toward the door. Kate, getting the hint, headed in that direction.

"You can't ride that motorcycle home," Kate announced.

Matt looked at the big Vulcan, then back at Kate with an amused expression. "I'm just a beginner, but I rode it all the way here from my house. It's almost four miles," he quipped.

"I'm referring to the whack on the head, smart guy."

"Actually, having benefited from the magic of your healing hands, I think this will be one of the less exciting challenges of the day," Matt held his ground with a smile.

As Kate continued her skeptical look, Matt picked up his helmet, spread it open with his hands, pulled it over his head — and winced with pain as the helmet closed around his head.

"Okay, that's it, tough guy. I can see there's no stopping you from riding, but I'm going to follow you.

By the time he had his black gloves on and the bike running, a late model silver-blue Subaru wagon pulled up with Kate at the wheel. "Lead the way, tough guy," she waved.

After winding several miles along the lakeshore,

the motorcycle turned onto Burke Hill Road. The road dropped down at first and across one of the many feeder streams to the lake, then under an ancient stone railroad trestle.

Matt twisted the throttle to climb up the hill from the abandoned railway. The big Vulcan pulled effortlessly. After passing through a little less than a mile of thick forest, a huge meadow opened up to the left. Matt swung the big bike onto a dirt and worn-grass drive that undulated through the field for another quarter of a mile and ended at Matt's chalet. The house was framed by a backdrop of huge white pines. Kate had never had an occasion to venture up this way and had certainly never been up to Matt's house.

Most of the area around Big Larch was rural, mountainous and beautiful, but the setting of Matt's cabin was in a different class. Stunning was the word.

While Matt pulled the motorcycle into the open bay of the detached cedar two-bay garage, Kate opened the door of the Subaru, stepped out.

The cabin was situated on the border between the forest and meadow. The cedar chalet-style structure was framed by massive white pines that gave way to a hardwood forest leading up the slope behind the cabin.

Neat stacks of firewood leaned against the pines and hardwoods as far as Kate could see into the woods. Looking to her left, Kate gazed across the broad meadow littered with fresh hay bales. Across the top of the trees on the far edge, sunlight danced on the waters of Big Larch Pond causing a glittering effect so bright she had her hand up as a visor to enjoy the view. Far to the left was town itself looking like a postcard captioned "Serenity."

"What do you think?" Matt asked.

"It's absolutely beautiful. I didn't know there was a place like this in the county."

Matt looked past her at the view. He had an easy, relaxed expression. "It does get inside you."

"Breathtaking." Kate was now looking at Matt as he stared off to the horizon.

"Well, Cowboy, you better hope it's healing here with that head and shoulder of yours," Kate blurted in a way that felt business-like to Matt.

He absently touched the side of his head. "Actually, I'm feeling much better already. I think it was the expert triage," adding a smile.

"I wouldn't rush things if I were you."

They stood silently for a moment.

"Well, I should be--" Kate said.

"Come on in."

"Where did you bag that trophy?" Kate was looking at a stuffed toy moose head hung on the wall.

The chalet was built into a hillside so they entered off a front porch deck that had a swing on chains. The chains were attached to the underneath of an upper deck that was clearly much larger then the lower one, wrapping around three sides of the cabin.

Kate went through the doorway and blinked her eyes to adjust to the relative darkness inside. The room she had entered was large, easily three-quarters of the footprint of the house. The walls were covered with honey-stained knotty pine. A light pine bed sat against one wall to the left. It was covered with a patchwork quilt that looked handmade. To the right was a massive wood stove sitting on dark green tiles of an otherwise wide pine floor. There were deer heads and antlers adorning the walls as well as a few wildlife prints, a pair of snowshoes and a rack holding a half dozen fishing rods. Toward the back of the room sat several pieces of exercise equipment, a few free weights and a red heavy-bag hung from a chain in the corner waiting for the next punch or kick.

Over the bed there was a faux moose head on the wall. It was like a child's stuffed toy complete with a stupid look on its face. A yellow highway sign announcing "Moose Crossing" hung next to the silly looking moose.

"Kingdom General Store, St. Johnsbury, 1995, one shot," Matt answered.

Kate nodded in mock admiration.

"This way," Matt said and bounded toward an open stairway just past the wood stove. The stairs went up to a landing, turned back on themselves and continued on up to the main floor of the chalet.

As he reached the top, Matt proceeded across the great room toward one of the three doors leading out onto a massive deck. "Make yourself comfortable. This will only take a minute," he announced over his shoulder as he stepped outside and disappeared around the corner.

Kate was standing in a large room with a fireplace at one end and a dining area at the other. The furniture was a tasteful mix of current as well as antique "camp" furniture inspired by the Adirondack and Green Mountains. The place was neat, orderly and spotless.

Matt came back inside holding a huge jar containing amber tea. The tea bags dangled in the brew suspended by their strings and were held in place by the jar's lid. The concoction had been sitting out on the deck in the sun. He held the tea between his two big hands as he crossed the dining area toward the kitchen. He was saying, "Ice tea, coming right up." Then he caught the entranced Kate. "I'm kind of a shutterbug," he half apologized.

Kate looked at Matt dumbly. "Shutterbug? No, I'm a shutterbug. This is something else all together," she replied gravely as she looked around slowly at the photographs on the walls. Hundreds of photographs. Some arranged in free form collages but mostly they were push- pinned to the walls. Some hung flat while others curled. Black and white, color.

There was not a single "snapshot" to be seen. Every

photo was special in some way. Either the composition was beautiful or the subject matter dripped with emotion. Joy, sadness, action, serenity, conflict, love. That and more all captured for a magic moment in time. Kate moved from one to the next. A wild turkey with its wings spread out and down to the ground as its chicks huddled under them, peaking out at the world. Two deer, does up on their hind legs fighting with their front hooves like boxers in a ring. Three deer, all bucks, walking in the tall grass of the meadow, twenty yards behind them a huge coyote hunkered down in the grass ready to strike the unsuspecting deer. There was a shot of the glittering lake just as she had witnessed it outside. There were shots of people and buildings in the desert, someplace in the Middle East. *Iraq?* In one, a woman and three children. The woman, head, burqa-covered, looked over her shoulder with apprehension; two of the children looked blank-faced as if shell shocked, while the third, a little boy, stood full face toward the camera with an unabashed smile of innocence. He was holding what looked like a stick of gum. There was a shot of a Humvee parked in front of a thick mortared building with a woman looking out a second story window. She also wore a black burqa covering all of her face, save the intense gaze of her eyes. The Humvee had a dozen children of all sizes standing on the hood and top. Two unarmed soldiers stood in desert camouflage, like sentries at either side of the vehicle.

In another area there were pictures of men in business

attire. One photo was of two men, one of which stood looking intently at a tablet — as if his life depended on the message it contained — while the other man lounged back in his chair folding his hands behind his head in a relaxed pose. Both men wore badges on their belts and guns in shoulder holsters.

On the next wall were photos of "regular" people, caught in magical moments. An old woman sat in a chair facing two small girls with their backs to the photographer. The old woman had her head thrown back in sheer delight at something the little girls had said or done. The old woman looked radiant.

There were two teenagers sitting on the dock at the gas pumps at Big Larch Pond. Their feet dangled down into a rubber boat with a gray outboard motor. A red gas can sat between them, and the planter around the gas sign was thick with red and white flowers. One of the boys had a tie-dyed tee shirt and the other was shirtless. Both were sun bronzed. On their faces were looks of pure contentment, illusive and seldom witnessed on the faces of any teenagers it seemed these days. Kate thought of Nick.

She turned back toward the big room and Matt was sitting at a long trestle table at the other end. In front of him sitting on thick coasters were two tall glasses of amber tea. Matt had quietly allowed Kate to be captivated by the pictures. "Sweet or unsweet?" he inquired.

"I'm sorry...." Kate was momentarily lost.

"The tea, with sugar or without?" he explained.

"Oh, the tea," Kate said as she moved toward the table. She reached for a yellow packet of sweetener in a bowl on the table and dumped the contents into one of the tall, icy glasses. Matt smiled and copied the action.

She sat at the table looking out the wall of windows, out past the deck to the lake a half mile below. She absently took a drink of the tea. Her eyes widened as she turned toward Matt. "Wow, this is <u>real</u> tea! You must not be from New England."

"Actually, I am from New England, but I spent some 'quality time' with some guys from the red states. They got me started on sun tea. There was no shortage of sun where we were at the time," Matt explained.

Kate picked up two CDs. One was Merle Haggard the other was Mozart's *Eeine Kleine Nacht Music*. "You have eclectic taste."

Matt watched her eyes as they traveled around the room and abruptly stopped on the top of his bookshelves where he had placed his gun and badge

"Okay, who <u>are</u> you?"

"You want to know who I've been, who I am or who I'm planning to be?"

"Is it that complicated?" Kate sounded skeptical.

"Actually, it is." Matt paused contemplating his next move. His life was built on playing his cards close to his vest. Mostly that had served him well, but he knew it could present problems going forward. That is, if he was actually going to dig out of the hole he found himself in. He decided to keep it simple but to also come clean -- or, almost clean.

"I'm a U.S. Marshall," he said. "I'm on an extended leave, but I still hold my badge."

Kate was confused but acted as if this made perfect sense. She nodded her head. "Lawman," she said noncommittally.

"Is that a problem?" Matt asked. There was something slightly defeated or maybe vulnerable in his voice.

Kate smiled softly, shaking her head. "No problem at all." Then she added, "You scare me a little bit, Matt.

"I don't want to do that, Kate," Matt said with deadly sincerity.

"You scare me, but maybe we can work on that." She smiled.

"I would look forward to that," Matt said.

Kate met his eyes, then she looked quickly at her wrist. "I'm late," she exclaimed as she stood and took a long drink of tea in one movement.

Matt was alarmed by the sudden shift. "Late?"

"Yeah." Kate was moving quickly to the steps. "I gotta go pick up Nick!" Then she disappeared.

Matt looked astonished at the empty stairway then quickly moved out onto the deck. Kate was scurrying toward the Subaru. "Who's Nick?" he yelled.

"My son."

Chapter 6

Kate drove as fast as she dared. Even though she had never actually seen anyone stopped for speeding in Big Larch, she was taking few chances.

By and large Kate went by the rules — it was part of who she was and it would be a great embarrassment to get a ticket. Especially if Nick found out, which he undoubtedly would in this little community that thrived on idle gossip.

On the far end of town she pulled into The Kwick Stop convenience store, braking just in time to miss two adolescent boys stepping out of the store into the drive-in lane, their arms filled with twelve packs of soda so high they could hardly see where they were going.

Jesus, I almost ran my own kid down!

"Hey, Nick, hey, Rami," she shouted out to the boys as she opened the door of the Subaru.

"Hey, Mom!" Nick smiled as he turned sideways to see around the soft drinks.

"Hello, Mrs. Halliard," Rami politely added.

"They put you two to work, did they?"

Both boys just smiled and turned toward the gas pumps where they started stacking their payload into a display of sorts.

Kate went on into the store. "Hi, Shuri," Kate said, greeting Rami's mother. "A little work will do those two no harm at all." She nodded her head toward the boys.

Shuri al Saeed smiled briefly at her friend Kate. "'Little' would be correct," she joked.

Kate heard paper rustling and turned toward the racks in the store and spotted a slight man restocking snack bags on the wire shelves. "Hello, Mr. al Saeed." Kate hoped her greeting wasn't as cool as it sounded to herself.

"Good day to you, Mrs. Halliard," Rashid al Saeed returned stiffly. He then went back to his task.

Kate turned back toward Shuri and noticed that she was being studied with a look of serious concern. "What is wrong, Kate? Your face and neck are bright red," Shuri inquired softly.

Kate's hand came to her neck unconsciously as her mouth dropped open slightly as if to speak. *God, do I always have to wear my feelings on my sleeve?* She looked toward Rashid and then out toward the boys. Shuri got the hint and headed out the door saying loudly, "Look, the boys are getting the display all wrong." Kate followed her out.

Shuri turned on her heels to face Kate. The boys were oblivious as they stacked the soda and argued about the process.

"What?" Shuri said simply. Kate had been thinking and reasoned that in this town, Shuri would know about the

Buck LaDue altercation including all the spin and hype of the local gossip mill. She might as well give Shuri a simple explanation.

"I had a little trouble in town with Buck LaDue. It was no big deal. It's over and I'm okay."

Shuri looked over Kate's shoulder through the glass of the store to see Rashid still working on restocking. She gave Kate a serious look. "He is a bad man," she hissed.

"He's a buffoon, Shuri." Kate paused, adding vaguely, "Anyway, I doubt he'll come around me after today."

Shuri now looked suspicious and glanced back toward Rashid, still at work. "What happened today?"

"Buck was bothering me and a man intervened. A big man." Kate was now turning beat red.

Shuri nodded her head with a slight smile. "A man."

"A man." Kate shrugged slightly and tilted her head as she confided.

"Shuriana, too much talk! Work there is to do!" Rashid had come out of the store bellowing. He stopped and fixed a cold stare on Kate.

Chapter 7

"It is not your place to question me woman!" Rashid slammed his hand down with finality. "Who I speak to, who I do business with is not of your concern."

"This Buck, he is a vile infidel" Shuri said.

Does this woman not know when to stop? Rashid brought his hand up threatening. "Hush, woman!"

When Rashid al Saeed had first brought his family to the United States from Pakistan, he was filled with self-importance at being head of a cell even if he was the only member of it, or so he thought. His brother-in-law, the great Peshawar warrior Abu bin Seidu, was rumored to be a top lieutenant in the most holy jihad, al Queda. And it was further rumored that bin Seidu had actually been in the person of the great man himself. Bin Laden, the lion.

Rashid, who was Urdu and not Pashtun, and not from the warlord controlled Kyber Pass area of Northern Pakistan, regarded bin Seidu with a sense of fear and awe. He knew little of bin Seidu's zealotry. Rashid wasn't even Wahhabist; he was Sufi and was raised in a more tolerant, easy Muslim culture. Relatively speaking, that is. He met Seidu's sister, Shuriana, at University in Islamabad where she had been sent by her warlord father Malik Haji Seidu.

Make no mistake, Shuriana Seidu was not being sent to Islamabad for her enlightenment.

Her wishes were of no concern to the great Malik. He just wanted her out of the way as violence in the border area heated up in the post Soviet Afghan-Pakistan era. The various tribes were now well armed and positioning for power. Haji Seidu didn't want the humiliation of having a daughter killed or kidnapped by a rival tribe. This would damage his hard earned stature. And besides, it was a badge of accomplishment to send a daughter off to university. In the Peshawar, status — and arsenals — were everything.

When Rashid met Shuriana, he was intrigued at many levels. Shuri was attractive enough but he was entranced by her background. It was as if a slicker from Boston met someone from the Wild West in 1870s America. There was adventure and excitement in the idea of it. When Rashid finally met Shuri's brother, the famed Abu bin Seidu, he saw his chance to be more than an unimportant face in the crowd. This was his ticket to relevance. Shuriana who had been treated, by and large, as an object with no soul or mind of her own, was predictably receptive to the advances of the smooth, cultured Rashid al Saeed. They married and a year later had a son, Rami. Rashid obtained employment as a government clerk in Islamabad and Shuriana was relegated to the traditional Muslim role of caretaker of her child, house and husband.

All the while, Rashid became more and more of a

pestering puppy dog to bin Seidu. He was a young man from a mundane background seeking adventure. Abu bin Seidu was disgusted that Rashid was not Wahhabist, not a true believer, and found the man to be weak and childish. But now he was family. Specifically, he was now the father of bin Seidu's nephew.

Had Rami been a female child, bin Seidu could have ignored all of them. But in the tradition of the Pashtun tribes, Abu bin Seidu felt a responsibility toward his nephew, the first male of the next generation of the family.

After growing weary of Rashid's constant badgering to be part of something important, bin Seidu finally relented in a way that shocked Rashid and Shuriana both. They would be sent to America.

Rashid was dumbstruck. He wanted to be part of some event that would pump him up into an important man of his community. He just wanted a little swagger, maybe a mysterious aura that would bring him respect and admiration. It had never occurred to him that bin Seidu would oblige him by sending him off to relative obscurity under the guise of some abstract, unspecified mission. But, bin Seidu had steamrolled him with the assignment. Rashid was trapped in his own web.

The cover story to Shuriana was that Rami needed to be raised in the American culture. America was the only superpower. It was the military, economic and cultural benchmark of the world. It would be a service to their tribe and their country for Rashid and Shuriana to take Rami to America. Because Abu bin Seidu had himself been sent abroad, albeit at a much older age, the concept seemed plausible to Shuriana. That there was an underlying scheme afoot she had no idea.

And so, after some rudimentary training in observation, clandestine communications and weapons, Rashid was sent to the United States. The first sleeper cell under the jurisdiction of Abu bin Seidu was being established. One pawn had been moved in what was to be a very long chess match.

Rashid had spoken to no one about this. It was fear as much as confidence.

"Well hey, Sheik, how's it hangin'?" Buck LaDue burst into the store. Shuri walked out.

Chapter 8

"Just cool it, Sport," Kate warned as she got out of the car.

"Hey Kate, did you bring the lamb for the slaughter?" Connie quipped.

"Please, not you too!" Kate begged. Kate had just pulled up to her house with Nick.

"Oh, has he been working you over today?" Connie came down the steps and casually placed a hand on Nick's shoulder as she spoke.

"Today, yesterday, the day before," Kate returned with mock weariness.

"Right, Mom," Nick added with disgust.

"Oh, you deny it, do you?" Kate then turned to Connie. "Get this, all he's talked about all week is he wants to get a gun! And wants to learn to hunt!"

"But Mom, all the guys at school are signing up for Hunter's Education classes," Nick protested.

"Going woodchuck on us, are you, Bud?" Connie enjoyed fanning the fire a bit.

"You don't understand!" Nick admonished both of them. He stomped up the stairs and into the house.

"Wow, what lit his fire?" Connie asked.

"I don't know, Connie," Kate continued in an introspective tone. "Is there not enough testosterone around here?"

"I'd say from the sound of it, Nick's going to have more than enough." Connie looked toward the front door that had just banged shut.

"Oh, Connie, you know what I mean. It's just me here. He's becoming a young man. I didn't really have a dad growing up, just my mom, two sisters...." Kate trailed off wistfully.

"Hey, ease up," Connie admonished. "He plays with other boys, does all that rough and tumble stuff. I mean, it's not like he's going around the house in drag, is he?" Connie now had a devilish smile.

Kate looked serious as she shook her head. "You know what I mean; I might be missing something here. What do I know about adolescent boys?"

"What are you saying, that he needs a man in his life?" Connie emphasized the word man with contempt.

Kate couldn't help but think of Matt Striker. "Would that be so bad?"

"Good God, woman, have you looked around this town?" Connie had her arms held out expansively. Then she added, "Men, can't live with them...." She paused. "Let's go shop for shoes."

Connie had done it. Kate was now laughing as she looked down at Connie's rag wool socks and Birkenstock sandals.

Connie Cutter was the proverbial trust-fund hippie. Family from Fairfield County, Connecticut, father was some kind of a big deal on Wall Street, mother was the grand-dame of the Greenwich charitable ball, which was as much a costume party for the rich as a fundraiser for the nearly non-existent poor of the town. Connie had gone off to school at Goddard College in Vermont, majored in Social Injustice or something like that, learned to grow everything organic, including a little wacky tobacco.

She settled into Vermont's Northeast Kingdom as the owner-operator of the ATO (All Things Organic) Fresh Market. And along the way, she cashed in on her parents' lifelong investment in her music lessons to snag a place as second chair cellist in the Vermont Symphony Orchestra. She was eclectic, sometimes weird, amazingly bright, talented, politically far left-wing bigoted, and a loving friend to Kate and Nick.

The two women put an arm on each other's shoulder and walked together toward the front door of Kate's house. Referring to Nick's imminent cello lesson, Kate quipped, "Let the battle begin."

For two years, Rashid and his little family had lived in the United States with virtually no contact with Abu bin Seidu. The email code and routing system had been tested a couple of times. Rashid had sent innocuous messages to a fictitious "friend in the United Kingdom" and had received equally mundane replies that indicated that the messages had been received and understood.

His assignment was to locate near the Canadian border and establish a stereotypical "foreigner in America" lifestyle. For Rashid, it was beyond easy. In fact, over time it felt real. He quit thinking of himself as an operative. He was established in business, in the community and was quite easily seduced by the decadent, soft lifestyle of the west. He had a nice little home, a car beyond his dreams, nice clothes. Rami was doing well in school, and other than her bothersome friends like Kate Halliard, life with Shuri was going acceptably well. At least in his opinion. And her friends were of no real concern since, after all, they were just women. He lamented from time to time that Shuri was adopting the uppity, bold, pushy ways of the American women, but he was confident that he could straighten his wife out when the need arose. He did regret that he could not slap some of the women customers who came into his store. It would give him much pleasure.

There was one source of pleasure that Rashid could avail himself of, however. His association with Buck LaDue was giving him an opportunity to feel like a power broker in the time-honored avocation of his country. Rashid was becoming a functioning member of the American black market. The many people he met through the store and the opportunities the store provided for unreported cash allowed Rashid to be both a buyer and seller of all matters of stolen property, making a tidy profit in both directions. And, if it came to dirty work, he had Buck LaDue to call on. Rashid had cash and Buck had a three-quart-a-week Crown Royal habit along with a need for two packs of cigarettes a day. It was a match made in heaven. He wasn't sure why his wife Shuri despised Buck so strongly, but he didn't care much either. He was enjoying his newfound status.

Then 9/11 came.

Chapter 9

"Do you see how they look at us, woman?" He was in a rant. "They act as if *we* attacked them!"

In the immediate aftermath of 9/11, Rashid al Saeed lived a life of abject paranoia. Would the government agents crash through the door at any moment, drag him off and subject him to unthinkable tortures? He was nervous and self-conscious in all that he did. With his family he was short-tempered and distant.

Shuriana thought that Rashid, while crumbling before her eyes, was doing so because of the fact that they were known Muslims in a mostly Christian society. People started staring at them. Teenage woodchuck boys drove by the store slinging epithets and slurs. Business dropped off at the store by half. She assumed that Rashid was just under the pressure of being singled out as a Muslim. Guilt by association. Or at least she hoped that was it.

While she was angry and disappointed in the behavior of some of the townspeople, in particular the cruelty of Rami's schoolmates, she was also aware of Rashid's idolization of her brother, Abu bin Seidu. And she knew in her heart that Abu bin Seidu was a fanatical Wahhabist and thus a hater of the West.

Often Shuriana tried to explain the difference between the Wahhabist and their hateful doctrine and the more tolerant, more numerous Sufi Muslims. As much as she tried to explain, her pleas had mostly invoked responses of suspicion or confusion, at best.

One glowing exception was with a relative newcomer to the town. Kate Halliard and Kate's son, Nick, held fast with Rami. For this she was deeply appreciative. Especially appreciative since she revealed to no one that she herself had grown up in a Wahhabist household, even though her father leaned toward a secular existence which accommodated his entrepreneurial pursuits as a warlord.

After she married Rashid, she gladly embraced the Sufi ways and even the Urdu language in place of the Pashtu language of the lawless hills and mountains in the north and west of Pakistan. She was civilized now, educated and a woman of the world. The old ways were those of the ignorant and the blackhearted.

For Rashid, the stares and crass comments of the townspeople were annoying — even maddening -- but in his paranoia he was surrounded by a cloud of guilt. While he knew Abu bin Seidu was a violent hardliner, it was inconceivable that he had had anything to do with the attacks of 9/11. But he also knew that given a chance, bin Seidu would gladly commit that madness and more. Rashid was soon reminded that he was a sleeper cell — in a way that affected him like cold water was thrown in his face.

Rashid had become complacent, lazy and disconnected. The assignment from bin Seidu seemed a lifetime ago, ancient history that no longer had relevance. He was living as an American, making money and purchasing modern conveniences, a car, a house. In his own country he would be seen as a man of means, a squire.

He liked this lifestyle in ways he had never imagined and embraced the societal freedoms. The "down with America" doctrine seemed old and worn. Sometimes he wondered if he had just been seduced by the materialism, but mostly he pushed those notions aside as nonsense. He liked some parts of freedom and opportunity. Not the parts that made his wife act unacceptably uppity, but some of it was okay. The wife he could handle.

Rashid finally stopped expecting a dark sinister encrypted message from bin Seidu.

As the months after 9/11 turned into years, Rashid's paranoia melted away bit by bit. The sweat above his upper lip dried up. His irrationality subsided. The suspicious hateful looks faded, the customers came back. Everything returned to normal.

Pakistan became an official ally of the United States in the war on terror. Even Rashid knew it was mostly hype, but he allowed the notion to take the heat off. He spoke of the alliance and the benefits therein to his customers often. Mostly the residents of the Northeast Kingdom who frequented his store were disinterested or mildly supportive. But the alliance gave him a stick with which to fight for his previous stature. Now he felt like he had a chance.

Then four and a half years after the strike against America, Rashid's world came down upon him with the first of several coded messages from bin Seidu.

The first message was simply reminding him to be ready to serve Allah. An important service would be required of him.

The messages looked harmless enough. The cover was that they were inquiries from a school chum now living in London. The identity was stolen and even though such a school chum existed somewhere, it was unlikely he was anywhere close to London. The encrypted messages looked like idle chitchat and trite remembrances, but the interpreted messages were not only sinister, but terrifying to the now fat and happy Rashid. It was as if he was living in a nightmare.

Rashid grew to blunt his fears with momentary clarity of intuition. He was a cell. He was for the most part a simple nobody. It was unlikely that he would be called upon to take some overt role in whatever was going on. In fact, it was unlikely that he would even be privileged to <u>know</u> what was going on.

Maybe he could even walk the fence by playing his minor role while clinging to his new lifestyle. As if to insure this fantasy, he brazenly decorated his entire store with little American flags. They waved above the chips, cupcakes, pretzels, soda, motor oil, road maps, magazines and even the slushy machine. Little American flag stickers adorned the gas pumps, the store windows and even the mirrors in the restrooms.

He even toyed with the notion of not responding to Abu bin Seidu's messages at all. Ignore them, maybe he'll just go away. But he knew deep down that to do so would risk being hunted down and butchered.

During his "orientation" back in Peshawar he'd seen the photos. He knew what these animals were capable of. The very thought made his blood run cold and his bowels go slack. No, he would play the game. But he would do it on his terms. If he was careful, he could exist in both worlds. He would just have to be resourceful.

Finally, the encrypted emails became more specific. Two rifles — AK-47s. Buy them, hide them, further instructions would follow.

Rashid was panic-stricken. He ran a convenience store in a foreign land; where would he get AK-47s? Rashid frantically started combing the papers. He had seen gun ads for the sportsmen's stores. Would they have such a thing as AK-47s? He started looking each week in the trader paper of private want ads that were on the racks at his store. What if he bought a gun from a federal agent? Rashid was not a U.S. citizen. Non-citizens were forbidden from the purchase of guns in the United States. What if he was deported, or worse?

Time gave way to reason and reality. Rashid had developed a lucrative little black market business and it would be the black market that might solve his dilemma.

"That goofy-ass raghead!" Buck said to himself.

At first, when Buck heard Rashid's request, he thought the the man had gone over the edge. He had supplied all manner of black market goods to Rashid in the past, everything from cigarettes and CDs to construction tools and riding mowers, to say nothing of all the stolen car parts. Rashid had cash and buyers; Buck had resources. And Buck was not beyond lifting the goods himself when he saw opportunities. Cut out the middleman, so to speak.

"You say you can get anything?" Rashid let an air of desperation creep into his voice.

"By God I can get anything, but I ain't likely to go to the slammer for your sorry ass! You need to be educated."

AK-47s were a different story. First, he had to explain to the simple foreigner the difference between fully automatic and semi-automatic. To the uneducated it sounds like a subtle difference. But in reality it is like night and day. A fully automatic is effectively a machine-gun. Hold the trigger down, it keeps firing. It doesn't stop until the shooter lets off the trigger or the gun runs out of ammunition. The firepower is awesome. Fully automatic weapons in the United States are restricted to military and police. There are, however, two exceptions. First is a specially licensed gun collector who has undergone rigorous background checks and is regulated by the feds, namely, ATF — Alcohol, Tobacco and Firearms. The second exception is the ones that are illegal. Smuggled or re-worked by home-grown gunsmiths. The illegal guns, by and large, are in the hands of organized crime and goofball backwoods militias.

A semi-automatic rifle, on the other hand, is perfectly legal in most parts of the United States. In fact, some of the most popular sporting rifles are semi-automatic rifles made by Remington, Browning and others. Whether the gun looks like a hunting rifle or an assault rifle (like an AK-47) is immaterial to how it shoots or how lethal it is. With all semi-automatics, the shooter depresses the trigger, the gun fires. The gun then automatically ejects the spent cartridge and cycles a new round in the chamber. The shooter then lets off the trigger and depresses the trigger a second time for a second shot. While firing fast, a semi-automatic pales in comparison to a fully automatic when it comes to firepower. Ironically, what many people believe are "assault rifles" in the United States are semi-automatic action, while the rest of the world is awash in fully automatic Soviet/Chinese style AK-47s. In some areas, AK-47s are so prolific that teenagers and younger are seen with them. And yet it is the United States that is seen as the "cowboy gun culture" in the eyes of the world.

When Buck finally made Rashid understand the automatic versus semi-automatic difference, he made sure that Rashid understood that "real" fully automatic AK-47s were out of the question. To Rashid, the reason given was that he wouldn't know where to start to find them — which was not totally true. He figured that Clyde Gash would be a starting point. His real concerns were twofold: first of all, machine-gun type AK-47s were so rare that the cost, he surmised, would be prohibitive. Buck himself had never seen one, didn't know of anyone who had seen one. Not for sure anyway. Secondly, even a woodchuck like Buck knew the difference between supplying an otherwise legal weapon to a non-citizen and supplying a totally illegal weapon to a non-citizen. One felony was far worse than the other. Buck didn't want ATF all over his ass.

"What you want something like that for?" Buck asked Rashid warily.

"I do not want them for me," Rashid returned. "I have customer who wants them."

Chapter 10

He needed tomatoes, carrots and celery. Maybe a few ripe berries. He turned into "All Things Organic".

Matt had been to the place a couple of times but wasn't particularly drawn to it. The produce was fantastic. And the store itself was rustic and outdoorsy in a way that left Matt feeling comfortable and nostalgic -- an old fashion vegetable stand! Great stuff. Good for you. Not bagged and tagged but fresh, like it came from your own garden.

The problem was the strange lady who ran the place. She was all Birkenstock and rag wool sox and her sweater looked like it was made from the hair of her dog. The dog didn't look all that clean and neither did the sweater. Instead of white, the dog and the sweater looked kind of yellowish, like smokers' teeth, and there were flecks of brown here and there. Tree bark? But anyway, it wasn't how she looked. It was how she looked at Matt. She was constantly sizing him up with a cold stare and pursed lips like a Sunday school teacher who just heard a poor, wretched student recite Genesis saying, "and on the sixth day, God decided to rest." Matt couldn't imagine what the problem was. He didn't know her, he was sure of that. His excellent memory was augmented with intense training to pay attention to faces and details.

Maybe she just didn't like his looks. Maybe he resembled her no-good ex-boyfriend who ran away with a bimbo who she thought was her best friend. Or maybe she had seen him inadvertently throw a plastic water bottle into the trash instead of the recycle bin, pegged him for an eco-trasher. In any event, it was clear that the lady had no use for him. Too bad. If she lost the "laundry bag" look and the attitude, maybe even smiled a little, she could pass for a mildly attractive sort.

Matt parked the Jeep in the pebble stone parking area and climbed out. He was pleasantly surprised to see that the wicked witch was nowhere in sight. In fact, the high school age girl tending the little store was all wholesome smiles and "May I help you?" Maybe the regular biddy got rabies from her dog sweater and wouldn't be around for a while.

Matt grabbed an empty peach basket and went to filling it with fresh goodies and whistling all the while.

The tomatoes were at the front edge of the porch of the store and as Matt stood there selecting the best and the brightest, Kate's Subaru pulled in next to his Jeep.

Matt recognized the car immediately and broke into a spontaneous smile --which was extinguished when the first one out of the car was the wicked witch. The lady returned Matt's withering smile with a look of disgust. Somehow Matt was able to resurrect his original look and added a note of confusion as Kate came out of the car next, followed immediately by a nice looking teenage boy.

As Matt shot glances from one to the next, Kate was saying, "Hey, Connie, I want you to meet my friend, Matt Striker."

Connie stopped and whipped around toward Kate with a "You've gotta be kidding me" look.

"Matt, this is my friend, Connie Cutter, and my son Nick."

Matt moved first to shake Connie's hand but she had turned toward the store again and threw a sarcastic "charmed" over her shoulder. Matt's handshake turned to a weak wave that was still in place as he turned back toward Kate and Nick.

Kate, also talking to Connie's back, was futilely adding, "He's the one I told you about!"

Meanwhile, Matt had regrouped and was saying, "Nice to meet you, Nick." Matt was impressed. For an adolescent, Nick returned a strong manly handshake and a polite "Nice to meet you."

Kate, shaking her head at Connie's rudeness, turned back toward Matt. She had the look of mild embarrassment which turned her cheeks a little red. She looked fantastic. "Hey Matt, how you doing?" She offered her hand to Matt who immediately decided where Nick had learned his handshake.

"I'm good." Between Connie's greeting, the presence

of Nick and the surprise of seeing Kate, Matt was feeling engulfed by a small tornado.

Kate turned to Nick. "Hey, Sport, could you go in and see if we can get some cold drinks?"

"Sorry about all that," Kate offered.

Matt waved it off. "No problem." His smile was now back in full force.

"How's the head and the shoulder?"

"Everything's great. Your son seems like a real nice young man."

The screen door slammed and Nick was on the porch. "She doesn't have any soda. You want papaya juice, kiwi juice, or rainbow juice?"

"Hon, could you see if she has some bottled water?"

Nick disappeared again.

"I was thinking...."

"Do you know where...."

They both spoke at once.

Matt smiled. "Ladies first," he insisted.

Kate hesitated a moment. "I was just going to ask if you knew where the little waterfall was by the lake?" Kate asked.

"The one on the little stream below my house?"

"That's the one."

Just before the stream that went across Matt's land met the waters of Big Larch Pond they cascaded over a little four-foot waterfall. The town had made the area a small park. It was a beautiful spot but seldom used as most area residents and summer visitors preferred the several beaches near town.

"Sure, I know it well."

"Well, I was just thinking that it would be a nice place for a picnic — you know, for you and me."

"Perfect." Matt jumped to her aid. "How about tomorrow? I'll pick you up!"

"Great! I work for an outreach program for Dartmouth Medical and my schedule is pretty flexible this week."

As she was giving Matt her address, Nick burst out of the store with three bottles of water. He passed one to his mother, then presented one to Matt. "Here you go, Mr. Striker."

Matt kept an amused expression under control. "Well, thanks, Nick, I appreciate it."

Kate looked back and forth between her son and Matt for a moment. "Time for us to get going, Sport."

Nick seemed curiously disappointed to release the moment. "What's the big hurry?"

Kate smiled at Nick. "The big hurry, Sport, is that you have a big exam this week and we're going to make sure you have time to study."

Not able to resist the jab, Nick retorted, "I wish you would have thought of that before the music lesson."

Kate jerked her thumb toward the car and with that, they were off.

Chapter 11

Buck's thoughts drifted to Kate Halliard and the big show-off flatlander who had stuck his nose in their private business. "Who the hell does that asshole think he is?" he hissed. "Mr. Showtime Judo Shithead. I'll show his sorry ass. I'll show them both." He blinked back to the present when he saw the turnoff to the compound. "Business first, though."

This was not Buck's first trip up the half-mile track from the dirt road he'd turned off of. But, he always shook his head in wonder and amusement. The wooded track was one vehicle wide. On each side of the little road were four strands of barbed wire running from tree to tree. There were no fence posts so the end result was a zigzag mishmash of barbed wire going from one tree to the next. Because the wire was so close to the path, there was nowhere to pull over if another vehicle was coming the other way. If it happened, some poor soul had to back out the entire path to the road or the compound to let the other continue.

Buck had been that poor soul on one occasion. He had raked the sides of his truck repeatedly trying to navigate the slim path going backwards. "Dumb bastards," he muttered.

Buck rounded a tight turn and was facing a big iron

gate that looked to have been made of an old car frame welded to a swing post. On either side of the gate were armed guards, one sitting on an old web and aluminum lawn chair that was pink and lavender. The other was sitting on an old iron tractor seat that was screwed to the top of a tree stump. The stump was too high and his feet didn't touch the ground. He was dressed, like the other guard, in a mishmash of wood camo, desert camo and show camo. He looked like a clown sitting on the chair of a carnival dunking booth. The one on the cheap lawn chair had an M-16 assault rifle across his lap while the other sported a Kalashnikov.

Buck snorted quietly, "By Jesus, where do they get these nut jobs?" He pulled up, stopped the old truck and cranked his window down.

"Morning, boys," Buck offered.

"State your business." The fellow with the M-16 was getting up from the lawn chair.

"State my what?"

"State your business," M-16 said more forcefully. Now Mr. Kalashnikov was coming around the truck from the back.

"Jesus, Ray, it's me, Buck." He stuck his head out the window as if they hadn't seen him. "Come up here to see ol' Clyde."

"Commander Gash ain't receiving no uninvited guests," Kalashnikov replied sternly.

Buck didn't recognize this clown. He turned back to Ray, Clyde Gash's nephew. "Goddamit, Ray, I spoke to Clyde in town yesterday and he told me to come on here to finish our talk!" Buck was uneasy and exasperated. "And who the hell is this 'Commander Gash'?"

"That's Uncle Clyde," Ray whispered conspiratorially.

This place is turning into a full-fledged looney farm.

"Well Ray, either open the goddamn gate or go tell 'Commander Gash' that General LaDue is up here to see him."

While Kalashnikov scowled, Ray bit his lip trying to decide what to do, then he turned and swung the gate open.

As Buck drove past the two men, he stuck his arm out the truck window pointing to the sky. "Fellas, watch out now, seen a black helicopter down to the lake yesterday," Buck razzed.

Buck looked in his rearview window. Kalashnikov was still staring after the truck. Ray was looking up in the sky. *Dumber than stumps and armed with machine guns.*

As he progressed into the compound, the area opened up to a series of rickety house trailers scattered up and down a logged-off hillside. Some had blue tarps hanging off them, some were roofed-over with corrugated tin setting atop rough lumber frames. Old rusted brush mowers, tillers and tractor parts littered the ground.

There was no grass, just work paths through bushhogged weeds. Rough planks were plopped down where the paths were muddy. Generators sat askew throughout the mess. An old school bus painted O.D. -- military olive drab -- was parked in tall weeds next to a rusty blue Ford Econoline van and a Chevy Suburban. ATVs and snowmobiles were parked or abandoned everywhere. It was hard to tell which.

There were several large nasty dogs chained to stakes in the ground. Old crates and 55-gallon drums on their sides served as crude dog houses. The mutts went into a frenzy as the truck advanced.

Buck pulled up near the biggest trailer. It had a massive deck built all along the downhill side. By the time he killed the engine and opened the truck door, a big man had come out of the trailer onto the deck. He raised a hand in the air and boomed, "Shut up!" Every dog fell silent and lowered its head in a cower.

"Hey there, Clyde, nice day, eh?"

The big man looked up at the sky as if to consider the question. He had white hair and a bushy white beard. He wore old greasy camo overalls and an old black ball cap pushed back on his head so the bill stood almost straight up.

"Reckon it'll do," the big man replied.

"Thought them pups at the gate might shoot me."

"They got their orders."

"Orders? Gettin' a little formal up here, ain't ya?"

"None of your goddamn business how we run things."

"Jesus, Clyde, just talkin' here. Ain't trying to butt in none," Buck said defensively. "Who's that new one down there with Ray?"

"Name's Willie Jones. Come up from down home."

Buck thought about that for a minute. He knew that "down home" was the coal country of West Virginia. Buck had never been there, hadn't been much of anywhere outside New England. As he looked around the rag-tag compound, he couldn't help but wonder why anyone would move to this place. *What kind of hell must West Virginia be?*

"Kinda touchy, ain't he?" Buck said.

"Ain't got his ground under him yet. He'll do," Clyde replied. "You didn't come up here to talk about Willie nor how we do things, noway. Let's talk turkey." Clyde waved Buck up to the trailer as the big man went inside.

When LaDue came out of Gash's trailer, he was carrying two Kalashnikov rifles — AKs — and a plastic grocery store bag with two extra clips and a brick of .223 ammo. Clyde followed Buck out, holding a roll of hundred dollar bills.

"Now look here, Buck, if you'd just wait another two weeks I coulda got yuns the real thing." The big man was referring to the two AK rifles.

"Won't be a problem at all. My raghead buyer won't know the difference," Buck replied.

"They'll find out soon enough if they go to puttin' AK47 rounds into those things," Clyde warned.

"Trust me, Clyde, won't make any difference."

"Trust you? Horseshit!"

Buck tried to look offended, but just managed to look even more slippery and insincere.

"You just make sure none of this comes back on me, or you and me are gonna do-si-do," Clyde threatened.

Buck wasn't sure what it meant to "do-si-do" with Clyde, but he was relatively certain it couldn't involve any new dance steps. He was about to speak when he heard gunfire up in the woods above the compound. First, what sounded like semi-auto shooting, then fully automatic machine gun fire.

Buck was relieved to change the subject and take the heat off. "Some of the boys up doing a little deer huntin', eh?"

Clyde just looked at Buck with a malevolent stare that communicated two things: don't change the subject and stay the hell out of our business. Buck could see that the big man didn't bite. "Jesus, Clyde, don't worry. I swear by the Blessed Virgin nothing will come back on you."

"You best be right 'cause if you ain't, won't the Blessed Virgin nor Jesus Christ hisself gonna be able to help you none."

Buck was already turned toward the truck and lifted the muzzles of the two rifles in his right hand in reply.

"Goddamn frog," Clyde ranted to himself referring to Buck's French connection heritage. It didn't matter to an ignorant bigot like Clyde that Buck was a second generation American and that his family was sixth generation Canadian dating back farther than most of the people on the North American continent. No, Clyde subscribed to a more simple logic. His name was LaDue. He was a frog.

Once Buck got his booty loaded into the old Chevy he was already thinking about how he would handle Rashid. The problem was that the two Kalashnikov rifles were chambered in American .223 caliber, also known as NATO 5.56 millimeter, and actual Kalashnikovs didn't come that way.

Western power armed forces' small arms by and large come in two calibers: .223 also known as 5.56 mm, or .308 also known by its NATO moniker of 7.62 mm x 52. During the cold war the Eastern block countries led by the Soviet Union and their star assault rifle engineer Kalashnikov, developed their own small bore and big bore assault rifle calibers. They were 5.45 mm and 7.62 x 54 mm respectively. Virtually all Western military assault rifle and sniper rifle development revolved around NATO 5.56 small bore and 7.62 x 52 large bore. In the Soviet empire, nearly all of the Kalashnikov assault rifles were 7.62 x 54 and a few were 5.54 mm. The idea of each side was to have standard caliber for small arms so that ammunition needs would not be complicated. The U.S., British, French, Italians, Israelis, etc. all had the NATO calibers while the

Czechs, Hungarians, East Germans, Chinese and Russians all had the Russian calibers.

The offshoot was that after the breakup of the Soviet Union, AK type or Kalashnikov rifles went from a Soviet/Chinese military mainstay to a black market commodity so prolific that in some parts of the world AKs became virtual currency. The Middle East had been literally flooded with AK assault rifles. They were now the weapons of choice for virtually all terrorist organizations.

Buck's problem was that the two rifles he had just purchased to resell to Rashid al Saeed were chambered for NATO 5.56 cartridges. They were bastardized by enterprising Americans who had gotten their hands on some of the flood of AKs and decided the American thing to do was "Americanize" the rifles. So they reworked the receivers and barrels so that they would only shoot the American .223 rounds. Buck now had two such rifles to resell -- for an attractive profit. He was in the process of deciding that he would deliver the rifles to Rashid and offer no explanation at all. See if the dipshit knew the difference.

The alternative was to wait for Gash to get "real" Kalashnikovs in the coming weeks and Buck figured that "a bird in the hand" was the preferred strategy. "What the hell, raghead won't know the difference till after I get my money."

But, before he delivered the rifles to Rashid, he intended to put one of them to good use.

Chapter 12

Matt steamed as he looked at the green truck.

He was up early. He wanted to get out to the range and back in time to get lunch together. The Kingdom Fish and Wildlife Club was just four miles from his house. After sitting by the window and watching deer graze in his front yard while eating his breakfast, he reluctantly grabbed his Browning A-bolt hunter and the .280 shells purchased at Wendell Gidding's store and headed quietly out the door of the lower deck. The deer heard him come out as he knew they would, flagged and ran into the woods. He listened to them bound through the dry leaves for a moment before going on to his Jeep.

The drive into the club was lined on both sides with towering white pines that continually laid down a blanket of pine needles on the roadway. The result was smooth quiet entry to the club that contrasted sharply with the inevitable "pops" of gunfire.

Matt took a long look at the truck and the man beyond it at the pistol range as he drove quietly by on his way to the rifle range.

He had seen this truck and the man previously and was hardly awash in fond feelings. But he shrugged it off and went on to a parking spot in front of an empty bench at the rifle range. The range area was basically a broad long meadow in the middle of a large pine-spruce forest. It was one of the flattest areas in the entire county to the point that a bulldozed earthwork was constructed at the ends and along the sides of both the pistol and rifle areas.

The rifle area was a series of benches on concrete pads with little roofs providing a canopy. Between the benches and everywhere on the range the grass was thick, lush and deep green. The area could have passed for a driving range at a posh country club. Behind the benches opposite the range was a long, low log building that was impeccably maintained. It contained restrooms, showers and the meeting room for the gun club. Behind the building was a rather open wooded area with a series of lifelike archery targets scattered throughout woods. It was adorned with silhouette targets of deer, bear, moose, turkey and coyote. A small maintenance building sat on the edge of the woods, the side covered with deer antlers and one set of moose sheds. Like deer, moose shed their antlers each year during the early winter. Occasionally, hunters and hikers were lucky enough to find them on the forest floors before they were gnawed away by mice, chipmunks and squirrel, all craving the calcium the antlers provided.

Matt backed his Jeep up toward the bench, got out and opened the tailgate and removed his gear. On the bench he set up his rifle rest, spotting scope and his gun bag. He set his three boxes of .280 ammunition next to the rifle rest and removed his ear protection and shooting glasses from the gun bag. He extended the legs of the spotting scope and sat at the bench and looked through the scope down range. Next, he walked a metal frame two hundred yards out on the range and set it up with paper targets, one to each side of the center of the frame. He then placed a small orange dot on the bull's eye of each target.

As Matt walked back to the Jeep he looked across the field to the man at the pistol range. The man had gone out to one of his targets and was on his way back to the shooting station. Matt noticed two things: first, the man had a shield on his khaki hat and second, the man was frustrated. He stomped more than walked back to the pistol-shooting stand. Matt was now sure that this was who he thought it was and it pissed him off.

When Matt got back to his Jeep, he reached in, took out his Browning A-bolt Hunter rifle and opened the bolt. He carried the rifle, bolt open and muzzle up, to the shooting bench. Pushing a button on the bottom of the action, he popped the magazine out of the rifle and loaded three cartridges into the clip and returned it to the rifle. He got comfortable on the seat of the bench, pulled the rifle firmly to his shoulder and looked through the Leupold scope. He dialed the scope up from four-power to the maximum nine-power and looked at the target bull's eye.

A properly sighted rifle of this and similar calibers

should be sighted point-blank at two hundred yards. In other words, at two hundred yards where the crosshairs of the scope are held is where one should expect a well-placed shot to hit. At a hundred yards, a .280 bullet is actually rising and the point of impact should actually be about two inches higher than the sightline. Between a hundred yards and two hundred yards, the bullet is pulled down by gravity back to the sightline for a point-blank hit. From the barrel of the rifle to the target, two hundred yards down range, the bullet travels in a slight arc, going above the barrel of the rifle and back to the exact level of the rifle.

Matt wiggled the stock of the rifle into the sand-filled rest and sighted on the middle of the tiny orange dot he had placed in the bull's eye. He took a long breath, exhaled and softly touched the trigger of the rifle. The gun boomed as it bucked against his shoulder. When the gun settled back on the rifle rest, he looked through the rifle scope. He could see that the orange sticker had been cut, but couldn't see it clearly. He opened the action of the rifle and the spent cartridge flew out of the gun. Leaving the action open, he scooted around the bench slightly and looked through his 24-power spotting scope. Now he could see the orange dot clearly. The shot was nearly dead center with orange showing all around the hole in the paper. He repeated the entire sequence two more times. Finally, looking through the high-powered spotting scope, he could see a little cloverleaf pattern of bullet holes all touching each other to the point where a single dime could cover the three holes at once.

"Damn fine shooting," a voice behind Matt said softly.

Matt glanced around to see the man from the pistol range standing behind him holding a pair of 10-power Steiner binoculars. The man was dressed in khaki green with a green ballcap with a yellow, orange and green shield that identified him as a fish and wildlife enforcement officer. A ranger. A game warden. He had a duty gun belt on with a Glock 19, 40 caliber in the holster.

Matt stayed on the bench and turned back toward the targets. "That's the rifle, not me. I've got it anchored on the rest," Matt replied coolly.

"Yeah, I know all about that, but it's still you squeezing off the shot, rest or no rest."

Matt didn't reply. He just flipped the magazine box out of the rifle, left the action open, got up and started striding smoothly toward the targets. When he got out to the target, he placed a new orange dot over the one he had shot up with his three-shot group. When he turned back for his walk back to the bench, the ranger was still standing there. When Matt got back to the bench, he didn't sit down—he just stared at the man.

"You looked like you were doing fine," the man blurted defensively.

"Thanks a lot!" Matt returned.

"Even from where I was I could see that you've had training and would be okay," the ranger continued feebly.

"So you decided not to do your job?"

"I'm a goddamn game warden, not the sheriff," the man said red-faced.

"You and I both know that you're an officer of the law everywhere in this state."

"Look, I've been on Buck LaDue's ass every which way you can imagine. I'm at the point where I've caught him at so much it's looking like harassment. He's got the prosecutor and circuit judge half convinced that I'm out for his ass. The dumb son-of-a-bitch doesn't know when to say 'when.' And I keep catching him. Poaching, hiding stolen property, assault, breaking into cabins. Jesus, he's practically a full-time job! If I'd gotten into your ruckus it would have looked like one more case of Sam Hood against Buck LaDue," the ranger rambled.

"It wasn't <u>my</u> ruckus," Matt interrupted.

The ranger looked quizzically, then a look of recognition came over him. "I know, it was that Kate Halliard he was harassing."

"Choking," Matt corrected again.

"What?" The ranger was incredulous.

"He was choking her. In the alley next to the ice cream shop." Matt was still hot.

"Jesus, I didn't know that. The goddamn piece of shit was choking her?" The warden looked truly surprised.

"You wouldn't have known that from down where you and your truck were," Matt pointed to the green fish and wildlife pickup truck by the pistol range.

"Jesus Christ, I'm sorry. Shit, I fucked up on that!"

"Where you get that mouth?" Matt asked with a slight grin.

The ranger suddenly went red in the face, embarrassed. "Army," the man said. "My wife's on me about it. I'm trying to clean it up."

"Well, it's going real well I see," Matt said flatly.

"Oh, shit, yeah," the man said, and held out his hand. "Sam Hood's my name. And I am sorry I didn't jump in the other day. Truth be told, I'm ashamed of myself."

"Next time, help a brother out, huh?"

"Brother? You the law or are you Army?" he asked.

Matt just stared back at the warden. Hood let the wheels turn a minute and then blurted, "Shit, you're both!"

Matt knew he was caught. He just nodded slightly and turned back toward the shooting bench. Hood stayed on Matt. "Where you learn to shoot like that?"

"Army," Matt said simply.

"Bullshit," Hood replied. "Not in the Army I was in. You went to sniper school." Then thinking of how Matt had handled LaDue he added, "Maybe more than that."

Matt tried to turn the tables. "What Army were you in?"

"Eighth Armored. I got some sand in my boots."

"You in-country in '90?" Matt asked, referring to Gulf War I.

Hood nodded affirmatively. "You, too, huh?"

Matt just nodded.

"What outfit, Rangers?"

"I had been with the Rangers, but had a different assignment during the war," Matt offered elusively.

Hood furrowed his brow. "Advisor?" he asked, referring to the Special Ops units that went in early to organize the Kurds or any other disenfranchised group.

"Something like that." He then pressed three .280 cartridges into the Browning magazine and clipped it into the rifle. Smoothly picking the rifle up and pointing down range, he shot three times in succession. Very quick succession.

Hood had his binoculars up looking down range. He let out a low whistle. "Can you do that every time?"

"I find that it's more difficult with a bee on the end of my nose." Matt was speaking as he looked through his spotting scope at the cloverleaf quarter sized pattern of the three holes in the target paper. He looked up at Hood and they exchanged amused looks.

Suddenly, the game warden had a look of deep thought. "You a deer hunter?"

"Have been. Thought I might wander around this fall."

Hood pursed his lips still figuring. "Can ya shoot a pistol?"

Matt was getting intrigued. "I do alright."

"Yeah, I'll bet. Tell you what," he went on, "I have to qualify with this damn Glock down at Waterbury next week and I have a problem." Hood held up a piece of target paper he had been using.

"I can see that," Matt said as he looked at the wildly scattered shots on the paper. "Was that at twenty-five yards or fifty yards?"

"Ten," the warden said, looking sheepish.

"Geez." Matt was chuckling now. "Did you have your eyes open? That can be real helpful, you know."

"Okay, okay." The ranger was starting to look stressed. "Here's the deal. I show you where to hunt, you get me ready for Waterbury."

Matt knew the ranger was referring to the state offices in Waterbury, Vermont, about ten miles southwest of Montpelier, the capitol. This got Matt's attention. No one spent more time in the woods than a game warden. They knew every hot spot and hell hole in the woods.

"I help you with that Glock, and you put me on a buck to write home about?"

"That's the deal," Hood responded, then adding, "but no guarantees; I can't hunt for you. You have to do that. I just put ya in the right neighborhood."

"Wouldn't have it any other way," Matt responded. Looking at the target paper in Hood's hand, he added, "I'm not making any guarantees either!"

Chapter 13

Buck was incognito. He didn't drive his old red International Scout much. The old truck was not only rough and tired, the engine was diesel. Unlike modern diesel systems, this truck was next to impossible to start in cold weather. This being Northern Vermont, the old rust bucket was virtually useless in all but the depth of summer. But Buck was having fun. He knew that everyone in the county recognized his old blue Chevy pickup, but most people didn't even know about the old Scout.

Buck knew that Kate worked — something to do with nursing, but he couldn't figure the schedule. She came and went at all different times of day. He couldn't pattern it. About the only thing he saw that resembled a schedule was when that hippie bitch from down at the foo-foo market came to the house to give Kate's whelp a music lesson. *Music lessons, by Jesus, the brat will be in a dress next.* Buck was disgusted. If that Kate Halliard would just smarten up, she'd see that he could fill all her needs. He'd have the boy drinking hard and runnin' the ridges in no time. He'd be a man or Buck would lay the wood to him. And he'd fuck that Kate so regular she'd walk around town with a perpetual smile on her face. Why, he'd make her nearly exclusive.

Buck drove past Kate's house and parked in the brush of the abandoned farm fifty yards past the Halliard house. He rolled the windows down, turned the old AM radio on softly and got out his beat-up binoculars.

Kate was putting the final touches on the food for the picnic. When she heard a truck through the open windows of the house, she was afraid Matt had missed the house. She quickly wrapped up her work and went out on the front porch. She looked down the road both directions.

Kate had on a light colored sundress with a belt pulled to a bow in the back showing off her figure. Her auburn hair was pulled back softly and held in place with a cloth bow that matched the sundress. Aside from the tan sandals, she wore no other adornment. No jewelry. No makeup. She looked stunning.

A truck came up over the hill near Kate's house. It was a dark green Jeep Cherokee. Kate was now turned toward it waving. The Jeep pulled into the yard and stopped. A big man got out.

"Hey, Matt," Kate said loudly across the yard.

"Hey, Kate. You look terrific."

"You clean up all right yourself."

Matt looked down at his faded, but thankfully clean golf shirt, his brown ranger belt and chinos. He was doubtful.

"Come on in. I need a good packhorse to carry this stuff," Kate continued as she turned back toward the wood screen door.

Matt glided across the lawn and up onto the porch behind her.

Kate passed a very large dog that was intent on cornering the newcomer. "That's Brutus; he's friendly when we want him to be."

"Is this one of those times?" Matt was regarding the passive animal.

"Absolutely. Come on back when you're done sizing each other up."

"Where do you keep the saddle for this pony?" Matt quipped as he knelt on one knee to greet the big slobbering hound. Matt started purring to the big dog. "Hey, big boy. How you doing?" he said as he scratched Brutus' chest with one hand and top of his head with another.

A moment later, Kate stepped out into the hallway holding a big stainless bowl in one hand and pinged it with a giant dog treat shaped like a bone. She looked as if she was playing an instrument. Brutus must have liked the tune because he jerked around and trotted back toward Kate and the kitchen. Matt followed.

"His weak point is his stomach," Kate explained.

"Mine, too," Matt said as he looked around the big country kitchen. "But a dog bone won't cut it with me, unless I'm <u>really</u> hungry."

"How about picking up that cooler and that picnic basket — full of dog bones," Kate ordered as she grabbed a blanket off the counter and roughed up Brutus' head as she passed him.

"Yes, ma'am," Matt saluted and grabbed the two items. "Lead the way."

"I love a man who knows who's in charge," Kate said as she headed toward the front door, Matt in tow. "Brutus, watch the house," she yelled over her shoulder.

Brutus tilted his head when he heard his name and returned an inquisitive look.

As they went out onto the front porch and down the steps toward the Jeep, Matt glanced around and then locked in on something to his right. "What's down there?" he nodded still holding the cooler in one hand and basket in the other.

Kate looked toward his gesture. She knew that an old abandoned homestead was next down the road, but she also knew that from her house the ruins were totally camouflaged by overgrowth. "Abandoned house," she answered. "Why?" She was looking down the road seeing nothing.

"No reason," Matt answered distractedly, still studying the landscape. "Thought I saw a fox is all."

Buck LaDue froze in his seat. He had been watching

toward Kate's house, seething all the while. At first he was relieved that they had reappeared on the front porch. He could hardly stand the thought of them together in the house screwing. They hadn't had time for that. Maybe just some kissy-face-grab-ass.

But now he was sitting stock-still. Buck was a hunter and a pretty good one at that. He knew that when observing prey, movement gave you away faster than anything.

He couldn't believe it when the big man stepped out of the house and looked directly at him. Then they were both looking at him. Buck held the binoculars to his face until his arms ached. Beads of sweat formed on his upper lip making it itch. But he didn't dare move. *Jesus, don't tell me the shithead has radar.* A bee flew into the open window of the old Scout and was buzzing around the cab. *Look away and get in the goddamn Jeep.*

Finally, the woman went to the vehicle and the big man followed. But not before looking over his shoulder one more time. Mercifully, the Jeep finally started, turned around in the yard and headed down the road the other way.

As Kate busied herself laying out the meal, Matt lounged on the blanket taking in the surroundings. He was in a near state of total relaxation when he heard the far off clatter of a diesel engine. The sound came closer and slowed to an idle. The engine revved again slightly and sounded like it was going away now, and then it shut off. Kate wasn't even aware of the sound as she prepared lunch.

Matt rose, stretched his arms above his head and announced he'd be right back.

As Buck rounded a curve in the road, he was suddenly struck by a thought. He was confused when the Jeep hadn't turned toward town. He was careful not to get close enough to be seen. He followed by watching for dust kicked up on the road. When the dust went away from town at the turnoff, he couldn't figure out where the shithead was going. Now he replayed the scene back at Kate's house — cooler, basket, blanket — the two lovebirds were going down to the town park by the lake at the end of the road. *Now ain't that ducky*, he thought as he rolled to a stop on the road.

Buck decided to back the truck up around the curve in the road and then go up on foot for a look around. When he got the Scout stopped, he opened the door quietly and picked up the binoculars and the assault rifle. He didn't think he'd shoot the bastard here, but carrying the weapon made him feel good.

As he crept forward, he contemplated the stillness ahead of him and thought of the blanket Kate was carrying. He felt his face get hot as he thought, *They're probably on that blanket having a good fuck in front of God, and anybody on the lake.* His hand tightened on the rifle.

When he rounded the curve, he saw a faint game trail coming off the hill to his right. He angled up the trail into a clump of white pines. The ground around the trees was covered with a blanket of brown needles. A few large rocks broke up the landscape.

Buck crouched down and moved silently forward through the pine needle carpet. He eased up behind a rock with a flat top and he knelt down resting his elbows on the rock as he scanned through the binoculars toward the park. He was just settled in looking at the top of the Jeep parked by the lake and some occasional movement near the big maple tree in the park. He was focused intensely on that area when he slipped a bit on the rock and the binoculars sagged down to the brush below him. Movement.

Buck switched the binoculars urgently to the undercover below him and out about fifty yards. He could see a person's head bobbing through the brush. Headed his way. His first instinct was to bring up the rifle but then he thought better of it. *Not here; not with my bright red truck parked out here on the road. Someone may already have seen it.*

Quickly, Buck slid back from the rock and scurried down through the pine needles. He stayed up on the wood's edge all the way to his truck. As he opened the door, it squeaked from age and inattention. He cursed himself softly for not hitting it with some WD-40. He quickly followed the binoculars and rifle he'd thrown into the truck. Fumbling, he stabbed the key into the ignition and fired up the engine, shoved the floor shifter into reverse and stepped on the accelerator. He continued that way for half a mile before he risked turning the truck around, so he could escape, driving forward.

As Matt moved up through the brush, he stopped periodically to look and listen. He was not being particularly careful and was already chiding himself for leaving Kate and going on this goose chase. The noise he had heard was probably some farmer out checking a fence or maybe even the town employee on the tractor that had mowed the park. He stopped for a moment thinking of cutting back up to the road where he could jog back to the park in a hurry. *How long had he been gone?*

Suddenly, Matt heard the creak of a car door then the sound of the diesel. He started sprinting sideways through the brush parallel to the road. He needed to see around the corner. Just as he thought, he saw a puff of dust and maybe a glint off of a vehicle. Red? He was stopped cold by a wall of needles. A huge berry patch, thorns and all, blocked his way. He stood still and listened to the diesel engine growing further away.

At first, Kate was pissed. She had everything ready and sat patiently estimating the time needed for a pit stop in the weeds. After tripling that time, she began to steam. *What the hell?* Anger began to fade to fear as the stillness around her settled in. She got up and headed for the brush where Matt disappeared.

"Matt!" she yelled. "Is everything okay?"

"Everything is fine," the voice came from behind her making her jerk, startled.

"Where the hell...." she began, but Matt was talking over her, smiling and holding out his hands.

"Look what I found! Dessert!" he said proudly as he displayed a huge handful of big blackberries.

"Jeez, Matt, I thought you fell in the lake." Kate was smiling, her fear and anger melting away.

Matt beamed as he dumped the berries onto the picnic basket lid. "Sorry, I couldn't help myself." He continued casually, "You know anyone with a red truck?"

Kate looked at Matt suspiciously and then back toward the road. "Yeah, about half the county. What's going on?"

Matt winced at his dumb question. "Nothing, I just thought I saw a red truck go by."

"Well, let's alert the media," Kate joked. "You always this hyper-vigilant?"

"Hey, I met a guy named Sam Hood. Game warden. Nice guy," Matt said.

This guy moves faster than I can keep up, Kate thought.

"Yes, I know Sam. I know his wife Sara better. When I first came up here she was pregnant and was one of our first patients. Prenatal care is a big piece of this project we're doing up here." She thought about Sam and Sara — and their little boy Josh and the new baby Jason. She thought about how loving they were toward one another and how close-knit they were. She envied them that. "They're wonderful people." Then she added, "It's a little hard for them, Sam being the game warden. Some people think he's sneaking up on them when they're in the woods, but he's just doing his job. They're very good people," she added again. "Where did you meet him?"

As they ate, Matt told Kate about running into the ranger at the gun range that morning. He told her the whole story, including the part about Sam being parked down the road in town during the altercation with Buck LaDue.

Kate interrupted Matt's story. "You mean to tell me that Sam stood there at his truck and didn't lift a finger?"

Chapter 14

How big of a lie should I tell?

Matt was lying on his back, looking up at the big white puffy clouds gliding by on the light breeze in the cobalt sky. He smiled to himself as he thought about the now soggy bologna sandwiches and warm cola in the Jeep and compared it to the feast he had just consumed.

The grilled margarita-marinated chicken, the <u>real</u> German potato salad, the soft multi-grain bread that was still warm in the tin foil wrapped around the warming stone, the split of Riesling to augment the tea and the soft chewy double fudge brownies, all floated softly through his head like the clouds in the sky. The red truck was long gone and no other alarms sounded.

Kate had been busy cleaning up, but was now stretched out on her side, elbow on the ground with her head in her hand as she looked toward the lake.

"You want to go first?" Matt broke the silence.

"Go first at what?"

Matt knew she knew. "Go on, tell me the whole story. And start from the very beginning. I want to hear it all."

Kate sighed as she laid back and looked up at the sky also.

They told each other their stories.

"Your Mom was a deputy sheriff?" Matt was a little incredulous. That must have been interesting in a household of three girls and a single mom."

Matt had been fascinated by Kate's story of growing up in an all-girl environment. Kate had told him about her father being killed in a car-train accident when she and her two sisters, one older, one younger, were quite young.

"Are you kidding," she said. "It was great. We got the skinny on everything happening in town. Elyria, Ohio isn't very big. We knew all about every punk and bully in town. Everyone in school came to my sisters and me for the real scoop. They thought Mom was really cool -- and she was".

"So, she carried a gun and the whole bit?"

"Sure, she would come home, unstrap the gunbelt, put it on top of the refrigerator, put on an apron over her uniform and start dinner. She was a great cook and really into discipline at the table. We used to sing, 'I fought the law and the law won,' drove her crazy."

Matt had heard Kate's description of her husband, a doctor at Dartmouth, passing away.

"So you came to the Kingdom to escape?"

"Something like that. I wanted Nick to be insulated."

"No man in your life?"

"Nick has been the man in my life. And what's your

deal?" Matt wasn't sure if he was being mocked.

"So, that's pretty much it. Blue collar home in Worcester Massachusettes, a little college, Army, now I work for the U.S. Marshall's office."

Kate was uneasy. Matt's story was plausible but full of omissions, she was sure. Like, how did he receive the bullet scars she had seen when she was patching him up after the Buck LaDue altercation? He was holding back. And she was scared -- scared for herself and for her son. She was intuitive, and her intuition told her that this guy was trouble.

Chapter 15

Should have shot the bastard right there at the lake, he boasted to himself.

Buck pulled his red truck into Rashid's store. He told himself that he didn't because he didn't want to hit Kate. She might have been there in the brush with the interloper. Positioning it this way made him feel almost gallant. And allowed him to push back the miserable truth. He was scared, afraid to pull the trigger. When he saw Striker's head coming through the brush, he couldn't see his hands. He might have been armed. If he missed the son-of-a-bitch, he might have been fired on himself. It was a sensible decision. Hell, he had been holding a rifle he'd never shot before. Not even one <u>like</u> it.

But now he had it worked out. He knew where the ambush would be. He smiled as he parked the little red truck and turned his attention to his need for a carton of Marlboros.

"He spend too much time with the infidels," Rashid complained to Shuriana.

Shuri wanted to laugh but knew it would lead to no

good. Here they were making a life among these people of the Kingdom. The closest mosque was in St. Johnsbury. Hardly a palace, it consisted of a space rented in an old strip shopping center. Linoleum floors, harsh fluorescent lights, white walls and a ragtag of regulars. Infidels indeed. If Rami, and for that matter she and Rashid, didn't spend most of their time with so-called infidels, who would they spend time with?

"But, Husband, there are no other followers of Islam here. What are we to do?" she skillfully put it back on him.

Rashid shook his head in frustration. He was under pressure. The cryptic e-mails were coming regularly now. All the needs, all the preparation. Did they think him a magician?

Shuri was spending time with these American women. She was being ogled by men coming into the store. Rami spent nearly all his free time with the pushy lady's son, Nick. And he himself was being seduced by this America. But these e-mails were like a dark, tormenting nightmare. If bin Seidu came now and saw how degenerate they were, they would <u>all</u> be killed. It was all spinning out of control. One day he was an accomplished, prosperous merchant; the next he was a peon, an errand boy to a nearly forgotten force far away. He thought his head would explode.

"Then the boy can spend more time at home — reading the Koran," Rashid continued lamely. "Why is he permitted to spend so much time in the home of a woman who does not know her...." He didn't have a chance to say, "her place," as his eyes locked on a red truck pulling into the lot. It looked like Buck LaDue driving, though he'd never seen him in that truck.

Rashid shot out the door before the truck stopped rolling. Shuri watched from inside the store. She had a worried look on her face.

Rashid didn't wait for the occupant of the red truck to emerge. He walked around to the driver's side and tapped on the glass. It was unlike him to be so bold.

Rashid slapped the window of Buck's truck.

"What the... Jesus Christ, Rashid." Buck tore the door open. "You tryin' to give me a fuckin' heart attack?"

Buck had just picked up his foam cup, then jerked and spilled coffee all over himself and the inside of the truck.

"God damn, look at the.... look at my truck," Buck ranted. "What the hell you doin' sneakin' up like that, you little..." He wanted to say ragheaded runt, but thought better of it.

"By God, you're lucky it was me in here. Some fellas would come out and stomp you to the pavement."

Rashid looked stunned. He ran over to the gas pumps and pulled a wad of paper towels out of the dispenser and ran back to the truck. He started to wipe coffee off Buck.

"Goddamnit, I'll do it," Buck roared as he snatched the

towels away. He took a couple towels and poked them at Rashid. "Here, you clean up the truck. I'll take care of me."

Rashid turned red. He was just starting on the seat of the truck. The rifles were behind the seat.

Buck jerked Rashid around with a heavy hand on the smaller man's shoulder. "Forget it, the damage is done. I need to get some smokes." Buck slammed the truck door, pushed a wad of used towels into Rashid's hands and started to the store.

"But...." Rashid was stammering as he followed Buck, his arms full of paper towels. He ran ahead of Buck and pushed his load into the trash container by the door of the store and turned to face Buck, blocking him. "I need those rifles."

"Don't worry, it's taken care of." Buck started to step around the little man.

Rashid sidestepped in front of Buck, stopping him again. "You don't understand. I need them right away and there are more things I need. Things that you will profit from."

Buck took the bait. He stopped and looked around to see if they were being watched. It appeared that everyone at the pumps and in the store was in their own worlds. He took Rashid by the shoulder and headed him to the gravel lot behind the store.

"What else you need and how much are we talkin'?" Buck asked.

"First the rifles," Rashid said.

Buck dropped his head and swore under his breath then looked back up. "I <u>told</u> you, the rifles are taken care of."

"I need them. Now!"

Buck didn't like being cornered. "Where do you want them delivered?"

Rashid brightened. "Up at the warehouse. Do you know where it is?"

Buck snorted. "That old Quonset hut was up there long before you came to town."

"I meet you there at four o'clock," Rashid looked anxious.

"Tomorrow," Buck said casually.

"Today," Rashid whined.

"Goddamnit, four o'clock tomorrow, and that's it." *Ragheads!*

Chapter 16

Pop, pop, pop.

He could hear the crack of a rifle.

Sam Hood liked to drive on the road that went past Matt Striker's place. There were several meadows along the road, including the big meadow in front of Matt's place where deer came out to feed on a regular basis. He told himself he was doing his job, but the truth was that sometimes he liked to sit in his dark green truck, sip coffee and watch the deer. Their behavior was fascinating. He guessed not too many people had seen two does rise up on hind legs and fight each other with front hooves like two boxers going at each other. It was quite a sight. As he sat there in the early light, he thought he could see a truck pulled off the side of the road. *Poacher? Could be.*

Sam was sweat-covered before he even started to move to the tree line.

Matt awakened at his house and immediately thought of the picnic the day before. His mood was both buoyant and mellow. He was willingly falling into this web called Kate Halliard. When he had dropped her off, he walked

Kate to the door and hopefully leaned toward her for another kiss. Kate had put her hand on his chest and said, "Hold that thought, Cowboy, and we'll have something to look forward to." They had both smiled and Matt had gallantly backed off. If the idea was to leave him wanting, it sure had worked. Everything he did this morning after was automatic.

He pulled on his running shorts and shoes, knocked down a bottle of Propel fitness drink and headed to the downstairs deck.

Each morning Matt would get up, get hydrated, do a few exercises on his front deck and then take a run up the mountain trail behind his house. When he returned he would work out on the heavy bag in the downstairs corner and expand that into a series of martial arts practice moves. Today, the day after the picnic, was no exception.

Matt walked out onto his lower deck and stretched his tall frame. It was a cool, crisp, beautiful northwoods morning. No deer in the field today, he observed. *Maybe they were here earlier.*

He walked to the edge of the deck, stretched up to grab the top of the end rafter and started on his pullups, bringing his head up between the joists of the floor of the upper deck.

One, two, three, four.

Whack, whack, whack. Wood began to splinter and explode all around him. The rifle cracks quickly followed each whack of a bullet traveling into the house. Matt dropped in a pile on the lower deck.

When Buck slid down through the woods in the near dark of early morning holding an assault rifle, he felt like a Ninja commando. He knew how to move quietly in the woods. A lifetime of hunting -- and poaching -- had taught him that. But he'd never done anything quite like this. As he got down close to the meadow that extended up one side of Matt Striker's house, he was startled by a bunch of deer that had winded him and were blowing as they turned and ran back up the mountain.

Buck recovered from the familiar sound quickly enough, but still had a bit of a shake going. It wasn't that he was cold. It was crisp out but not cold by any stretch. Was it fear, or anticipation? He didn't spend much time sorting it out, but he knew if he didn't calm down, he wouldn't be able to shoot worth spit. He took a deep breath and settled in behind an overgrown stone wall at the edge of the woods and meadow. He sat very still. Jesus, he'd like a smoke. Couldn't chance it. He was settled in for the long haul, but thought this bugger might be a health nut and could be out sooner than later. He looked the type.

Buck wasn't disappointed. He had barely gotten settled in when he saw Matt come momentarily into view then out of view at the corner of the front porch. He could see the bastard was struttin' round in nothin' but a pair of shorts like he was some kind of big he-man or something. *Jesus, this guy is full of it!*

Buck wiggled a little bit and got a rest on one of the wall rocks for the assault rifle. He was bringing the shithead into his sight picture when his hands started to shake again. *Damn it! Settle down. He don't have no weapon. He's putting both hands up on the rafter; can't hurt ya now. Shoot the bastard.*

As Buck squeezed the trigger, the little rifle bucked. He pulled the trigger two more times quickly. He thought he saw the man drop. *Got 'em, maybe.* He shot three more times at the corner of the house where the man disappeared, waited to see if anything moved, then sprayed three more rounds.

Sam Hood heard a total of nine shots and knew this was no hunting rifle that was firing. He hunched even lower and pulled his Glock 40 from its holster. Should he go back to the truck and get his rifle? *No time. Keep going, go easy.*

Just as he started to move again, he saw a figure on the porch of the house at the end of the meadow. Striker's house. The man was wearing blue shorts, running shorts, and was moving quickly off the end of the deck away from him.

What did he have in his hand? What the fuck's going on here?

He continued to move on up toward the spot where

the shooting seemed to be coming from.

When Matt hit the floor of the porch, he instinctively rolled toward the house and scrambled back toward the door. Using the doorframe as cover, he quickly stretched up to a shelf above the inside of the door and pulled down a strange hunk of plastic and metal. He reached up and grabbed a long black narrow object and then dropped back to the floor. He was counting the shots. It was nine now. Assault rifle. Or someone very good and very fast at slapping clips into a hunting rifle. But they had missed clean. Assault rifle.

Matt was working this out as he levered what looked like a trigger guard on the strange mass in his hands. As he did so, the little object folded out neatly into a small assault rifle. A KelTec Sub 2000, nine millimeter. He slapped home the long narrow object, a Glock 32 round magazine, pulled the bolt to jack up the first round, and scrambled off the porch away from the gunfire. He would flank the shooter in a wide arch keeping a rocky ridge-back between him and the gunfire. He was sprinting now, his soft running shoes making little noise on the packed trail. The shooter was silent now.

Was he on the run now, or reloading?

When Buck squeezed off the last three rounds, he was a basket case. He was hitting the side of the house, but that was all he was sure of. There was no response at all. Everything was strangely quiet. Buck's stomach was feeling queasy.

Jesus, had he actually killed the dumb bastard?

He was barely through that thought when he was up running. Running faster than he ever had in his life. As if getting away from this place would free him from the thought that he'd killed a man.

It was the dumb bastard's own fault. If he just hadn't been such an asshole, humiliating me in front of the whole town—and in front of that bitch, Kate Halliard. Hell, it was partially <u>her</u> fault too!

When Buck slid up to the truck, he flung the rifle through the open window and was in starting the truck in a split second. A moment later he was gone.

Matt had curled up around to a trail above where the shooting seemed to be coming from. He stopped to listen. He could hear faint sounds of movement up the trail away from the ambush site. A moment later he heard movement in the brush down the trail toward his house where the shooter had probably set up. He moved silently down the slope. He had gone about fifty yards when he saw a shape silhouetted by the meadow near his house. The man bent over behind the rock wall at the wood's edge. His back was to Matt — and he had a gun in his right hand.

Hood was moving cautiously up along the wood's edge. He followed an old rock wall for a hundred yards or so toward the gunfire. It was silent now.

What was the shooter doing? Who was the guy in the blue shorts and where was he?

The ranger's palms were wet with sweat in spite of the brisk morning. Beads of sweat formed on his upper lip and he wiped them away with his sleeve. He should have called in before he started up the hill. No one even knew where he was. Jesus, he wished he had his rifle or even a shotgun. Just as he had convinced himself to go back to the truck and call in for help, he spotted something shiny on the ground.

Empty cartridges. He was standing in the middle of them. They were all around him. He bent down to take a closer look. They looked like .223 caliber. The load used for varmint hunting rifles -- and for light assault rifles. Every western military used .223 cartridges by the ton. This was no varmint hunter or poacher for that matter throwing lead left and right. He was deep in thought when he felt cold steel pressed to the back of his head. A hard voice commanded, "Don't even twitch."

Matt had the drop on the guy, but there was something seriously wrong here.

Where is the rifle? Are there two men? Is the rifleman lurking around here? This guy is all dressed up in dark green.

He had laid his Glock on the ground as he was told.

"Oh, shit, Sam, is that you?"

"Matt? Good Christ, I thought I was dead." Sam's voice was shaky.

"You came damn close. What the hell are you doing up here? Stand up and turn around. I'm not gonna shoot ya."

"I heard shots, thought there was a poacher. Nice outfit."

Matt looked down at his running shorts and shoes. "Uh huh. You see anybody here?" Matt turned to look around and Sam imitated the action.

"No, I think we just missed him. But he left his calling card." Sam pointed to the empty shell casings on the ground.

Matt bent over and picked one of them up. "It's a .223. AR-15 maybe."

"That's what I was thinking. Did ya get hit?" Sam was looking at blood on the palm of Matt's left hand.

Matt absently turned his hand over. Splinters were sticking out of the meaty flesh below his thumb on his palm. Blood oozed out. "One of the rounds must have hit the rafter I was holding onto."

Sam nodded like he understood. "You think it was

a prank?"

"Maybe," Matt lied. "What do you think?"

Sam Hood knew his business. He looked at all the shells, Matt's hand and then down toward Matt's house. Even from here the pockmarks of bullets on the side of the house were visible.

"No way." Hood started toward the road and his truck.

"You gonna have to call this in?" Matt was hopeful he wouldn't.

"My ass if I don't. Don't touch anything. I'll meet you at the house." The ranger hadn't even stopped or turned around. Matt watched Hood's back and slipped one of the .223 casings into his pocket. He started toward the house, reaching for his knife. He wanted one of the slugs out of the side of the house before the cavalry showed up.

Matt was sitting on the lower deck, mission accomplished, when Sam Hood's green pickup came up his drive. The ranger walked up near Matt but kept his eyes on the bullet holes in the side of the house. "Inside of the house messed up?"

"A little. Not bad. Spackling and paint."

"I called this in as vandalism. It went to the sheriff, not the state police."

"Thanks." Matt knew Hood was trying to

accommodate him.

"Look, the sheriff here isn't stupid. It won't take him long to figure this was more than vandalism." Hood wanted to cover himself. "You get a slug and a casing?"

This ranger was pretty sharp. "Yeah, I got them."

Hood shook his head affirmatively. "You'll get faster results than the locals. But I'm warning you, you can't go Lone Ranger on this. I don't see a federal crime here."

"I know how it works."

"So, are you on duty now or still off?"

"Off," Matt replied definitively.

"Suit yourself. But you gotta show your shield to the sheriff when he gets here."

"Like I said, I know how it works."

"So. Buck LaDue?" the ranger asked.

"Who else?"

Chapter 17

When Buck rolled into his house, he was covered with sweat. Without breaking stride he went straight for the phone and dialed. "Got your delivery," he told the person who answered. "Meet me in twenty minutes."

"We said four o'clock," Rashid sounded bewildered.

"Goddamnit, yesterday you were on my ass about these things, now you want to wait. Do you want them or not?"

"Yes. And I have other needs as well." Rashid was being pressed by the e-mails so he pressed Buck in turn.

"Yeah, yeah, yeah. Twenty minutes."

When the sheriff's car pulled into the driveway at Matt Striker's cabin, it wasn't the sheriff who got out of the car.

"Hey, Sally," Hood smiled as he greeted Sergeant Sally Munson, Sheriff's Deputy, Kingdom County. He took it as a good sign that the sheriff himself hadn't come out.

"Hey, Sam, what we got?"

The game warden introduced Sergeant Munson to Matt and Matt showed his credentials. The deputy looked him over carefully and listened to their stories. They walked her up to the shooter's nest where she picked up spent cartridges using her pencil and placed them in a baggie. She pointed to a worn trail going up from the ambush site.

"Where's that go?" The sergeant looked at Striker.

"Up to a neighbor's farm. A small fork goes out to the road."

"You guys go up the trail, talk to the neighbors, look by the road?"

Hood jumped in. "Nope. Didn't want to mess things up for you folks."

The deputy nodded, looked up the trail, then back down at the house. "Let's survey the damage."

Back at the house, the sergeant made a sketch of the side of the house, marking where the bullets had hit the house. When she finished, she walked over to where Matt and Sam stood watching the officer.

"Eight hits to the house."

Matt and Sam stayed silent.

The deputy looked around as if she expected help from some quarter. She looked back and fixed a stare on Matt Striker's hand, looking at a fresh bandage.

"Hurt yourself?"

"Slipped when I tried to flank the shooter," Matt said. He didn't want the deputy to know that he had been shot at. Then it would be attempted homicide. Call in the cavalry. Lose control.

The sergeant eyed Matt suspiciously and then turned slowly to the game warden. "What were you doing here?"

"Lots of deer in these fields in the early morning. Poachers know that too."

"So you just happened along?"

"Parked out by the road. Had my window down to listen."

The sergeant nodded. Made sense enough she guessed. She looked back at Striker. "Been here long enough to piss anybody off?"

Matt and Sam Hood exchanged glances. Matt knew he would have to tell the deputy about his run-in with Buck LaDue. She was going to find out. Might as well be *his* spin.

The sergeant listened to Matt's short, simple version of the story and wrote notes. When Matt was finished, she got Matt's phone number and closed her book.

"I'll backtrack the trail then see if the neighbors know anything," the sergeant stated, all business. Then added, "Assault rifle maybe, ambush, inhabited dwelling." She looked hard at Game Warden Sam Hood. "And you called this in as vandalism?"

The warden flushed and shot a hapless look at Striker. "Could have been more," he said lamely. Hood already had a bit of a reputation when it came to LaDue. This was just going to make matters worse.

Munson snorted and started for the car. "Stay put a minute; I gotta talk to the sheriff."

In less than thirty minutes, a white Jeep Grand Cherokee pulled up to Matt's house. The man that emerged was a stocky man, well past middle age. He wore jeans, Rocky boots, a dark blue hooded sweatshirt and a ball cap from L.L. Bean. The hat had a small gold pin just above the bill. It was in the shape of a star and in tiny letters it said Sheriff. It was the only mark of I.D. that suggested the man under the cap was Sheriff Dick Drew.

Sheriff Drew spoke alone to Sergeant Munson and then approached Striker and Hood. Munson was now walking up through the field toward the shooter's nest by the stone wall.

The warden introduced Matt Striker and Striker showed his badge. The sheriff looked at the I.D. and Striker carefully. Hood started to speak again. Sheriff Drew held the palm of his hand up to stop him as he walked past the two men and positioned himself to look at the side of the house. Matt and the warden stood where they were as the sheriff alternately inspected the house and looked up the field where Sergeant Munson had gone. He pulled up the side of his sweatshirt and unclipped a small radio hanging on his belt next to a pearl handled Colt 45 automatic resting in a Desantis holster. He fingered the radio then walked back to Striker and Hood.

"Let's sit," the sheriff was smiling and nodding toward the porch. Before he sat on the edge of the porch, he added, "The sergeant's gonna back-track that trail up there. She'll be gone a few minutes." The smile on his face faded as he continued. "I got attempted murder, maybe; assault on a federal officer for pretty sure. And Munson says you guys are talking vandalism. So how about we cut all the bullshit and you two tell me what's going on here."

Hood gave Matt an affirming nod and Matt returned it. They told the sheriff everything.

"A shooting, right?" he said, referring to Matt's leave.

Matt seemed to cloud over slightly as he thought back to the last arrest warrants he and his team had served. And of the woman he had killed. He nodded, said nothing.

The sheriff studied him carefully before he turned back to the warden. Hood knew it was his turn.

"A, this guy was doing fine with LaDue and B, I've got a history with...."

The sheriff cut him off.

"Yeah, yeah, with Buck LaDue and you harassing him and all that happy horseshit! But I want to tell you, Hood, it wasn't my people who came down on you, it was your own. And I don't give a shit about what you do outside Kingdom County, but inside, you're the law same as me and I expect you to act like it. You have a problem with Waterbury or Montpelier, have 'em talk to me," referring to the State Police, DNR (Department of Natural Resources) and then the legislature. He continued his rant. "We got miles and miles of wilderness up here and lonely back roads and trails going every which way. I got limited resources and you." The sheriff was now poking Hood with a finger. "You <u>are</u> a law enforcement officer. I need you to act like it."

Hood, duly admonished, just nodded.

"And as for you," the sheriff turned back toward Matt softening his voice, "I'm a fair judge of character. I'm going to guess a good shooting?"

Matt looked a bit dully at the sheriff as he replied. "Good, maybe, but ugly."

The sheriff had been in his business a long time. Without the details he knew what that meant. He had an emotional tug that he concealed as he looked at Matt. "Part of the territory."

The sheriff walked back to the porch. Munson was with him now.

"We're going to go for a warrant. Pick up LaDue. See if we can find the rifle. The casings will go to Waterbury and we'll need to dig the slugs out of the side of the house. If anybody heard the sergeant on their scanner when she called me this morning, this is going to be in the paper. Maybe even television and radio. Depends on what they smell. But we're not going to call in the state and if the feds are coming in, that will be your call." The sheriff was looking at Matt. "Let's go a step at a time. See what shakes loose." He tipped his hat and waved at the sergeant to leave. He said over his shoulder, "Don't mess up the scene." In fifteen seconds he and the sergeant were driving out.

Chapter 18

Matt walked out on his upper deck to improve the spotty reception of his cell phone. In most of the remote Northeast Kingdom, cell phones were useless.

"What?" came the terse voice on the other end.

"What kind of greeting is that for your old partner?"

"Kemo Sabe?" The voice perked up considerably.

"Hey, Detto, where the hell are you? You sound out of breath."

"Yeah, we're running a little deal over here at Norwich."

Norwich University in Northfield, Vermont, was the oldest private military school in the country. While it had its fair share of great warriors as alumni, including several Congressional Medal of Honor recipients, it was uniquely known for its leadership development in both the military curriculum as well as the civilian side of the program. In spite of the inevitable and rare occurrences of hazing, harassment and horseplay, the university had provided a steady supply of great thinkers, doers, captains of industry and inspired military leaders. One of the institution's products was four-star General and former Army Chief of Staff Gordon R. Sullivan, now Chairman of the University Board of Trustees.

There was truly something special about Norwich, and a few hours on campus made it impossible not to detect it, even to the most oblivious.

Major Vito Debenedetto, or "Detto" as he was known to his friends and colleagues, was a periodic resource to Norwich. His considerable expertise in counterterrorism came from real-life experience in "Indian country" across the globe. And not only had Matt been there for most of it, Matt had been the ranking member of the team.

Some of the exploits of these two men would never, could never be known lest they trigger any number of international crises, protests, or congressional investigations. Hell, they would have been hanged by some in their own country if the complete truth were told. Neither man was brutal or cruel in nature, but they had created murder and mayhem in backcountry corners of the world in the name of domestic security.

They were proud to serve and protect their country. But they were both affected over time, each in different ways. For Vito Debenedetto's part, he was overwhelmed with an ever-increasing sense of urgency about stopping international bad guys. He was never satisfied with the progress, nearly paranoid that the slack-kneed politicians would give up, walk away or go into a bargaining stance. Debenedetto had seen the threat up close, and to say that he had a regard for the dedicated ferocity of the enemy would be an understatement in the extreme. He knew they would never stop in his lifetime and his answer <u>always</u> was to strike first. It consumed him.

Matt, on the other hand, was afflicted with a constant obsession to be the guardian of all good things around him. His country, his men, his foreign allies, and his friends alike. And he carried this self-perceived responsibility like a backpack full of rocks strapped to his shoulders. Every botch in a mission, every missed opportunity, every lost or wounded comrade weighed heavily on Matt as a personal shortcoming. The constant accolades from up the chain of command heralding his many successes were little consolation to his perceptions of failing those around him. Only he could see it. Most people around him were unaware of his torment.

Matt knew his biggest personal failure was the inability to create a balance to his life. Even Detto had a wife, two great kids and an extended family that was wacky and terrific at the same time.

Matt was conflicted beyond words. He longed for a "real" life. But in his warped view, a serious relationship was more guardian responsibilities, more rocks in the backpack. He feared it would bring him to his knees.

He stayed conflicted, yet took on more and more. Until one day he contacted the colonel running the Delta unit he was unofficially assigned to and, in essence, said he had to take the bag of rocks off — at least for a while. So here he was at his childhood haunt in Vermont's Northeast

Kingdom, doing what?

"How committed are you over there?" Matt asked.

"We finished this morning. Sully's gone and the Admiral's packing up. Season's over, everyone's gonna be outta here," Vito explained.

"Got your black bag?"

"Always." Detto was a little indignant.

"When can you be here?"

Chapter 19

Matt spent the afternoon watching the crime scene team from Sheriff Drew's office take measurements, look at angles, dig bullets out of his house, take pictures, and write notes. In about two hours they were packing up.

Matt strolled out to a burly man in a deep rust-colored sport coat.

"Can I patch her up now?" Matt pointed to the house.

The big man looked around and thought for a moment. "Sure, we got all we need."

Kate Halliard picked up her phone then put it down. Picked it up again, then put it down. Connie Cutter had called her.

Normally there was a considerable lack of excitement in the Kingdom. Opportunities to be breathless just didn't present themselves. But to increase the prospects of vicarious thrills, half the households it seemed had a police emergency scanner, and half of these households actually listened to the chatter from time to time. Two different people who had heard that something was going on with the sheriff up on Burke Hill, came into Connie Cutter's organic market clucking about it.

Kate looked at the phone one more time, then the clock, then her car keys.

And then what? Say, "I know I'm not your real mother but I wanted to check on you?"

She took a deep breath and sat down.

Chapter 20

Matt heard the crunch of gravel again in his driveway. He blinked his eyes and looked down toward the road. At first he didn't recognize the car. The sleek black Monte Carlo was gliding along the drive as if it were a magic carpet. Except for a little wheel spray on the rocker panels, the black paint gleamed like it was three inches deep.

Gigi's car. What is Detto doing with Gigi's car?

Matt was up at the rail of the upper deck when the car stopped. A short, wide man with wavy black hair combed straight back emerged from the car and stood behind the enormous driver's side door.

"Kemo Sabe!" the man yelled up to Matt.

"Hey, does Gigi know you have the Batmobile?"

"Jeep wouldn't start and she's in Vegas with her sisters." The short man then grew very serious. "And don't you tell her neither!"

Matt held out the palms of his hands and smiled. "When did I ever sell you out?" As Vito Debenedetto started around the car door, Matt was changing the subject. "What's wrong with the Jee...holy shit! What the hell happened to you?"

Detto stopped and looked down at himself. He was so covered in mud and dirt it was difficult to see the fatigues and boots he was wearing. He smiled broadly for the first time.

"Dog River Run over at the school. Whenever the corps ends a semester or a special training, like we did this week, the corps, the instructors, even the Admiral takes a run down the Dog River," Vito explained gravely.

"So you did it too?"

"No, shit for brains. I stopped at a hog farm down the road and wallowed around before I came here. Yeah, I ran it too. And I'd a won except for I fell in a deep hole in the river which I did not know was there, but the smart-ass cadets did know." He got a look of admiration on his face. "They got some good kids over there. Smart. And some of them will be pretty tough warriors." This was high praise from Vito Debenedetto.

"They do good work over there," Matt added.

Detto returned to his caustic self and started marching toward Matt's house again.

"Hey!" Matt yelled. "You can't come in here like that!"

"I thought this was a manly, guy's cabin-in-da-woods kinda deal?" He was still marching forward almost to the house.

"Not even on the deck, Detto! Stop in the yard."

"No shit?" Vito looked genuinely disappointed.

"I shit you not," Matt barked an order to his former

subordinate. "Strip 'em there, soldier."

"Here?" Vito looked around the acres of green field in front of him.

"There!" Matt commanded. "Besides, when did you get modest?"

"When I became an adjunct assistant professor...." Detto was referring to his occasional training role at Norwich University. Major Vito Debenedetto, Retired, was a counter-terrorism expert of the highest caliber. "I got my reputation to consider."

"Yeah, I'll bring you some clothes. Drop that muddy mess where you stand." Matt disappeared into the house and reappeared on the lower deck. He had a bundle of clothes in his arms. O.D. colored sweatshirt and pants. He alternately looked at the pile of muddy boots and clothes and the black Monte Carlo.

"Why did you get in the car with all that mud on you? Gigi's gonna have your ass."

"Did you or did you not tell me to get my young ass up here A.S.A.P.?" Vito looked truly exasperated as he looked back at the car.

"I did say A.S.A.P.," Matt confessed. "But...."

"No 'buts,'" the stocky man held up a single finger. "I don't wanna hear no 'buts.' A.S.A.P. is A.S.A.P. It don't mean take a nice shower, pour a little scotch, sit on the porch, light a cigarette, all of which I would very much like to have done," Vito wagged the finger he still held up.

"No, it means get your ass over here, your buddy needs you."

Matt was actually starting to feel responsible. "Jesus, Detto, I didn't know you had Gigi's car." Vito was pulling the sweatsuit on as Matt was speaking. "How bad is the inside of the car?"

"Bad."

"You got a plan to clean it up?"

Vito shrugged. "No, but I will before I head back to Brooklyn, you can bet your ass on that!"

Matt began to snicker. He was six foot three, Detto was five foot seven. It was quite a sight to see Detto in Matt's sweatsuit. The sleeves and legs flopped but the chest, shoulders, thighs, and upper arms were stretched taut as a trampoline. Detto looked at Matt laughing.

"What?" he looked down at himself. "Shit, first I'm a mudball, now I'm one of them dwarfs. Sneezy, Sleezy...,"

"Dopey," Matt corrected.

"Yeah, whatever -- asshole."

It took three Rolling Rocks each for Matt to tell Vito what had gone on at Big Larch the past couple weeks.

Vito Debenedetto was an internal processor. He liked to roll things around in his mind awhile then boil them down to the lowest common denominators.

"Sooo, lemme get this straight. Some bumpkin, out here in the middle of Podunk, gets between you and a Dinktown Dolly," pause, "and you decide to call in the cavalry, which would be me, to straighten out this chickenshit mess you got yourself into."

"Stop, your sympathy for my predicament is overwhelming. Besides, she's not a 'Dinktown Dolly,' and did I mention my gunshot wound?" Matt held up his bandaged hand.

Vito had heard all about the splinter in Matt's hand and dismissed it with a wave.

"Are you saying you're head over ass over some backwoods maiden? I have observed your previous adventures in dis area so lemme guess, she has an ass you could serve drinks on, am I right? Because only <u>that</u> could explain you calling me up here. Have I missed anything?"

"Hey, do I talk about Gigi like that? Have a little respect here, will ya?"

"If you talked that way about Gigi, she'd kick your butt—besides, she has an ass like a shovel. But ya gotta admit, her boomers are first-rate!" Detto had a wistful smile on his face.

"Hey, could we reel this thing in to *my* problem at hand? Which by the way is that some dickhead is running around the woods spraying my house with bullets." Matt tossed a baggie with a shell casing he found in the ground and a bullet he dug out of his house. Vito caught the baggie and started examining it closely.

"Two twenty three. AR 15 or maybe a Ruger Mini," he observed flatly. Then he looked at the bullet. "Bigger, hard nose. Maybe a 62 gram?" Detto was all business now.

Matt had a functional knowledge of nearly anything that would shoot, but Vito Debenedetto made a science of it. He loved ballistics.

"Look at this." Vito turned the bag and pushed it in front of Matt's face.

Matt studied it closely but couldn't see whatever Detto could apparently see. "What?"

"Look at those extraction marks on the shell casing. Ever see a .223 look like that?"

"Hell, Detto, I don't know. What about them?" Matt was getting cranked up for some profound insight. Detto tossed the baggie on the table between them.

"Just looked a little different is all."

"Geez, Sherlock, I thought you were headed somewhere with that," Matt said.

"I'll send 'em down to the office. We'll take a close look at them down there. See if there's anything helpful."

"Down there" was ATF—Alcohol, Tobacco and Firearms in D.C. The shell and casing would go through their forensic lab for analysis.

Major Vito Debenedetto, Retired, was playing the same game that Major Matthew Striker, Retired, was playing.

The Defense Department had no domestic arrest capabilities. So, Vito was ushered over to the ATF and Matt to the U.S. Marshall's office. Both were appropriately deputized. The program had been cooked up by the CIA and Defense who were frustrated with the FBI's necessity of protecting jurisprudence in all situations.

The President had signed off on it. By planting two ex-Delta guys with federal law enforcement agencies, two purposes were served. The first was the overt and obvious advantage to those two agencies in running down terrorists that had entered the country -- or even homegrown ones -- with the aid of the best in the world at that activity. And covertly, both Vito and Matt -- as well as others like them sprinkled through other federal law enforcement -- could coordinate with the CIA and Delta when their pursuit of terrorists led back to domestic soil—without passing off to the FBI.

Many things changed after 9/11, including the broad umbrella of Homeland Security, the naming of a National Security Director and now, information was shared in new and effective ways between the agencies. But the CIA and the Defense Department's Delta unit were clandestine agencies, and when months of clandestine work led them back and forth across the U.S. border, they wanted their own assets in place for continuity and unquestioning commitment to the mission — whatever it was.

Vito and Matt were planted in their positions. The President knew, NSA knew, the heads of DEA, ATF, the U.S. Marshall's office, Secret Service, and D.O.E. knew, and yet there wasn't a shred of paper or an e-mail anywhere that could reveal it. The entire arrangement was accomplished by private meetings and whispers in ears.

And it worked. Some of the best assets behind the fence at Gitmo were picked up on domestic soil by Matt, Vito and several others like them. They were foiling plots, saving lives and getting key intel on a complicated web of brutal terrorists who knew no bounds. It was a system that was effective. The bonus was that Debenedetto had access to ATF's resources and Matt had the resources of the Marshall's office. They operated in a gray area, but that had been true for years in Delta. They were literally on the front line of national security. While opportunistic politicians railed against covert operations, black-ops as it was called, both foreign and domestic, a large portion of Americans went to bed at night and prayed that there was someone protecting them and their families. Someone like Matt or Vito.

"So, what do you want to do about this shooter in the meantime?"

"I don't want to do anything messy. This isn't a wet-work problem and we are in the U.S.A."

Debenedetto was looking disappointed. Matt looked at him and held up a hand like a traffic cop.

"Don't look at me like that. You said yourself that this was Podunk and the guy was a bumpkin. Let's not go over the top with this."

"Guy tries to shoot your ass and you're worried about going over the top?" Detto was incredulous.

"Vito, we're not going to whack this guy. This isn't Indian country. Besides, I've got some things going in this town."

"Oh, yeah, I forgot, the chippie."

"So what's the plan?"

Chapter 21

Rashid had a knot in his gut wondering where all this was headed.

The store was not "in town," but rather on the fringe of town out by the highway that went to Burke then down to St. Johnsbury. Burke was a "ski-town," a playground for tourists, while St. Johnsbury was a <u>real</u> Vermont town with every form of quaintness and atmosphere. Not a made-for-tourist movie set.

Rashid fidgeted around the store. He had told Buck LaDue he needed him for another job. He'd tried to call Buck on several occasions to follow-up and had driven by his place a couple of times. He needed this loose end taken care of. The e-mails were smothering him. He wanted everything checked off the list so he could set it all aside and resume a normal life.

Will my life ever be normal? Will there be no end to Jihad?

He knew the answer but couldn't face it.

Where in the name of Allah is Buck LaDue?

Buck was out of the shower and in the middle of pulling on his cleanest dirty clothes when he heard a vehicle stop outside. He padded quietly across the room in his socks, picked up an old rifle and stood with his back to the wall next to his front screen door.

"Hello, Buck. Are you there? I must be speaking to you!" Buck recognized Rashid's voice and accent.

"Boo!" Buck jumped into the frame of the screen door. Rashid jumped up and back, almost falling off the porch. Buck was in a fit of nasty laughter.

"What you get," Buck snorted, "for scarin' me in my truck, dumbass."

Rashid was wild-eyed, holding his chest with both hands. As tight as he'd been wound lately, it's amazing he hadn't had a heart attack.

Buck stepped out on the porch, took a cursory look around and pulled Rashid into the house. "What's on your mind there, Sheik?"

Rashid quickly told Buck what he wanted and in spite of the speed, he added a melodramatic gravity to the proposition.

Buck's reaction was cavalier. "That's it, an ATV?"

"Side by side!" Rashid shook his head affirmatively.

"And for that you'll pony up ten thousand dollars?"

Rashid didn't understand the "pony" part so he just said, "I pay you ten thousand dollars."

"I pay you, I pay you," Buck mocked. "Jesus Christ, Rashid, how long you gonna be here before you learn how to talk right? It ain't 'I pay you,' it's 'I'll pay you.' Don't you watch TV or nothin'? You ain't gonna amount to dog shit if you don't talk right!" He added a son-of-a-bitch under his breath.

Rashid momentarily choked down his pride at being lectured by this dirty infidel and responded evenly, "I <u>will</u> pay you ten thousand dollars."

Buck grabbed his hand, shook it once hard, then started pushing Rashid out the door. "Deal!"

Chapter 22

Clyde Gash rode through town with two of his idiot goons from the compound. The two men didn't know why the "Commander" had pulled them away from playing with machine guns and "maneuvers" up at the compound, but they had learned to follow Gash's orders. He was their meal ticket and they figured they had nowhere else to go. It was a long way back to West Virginia. Clyde spotted Buck LaDue's pickup truck.

"Pull over," he ordered.

They got out of their camo-painted pickup truck and stood on the sidewalk. Tweedle Dee and Tweedle Dumb stood and looked around at nothing. Clyde on the other hand, looked at the position of Buck's truck and the proximity of Wendell Gidding's store. The store was two-thirds of the old white clapboard building they stood next to. The final third, the closest part, was a forlorn little real estate office. There was a light on but it looked like no one was around. At the end of the building there was an alley and a white congregational church where again no one was around. Clyde motioned the two men into the alley and pointed to a woodpile. It was the same woodpile Buck LaDue had picked a weapon from a few weeks earlier.

Clyde didn't know about that and could care less.

"Sit," he hissed, "and be ready."

The two men sat on the edge of the pile and acted ready — for what they hadn't a clue.

A few minutes passed when Clyde rousted his two thugs.

"Get your asses up; here he comes."

"What are you old coots lookin' at?" Buck LaDue was in a foul mood as he wandered around Wendell Gidding's store picking up some of life's necessities: Marlboros, bologna, a twelve-pack of Bud, and a big twelve-pack of toilet paper. When he got to the counter, he dropped his booty on it and pulled out his old, ratty hand-braided wallet. He had made it himself fifteen years ago with one of those mail order Tandy kits. Now it was falling apart from sweat, motor oil and general abuse. He looked carefully at the contents, then studied the loot on the counter. He picked up the big package of toilet paper and took it back and was returning with a two-pack when he looked over at the two old hangers-on, Cecil and Howard, standing huddled together next to the checkerboard.

Buck knew the whole town had heard about the shooting out at that shithead Matt Striker's house. And he knew that he was suspect number one, even though nothing could be pinned on him. The sheriff and deputies had come out with a warrant and had turned the place upside down making a mess of everything. Everything that wasn't already a mess. But, by God, it was his mess and they didn't have any call to rip the place apart the way they did. Then they walked away empty-handed. The sheriff looked none too happy and Buck had huffed around about his rights and gettin' a lawyer. Sheriff Drew ignored him other than to turn and point a finger at him for a long time. Didn't say a word. Just pointed. And Buck shut up and went in to kick around the mess and hope that he'd dodged the bullet.

But around town, folks knew about the fight in the street and Kate Halliard. Buck liked to think of it as a fight, not the ass whipping that it was. His internal histrionics already had him "holding his own" against the big man. In this town he was Buck-by-God-LaDue and he meant to continue filling his role.

"Good Christ, Wendell, why you let those geezers hang around here? Hell, it's bad for business. Don't they have homes? Shit, they ought to be committed to the state facility down at St. Johnsbury. They're a menace."

Wendell Gidding ignored the rant and rang Buck up as fast as possible. He wanted him out. Hell, he might start shooting this place up, crazy bastard.

Buck picked up his bag and started to turn away.

"Always a pleasure, Buck."

Buck LaDue hit the sidewalk and menacingly headed toward his truck, still swearing to himself and daring anyone to get in his way. It was a cheap dare as the streets were virtually empty this weekday afternoon. As he cleared the building the store was in, he had his eyes fixed on his truck up ahead. He was going to jump in and go see raghead Rashid. There had been talk of more money. He was already spending it in his head.

Maybe a fancy new rifle, a new chainsaw, shit maybe one of them big screen TVs.

His lusts were soothing his anger with each step. He loved easy money.

Suddenly, Buck was jerked sideways violently. His sack of provisions hit the ground. One of the Budweisers exploded from the impact.

"What the f…." He didn't get the word out. He was slammed down with his back on the woodpile. His wind was knocked out and he made a big "humph" sound. He was being held by two big hillbillies in bib overalls. Before he could get oriented, there was a big bearded face one inch from his own. The face was hissing something and spittle was spraying Buck.

"Goddamn you simple little frog. I told you to stay the hell out of trouble with them rifles. But you, you simple son-of-a-bitch, you go out and shoot a man's house. I've a mind to take you up to the house and take the horsewhip to your hide. How can you be so goddamn dumb?"

Buck heard some of what Clyde Gash was yelling, but couldn't concentrate on it because of Clyde's horrible breath. It was like liver and onions—or onions and some other vile mess. Between that and the thump from the logs, Buck wasn't feeling too good.

"Clyde, if you don't get your breath out of my face, I'm gonna puke, I swear to God!"

This just served to infuriate Clyde further, and with a swiftness that belied the cumbersome size of the man, Clyde rolled up a big paw into a fist and slammed it into Buck's gut.

Then Buck did get sick. Clyde was just able to side-step Buck's eruption.

Get 'em down," Clyde ordered his thugs, who instantly held Buck on his knees with the side of his face pushed down in his own puke. One man had the back of his hair and one of Buck's arms locked up on his back. The other had him by the back of his belt holding him still.

"Goddamn, Buck, you're a pain in the ass!" Clyde continued unabated. "Now let me revise our earlier discussion. If this rifle thing comes back on me, you're dead." Clyde gave a signal and Buck was pushed down further in the alley and left alone.

In a few minutes he was able to stumble to his feet. He cleaned off the side of his face with the sleeve of his greasy flannel shirt. Then he looked around. Nobody. He stumbled over to his sack of groceries and viciously kicked it.

"Fuck, fuck, <u>fuck</u>!" Another Budweiser exploded. As he went through his tantrum and then scooped up his remains to head to his truck, two sets of eyes watched from inside the little restaurant across the street. Buck never saw them.

Chapter 23

Sheriff Drew rolled up Matt Striker's long driveway and came to a stop next to a sleek black Monte Carlo with New York tags. He got out and went one lap around the big car, took mental note of the license plate, then strolled up to Matt's door and knocked.

"Come on up!" Matt shouted.

Sheriff Drew's head popped up from floor level and continued to rise.

"Got company?" the sheriff asked.

"Old buddy," Matt responded, then added, "Army."

The sheriff nodded his understanding. He was thinking that it was coincidental that a buddy would show up when there had been trouble. Sheriff Drew didn't like "coincidence." In fact, he mostly didn't believe in it. He could hear a shower running.

The sheriff nodded toward the big camera rig. "Going on a surveillance trip?"

Matt looked down then back up at the sheriff. As he did so, he pointed to the walls around the room adorned with dozens of photos. "Wildlife," Matt explained. "I like to photograph wildlife. Some of the best shots are from right there on the porch." Matt nodded outside.

The sheriff looked at all the photos, then followed Matt's look out to the porch and felt a little foolish. "We got a warrant and tossed LaDue's place. I mean we went over it with a comb. There wasn't a thing. Not one damn thing. He's got an old Savage .300, a Marlin 22 bolt and an old model 10, .38 special. That's it. There wasn't an assault rifle anywhere. There wasn't a .223 cartridge or a casing out on the grass or anywhere else. It was clean."

"So what are you telling me?"

"I'm telling you there isn't any evidence. Not a speck, at least so far."

"But, it sounds like there's a 'but' in there somewhere."

"But, he's probably your shooter."

Chapter 24

Matt looked up from the dog.

"So, Sport, how's life for you these days?" It was a far too open-ended question for a kid and Matt regretted it right away. Predictably, Nick looked like a deer in the headlights. Matt was floundering. He hadn't tried to talk to a kid this age in a long time.

"Okay, I guess," was all Nick could come up with.

"How old are you now?"

"Thirteen. Well, almost. Old enough to go to Hunter's Safety Class."

Matt nodded sagely. He knew this was big stuff for a near thirteen-year-old. "Got any experience yet?"

Nick looked a little downtrodden and glanced down the hall before answering. "I haven't shot a real gun yet." He brightened with hope. "But Ricky Lanky, Bart Wheeler and Billy Bowhan have."

"It's serious business. You have to be real careful." Matt had a taskmaster look on his face. "Have you signed up for your class yet?"

Nick looked down the hall and his mother was on her way out. Matt followed his gaze and Kate was emerging, looking fantastic from head to toe. "Not yet," Nick finally said quietly.

Kate looked at both Matt and Nick with a trace of suspicion. "You two getting to know one another?"

"Nick was just giving me the run down on some 'guy stuff,'" Matt responded conspiratorially. Nick was on his way over to a set of steps that probably led up to his room.

"You two have fun. Come on, Brutus!" The big dog looked at Kate and Matt then back at Nick, who slapped his hand to his thigh. The dog bounded up the steps obediently.

"Guy stuff?" Kate turned to Matt.

"Nothing, really." Matt held a hand up then used it to point toward the door. "Ready to go? Your chariot awaits!"

"What, you painted 'chariot' on the side of the Jeep?" Kate headed to the door, with Matt in tow.

"Thanks, Connie!" she yelled over her shoulder. "We won't be late."

Chapter 25

"But Connie, you had a hamburger at McDonald's. I saw you." Nick was pointing out the inconsistency of Connie's

position. The two had been locked in battle over Nick's obsession with being able to go hunting the coming fall. "And I saw that organic beef at your store, too."

Nick was right. Connie was an importer of organic grain from Montreal, and she supplied a couple of dairy farmers who had taken a state-funded dairy herd buyout and converted to raising organic "angus" quality beef. Now Connie had a small cooler in the store and sold it there. In a weak moment, she had even taken a small package of filet home. She had rubbed it with pepper grains, sea salt and fresh garlic, then cooked it medium rare on the grill. She paired it with an organic red from Napa Valley. The result was bliss, and she reflected on the indulgence to herself now.

"But I don't go running around trying to kill cows, Nick!"

"Someone kills them. It's not like getting an egg from a chicken!"

God, this kid is smart—and tougher and tougher to argue

with. Connie was thinking she needed to pack a little more ammo the next time she engaged in this battle. "Yeah, well I'm sure you and your mom will get it all worked out."

Nick was immediately deflated. He had hoped he was building an ally, not a spectator.

"Come on, let's go work on that music. Something good for the cello. Maybe the Brandenburg."

Nick slumped. Good for the cello usually meant hard. And he knew the pace of the Brandenburg Concerto went up to what he estimated to be about ninety miles an hour. His fingers hurt thinking about it. "How about Vivaldi?" He was thinking smooth, soft and slow.

"How about the Brandenburg?" Connie said, flatly, unwavering. There would be no negotiation.

"So, that's it. I just don't think I can deal with Nick going hunting, of all things. Hunter's Safety Class or none."

Matt had been sitting across from Kate in a knotty pine booth in the corner of The Bull Moose Brewery in St. Johnsbury. The conversation had been easy, pleasant and all over the board, but had stiffened when Kate confided that she had heard Nick talking to Matt back at the house. She had explained that the little family had been torn apart by loss when Stephen died and how she needed to protect Nick from danger. If she lost him, she would lose herself, she was resolutely sure.

At the same time, Kate fretted over the need for Nick to slowly, progressively become a young man even though he was mostly surrounded by women. She made it clear that she wasn't a rabid anti-gun type. Her mother, after all, carried one. And she knew about the "open carry" laws of Vermont which stood in stark contrast to the liberal bent of the political landscape. She knew that much of Vermont, practically all in fact was rural and that hunting was a tradition that went back generations and crossed virtually all lines of society including gender, age, religious and political persuasions, income, etc. Strange as it seemed, the state even held a "rifle season" for northern pike. Fish! She knew all those things. She knew that the first day of deer season was a no-school day, for God's sake. And in spite of it all, she could not bear to think of Nick being exposed to the dangers of guns. She had worked in a busy trauma unit of Dartmouth. She knew the grisly possibilities. So when she made her pronouncement, she sat quiet, looking away toward the bar and the big copper brew tanks behind it. Matt said nothing, but he studied this beautiful woman, this conflicted single mom.

Then Kate turned directly toward Matt. "You think I'm wrong."

Matt shook his head and held up the flats of both palms. "None of my business. What I think doesn't matter, Kate."

Silence. Kate nodded her head to the side and took another drink of her Vouvray. She had had grilled salmon on a cedar plank and Matt had ordered the Maine lobster. The French wine was light and breezy and went down easy. Perfect with the seafood. Matt was going slow on the wine.

"So, how do you think your friend, Mr. Debenadetto, is coming along tonight?"

Matt smiled, threw his napkin on the table, slid out from under the table and said, "Let's go see!"

Kate hesitated a moment then turned out of the booth herself.

Matt was smiling broadly as he added, "Got some Ben and Jerry's Chocolate Chunk in the freezer, too!"

Chapter 26

It wasn't like Clyde Gash puzzled through all the pros and cons of killing Buck LaDue. It was more that he woke up one too many mornings worried that the dumb sumbitch was going to get his tit in a wringer he might not get shed of. It just sort of struck him that Buck was his main worry and didn't need to be.

Nor was the plot to kill Buck all that intricate. He just pulled his nephew Ray and the newcomer Willie Jones in and laid it out.

"Shouldn't be too tough," Jones said. He had been steady when they kicked LaDue's ass.

"Yeah, no problem, Clyde," Ray interjected.

Clyde ignored his nephew and looked directly at Jones. Jones would be the brains. Ray would do as he was told. "But there's somethin' you ain't sayin'. If you got a burr up yer ass, spit er out," Clyde said.

"Gonna lead back here if anyone seen us whup up on LaDue," Jones stated flatly. He wasn't afraid, it appeared, just reasoning.

"I didn't see no one," Ray offered helpfully.

Clyde was quiet, contemplating. "How 'bout you, Willy, see anyone that day?" Clyde was more apt to rely on

Jones than his obsequious nephew.

"Reckon not, Clyde, but can't say who might-a seen us, neither."

Clyde thought a few more minutes. Jones had brought up a good point. He wasn't about to make things worse. "Tell ya what," he finally piped up. "Let's go into town tomorrow. See what's what."

Ray smiled and Willie Jones nodded assent. They both liked to go to town, but for very different reasons.

Chapter 27

When Buck LaDue's truck passed Matt's Jeep on the highway in the dark of night, neither of them knew it. Matt was focused on his easy conversation with Kate, and Buck was mentally spending money that he did not have, though he expected that to change soon. Very soon.

As he cruised down the highway pulling a small trailer, he was already thinking about the dumb-ass uppity tourists down at Burke, with all their fancy SUVs -- that had never been off on a dirt track, he was sure -- and their trendy catalogue company outdoor wear, and their toys. It was their toys that got him most excited. Snowmobiles, bass boats, jet skis, ATVs, motorcycles.

It was like a candy store. And the dumb bastards were so star-struck with "country living" they thought they had gone back in time or something. Leaving their doors unlocked, leaving their cars running at the convenience stores, not locking up the toys at night. This was almost too easy. Over the past two years, Buck had gotten one jet ski on a trailer -- the one he was now pulling -- and two snowmobiles. And countless small power tools — chainsaws, drills, sanders, air compressors and the like. Yeah, it was a candy store.

Buck had seen the fancy two-seater ATV, a side-by-side, a couple weeks previously when he was scouting for goods. They were new and a bit rare, which he had made Rashid understand clearly when they were talking price. He knew he could gouge Rashid another thousand on delivery if he wanted to. He'd see how things went. Might need Rashid going forward. The little twerp.

The old blue Chevy truck and trailer breezed through the town of Burke with no notice. Looked like any other woodchuck going through town. Buck continued on up to a turnoff from the mountain road that led to a labyrinth of little dirt roads sporting ten acre lots and mountain homes. Mostly second homes, owned by rich Bostonians, New Yorkers and flatlanders from Connecticut. They were all full of more hoity-toity crap than Buck could choke down at times. But he loved their toys.

After winding around and taking a couple forks in the dark road, he came to a driveway that went uphill from the road. He squared the trailer to the bottom of the drive, then walked up to the new Yamaha Rhino that was backed in the drive.

Backed in, by God. Morons.

He slipped the little brute out of gear, pulled a block out from in front of one of the tires and it immediately started to roll. He jumped behind the wheel. Silently, except for the faint crunch of fine gravel, the ATV rolled down to the trailer. Buck feathered the foot brake as the machine rolled onto the tail ramp and on up into the trailer. After the tail ramp was pushed up and secured, he was back in the truck and headed the twenty-five miles home.

Slicker'n shit. Might even help the poor bastards out. Teach 'em to be more careful with their stuff. Buck snickered to himself. *Ten thousand dollars for one night, not bad. Who knew how long it could take to piss away that kind of money?*

"Okay, Cowboy, I sweet-talked Connie. She's staying ten more minutes. We gotta go! It was terrific meeting you, Vito. I really enjoyed our talk." Kate had breezed in like a tornado and was already on the move toward the stairs. Matt and Detto jumped to their feet like the bugle had been blown.

Detto rushed over to shake Kate's hand. "It was a pleasure meeting you, Kate."

On the way to Kate's house, Kate put her hand on the console of the Jeep. Matt covered it with his big hand and they interlocked fingers. It was comfortable, natural, and exhilarating to both of them.

When they arrived at the house, Connie Cutter was sitting in a rocker on the front porch. "At long last," she said, standing up.

"I'm sorry; I didn't realize how late it was when we stopped over at Matt's."

Connie's eyebrows went up, which Kate noticed so she

felt compelled to add, "Where we met Matt's friend Vito."

To Connie, it sounded like a character out of the Sopranos. "Well, it was actually no problem. Nick had a wonderful time working on his music — and then we played poker."

"Poker?"

"For matchsticks only, although we came out of it with a 'no bitching' music lesson next time around. Your son is kind of a sore loser. Toodles!" and Connie was off the porch and walking toward her Volvo.

Kate, looking slightly agape, turned toward Matt who was smiling with unabashed amusement at the whole scene. They both laughed quietly. They didn't want to wake Nick.

Chapter 28

Kate knew tonight was the night. "Well, Cowboy, how about a drink?"

"Beer?" Matt answered hopefully.

"You got it!" Kate went into the house and a half-beat later Matt followed.

The big country kitchen was warm and inviting, lit by soft lights under the bead-board pine cabinets. Kate turned from the refrigerator to find Matt leaning against the butcher block island smiling at her.

She was attracted to this man like none she could remember. There was a break in the wall — and she was glad.

Kate moved toward Matt holding two amber bottles. She got much closer to Matt than she needed when she offered him one of the beers. Matt gently took the bottle. He set it on the island without taking his eyes off Kate's. Then he took her beer and set it aside as well.

Matt slipped his arms gently around Kate's trim waist and held her to him. At first, his kiss was soft, almost teasing. But when he eased back, Kate pressed forward. Soon they found each other's tongues and their grip on one another intensified slightly. Within a minute their faces, ears and hands were feeling richly warm and Kate's hand was fumbling with the buttons on Matt's shirt.

"What about… Nick?"

"Sound sleeper… No problem."

"Brutus?".

"With Nick…. Door shut…. Sound sleeper too."

Then Kate reached to the side of the island, flipped a switch and the under cabinet lights went off. The room was bathed with just the soft light of a full moon and a small pole lamp out between the back of the house and the garage.

Soon Kate had Matt's shirt off and Matt was pulling her white lace blouse over her head. As Kate worked on the buckle of Matt's jeans, she was looking at his handsome strong chest—and the array of scars. She could have shuddered at the scars and the violence they represented, but she willed the thoughts away like the proverbial "willing suspension of disbelief." All was good.

When all the clothes were off, Matt could see the silhouette of Kate's beautiful body in the blue glow of the moon. Her skin was silky smooth and his fingers ran softly over the perfect curves of her full breasts, back and hips. He was in a trance fascinated by the perfection. Then Kate's hand slid gently down Matt's chest and kept going. She leaned her lips to his ear.

Almost desperate, almost apologetic, she whispered, "It's been a very long time, Cowboy."

Later, they lay in Kate's big four-poster bed with a valance around the top. The second time they made love was much slower, each of them taking time to enjoy and give joy. They were relaxed, confident and skilled. It was as if they had been lovers for years. And they were both transformed by it.

Kate was on her side with her arm draped over Matt's chest and they were chitchatting like a married couple.

"You're lucky to have Vito. He's a nice man."

Matt thought about the many times Detto had been there for him, as well as the times he had covered Detto. They had a mighty bond. But he couldn't resist.

"Trust me, I'm feeling very lucky at this moment, but I can't say Detto is much on my mind," he quipped.

Kate slapped him gently on the chest. "You know perfectly well what I mean. But, thanks." She cuddled closer to Matt and remained quiet a few moments. Then she said, "You think I'm wrong about Nick, don't you?"

Matt lifted himself up on one elbow to look at Kate. "What are you talking about?"

"The hunting. The Hunter's Safety Class."

"Hey, listen kiddo, I'm not standing in judgment of you and your son. Looks like a fine kid to me! Besides, what the hell do I know?"

Kiddo, she liked that. "Matt, you're a gentleman for not butting in but now I'm asking you. I know you have an opinion; I could see it on your face at dinner."

Matt was silent. Obviously reluctant. For one thing, he didn't want to break the magic.

"Please," Kate said with a soft desperation.

Matt stayed quiet for a moment longer, then brought his fingers up to the nape of Kate's neck under her thick hair. He gently stroked her neck.

"I think boys, for all of time and in every part of the world, seek the passages to manhood," Matt began. "And in many cultures and over the ages, there have been rituals of that passage provided to boys. Usually provided by the man of the family, or men of the clan or community. I think the lack of these rituals in many modern societies robs boys of wholesome ways to approach manhood. Unfortunately, boys are then down to self-made, unsupervised and usually unwholesome passages of their own. Fast cars, drinking, drugs, street violence, vandalism, you name it."

"But I brought Nick up here to keep him from all that," Kate protested.

Matt stopped stroking Kate's neck and grasped her upper arm.

"Kate, there's no escape, no immunity. Just look at Buck LaDue. He's a product of this rural sanctuary. It's not just about what's around. It's about what's within." Matt stopped talking. Kate looked very thoughtful for a moment, then slumped down into the crook of Matt's big arm. He wrapped it around her and held her close.

Kate started running her fingers up and down Matt's side and inevitably down toward his belly button.

"Oh, my, Mr. Striker, you are a horny devil."

"I blame it all on you, you floozy."

Chapter 29

When Matt finally got back to his place, Detto was sitting in an Adirondack chair on the lower porch. Matt wasn't exactly sure how to describe the look on his buddy's face but "shit-eating grin" came to mind.

Matt was silent as he walked past Detto to go in and put on fresh clothes.

"Can't say I blame you. Not one bit." He heard Vito's voice as he moved on inside the house. Then a chuckle and something about, "We have to talk."

When Matt returned, Vito was in the same position, in the same chair with the same look on his face. "Speak to me," Matt opened.

"We gotta talk about our little operation. I went out and did a little more recon last night."

"After we left?" Matt was impressed.

"Well one of us had to focus on the mission."

"Funny. What'd you find?"

"Couple of things. Lives alone, no dogs, or security of any kind, easy locks. The mark is clueless. It's a piece of cake. I think we should move on his sorry ass tonight."

Matt thought for a moment and couldn't think of a reason to delay. They'd been over it and over it. Now Detto had the latest intel. "It's a go as far as I'm concerned."

Detto chuckled. "Let's do it."

The phone rang. Kate picked it up.

"Hey, lady, how are you this morning?" The question was dripping with innuendo. It was Connie.

"I'm fine." Kate was a fortress.

"I'm fine? What kind of crap are you spooning up here? Come on, I want details here!"

"We had a very, very nice time."

"You did it, didn't you? I can tell by the way you said 'very, very.'"

Kate tastefully threw some crumbs to Connie, referring to "romantic" and "connecting" and "role model for Nick" and so forth. Finally, Connie could see it was no use.

"Okay, you're no help. I'm going down to the store and get a cucumber."

"Oh, Connie, for God's sake!" Then the phone went dead. Kate looked at the phone in dreaded wonder. She thought she was going to have a nice, private relationship with Matt Striker. It might be nice, but private was definitely out of the question. Kate could sense her world turning upside down. And she was giddy.

Chapter 30

Buck LaDue finished the last cigarette in the pack pushed in the pocket of his old red checkered flannel shirt. He started looking around the room. *Shit.* He didn't want to get up. He was enjoying the monster truck show on his big screen TV. He'd delivered the stolen ATV to Raghead Rashid, gotten his money and went straight to Eddie's Pawn Shop in Newport and bought the big television. Eight hundred bucks, by God. Eddie had started at nine hundred, but Buck had weaseled him down. *Christ, it wasn't like I haven't supplied Eddie with enough goods over the years.* A good half of what Buck stole ended up at Eddie's. Although the little A-rab was getting to be a pretty steady buyer, a fact that Buck wasn't averse to using as leverage on Eddie.

Just when the trucks with the gigantic tires were down to the final round of destruction and mayhem, Buck was out of smokes. He pawed around his pockets. Nothing. Walked across the room to grab his coat, never taking his eyes off the trucks. He felt around the pockets of the coat. Nothing. *Fuck.* He threw the coat down and went back in front of the TV. Standing for the final round. He fidgeted until the trucks finally took off. The big trucks ran over cars, school buses and then over big prone concrete figures in the shape of Osama bin Laden. The crowd cheered with delight. Finally the big black truck named "Bad Dream" flipped over backward and the "Purple Onion" raced to the finish and another cheer went up from the crowd.

For a moment, Buck fantasized about turning the old red Scout into a Bigfoot stomper. *Hell, I have a little money. I could drive one of those rigs. Nothing to it,* he deluded himself. *Where in Christ are those cigarettes?* He'd bought a whole carton at Gidding's. He went to the kitchen and slammed cupboard doors in a futile search. *The truck. Probably left them in the damn truck.*

When Buck went out through his front door, he didn't bother to turn on the porch light. There was a full moon and the light drew mosquitoes the size of helicopters anyway.

Suddenly, as Buck stepped out onto the yard, everything went black and he was falling. He wasn't able to bring his arms up to break his fall and he thumped down hard. He didn't realize at first that he had broken his nose. He was more concerned with trying to get air into his lungs since something had fallen with him from behind, pushing all of the air out of him.

Gasp, gasp. "Fuck, Clyde!" gasp "Told you..." gasp, "wouldn't talk." Gasp "Holy Jesus...," gasp "broke my nose." Gasp "Let me..." gasp "let me up, Clyde." Gasp "I'm bleedin' here." Gasp "Take this thing off my head, for Christsake!"

Now Buck's hands were jerked behind him and he could hear the snap, snap, snap of a big cable tie and he was bound tight. Hood over his head, nose bleeding, hog tied. Buck jerked, struggling hard.

"What is this bullshit?" he screamed, lungs working full force.

"Shut-da-fuck up."

Buck was barely able to process the fact that the voice was totally strange when something slammed into the side of his neck and everything went black.

The next thing Buck was aware of was being in a god-awful uncomfortable position. And he was moving. Through the fog he realized he was in a car or maybe a van. No, it was a car and he was on the back floor squeezed down between front and back seats. Something was pushing down on him. He started to lift up slightly when he was violently pushed back in place by the two boots on his back.

"Sleepin' Beauty awakens!"

"Who are you? What do you want from me? I ain't done nothin'!"

"Ain't done nothin'." One of the boots kicked him. Not viciously, but hard enough to get Buck's attention. "Hear dat? He ain't done nothin'."

Whoever the abductor was talking to, maybe the driver, maybe there were others, didn't bother to answer.

Buck was baffled and becoming terrified. This guy

sounded like the mob or something. *Hell's Angels?* They were big just across the border in Sherbrooke, Quebec, and they had some play in Newport and Burlington. But, there wasn't much for them in the Kingdom. Besides, this guy sounded New York or New Jersey mob, like the guys on TV. *What do they want? What are they going to do to me?*

As if reading Buck's mind, the voice said, "Don't worry, asshole, in a little while you'll be squealin' like a girl, tellin' us all about it."

Buck didn't say anything more, but he began to shake. He could feel the car turn from time to time, but he had no idea where he was or where they were taking him. *How long was I out? I could be anywhere.* Suddenly the car stopped.

"Showtime!" The voice sounded delightedly macabre.

A door opened, then another. Someone had Buck by the ankles and he was being dragged out of the car. The side of his head hit the rocker panel and then thumped on the ground.

Now he was sliding across the grass feet first on his side. Sometimes he rolled to his belly and his broken nose bumped the ground and he screamed out. Finally, he was jerked to his feet and something was shoved under his arms tied behind his back. A bar of some sort. Then another cable tie went around his ankles.

"Please, don't. I'll do any...." The bar came tight up under his arms with a painful jerk and he was being hoisted off the ground. Buck lost control of his bladder. Piss ran down the inside of his pants to his shoes.

"My, my, dat don't usually happen 'till later. Maybe we won't have to work on you all night."

"Anything." Buck was in pain from his full weight pulling down on the bar between his bound arms and his back. "Just tell me," he groaned.

A strong hand grabbed Buck hard by the cheeks through the bag over his head.

"You got any fuckin' idea who we are, dirt bag?" the voice growled.

Buck didn't know if he was supposed to actually answer or just listen. He guessed wrong and didn't say anything.

"I asked you a question, asshole."

Now the hand was squeezing his cheeks so hard he could feel his teeth starting to cut the insides of his mouth.

Buck started shaking his head rapidly up and down.

"Dat's better."

The hand came off his cheeks.

"So, do tell."

"People you don't screw with. People that don't take any shit." Buck didn't want to guess wrong and suffer whatever the consequences were, so he decided to stay general and as obsequious as he could.

Now the hand was slapping him firmly on his right cheek.

"Good boy! You ain't as dumb as you look! Now, Buck — your name is Buck, ain't it?"

Buck shook his head.

"Wouldn't want to snatch the wrong guy." The man started to chuckle.

Buck thought he could hear someone else stifling a laugh.

"Okay, enough frivolity."

Something cold and sharp came up to the side of Buck's neck. A knife.

"Tell me, Buck, why are we all here this evening?"

Buck was thinking hard and fast. He wasn't sure what to say. It seemed like a no-win question.

"I'm sorry, I'm sorry," Buck said, opting for a vague apology covering all recent sins.

"Sorry for what, dipshit?"

"The ATV?" Buck was desperate. "I can get it back for you, I swear to Jesus." *Must have been a mobster's part-time house. What a fuck-up.*

The knife dragged across his neck and he began to bleed. Now the voice was really angry and another hand grabbed the front of Buck's belt.

"ATV? You fuckin' moron, I don't give a shit about some ATV. Now you tell me what you're really sorry for or I start cuttin' your balls off and feeding them to you."

The hand on his belt started jerking it violently. Buck was so terrified he couldn't think. Finally, the shaking stopped.

"Try again, asshole."

Buck was thinking feverishly. *Are these friends of Clyde's? Rashid's? No, can't be.* Then it finally hit him. *It's Striker. That's it. That's why the guy hadn't taken any shit from him. He's fuckin' connected. Holy shit! That has to be it.* He started blurting.

"I didn't know, I swear to God. I'm sorry I bothered him." Shit, he'd tried to kill him. "I didn't know. I just shot at the house. I swear to Christ I didn't know. How can I make it up? I'll do anything. I got connections up here. I can get stuff for you, anything." Buck was pleading at light speed now.

"Bingo."

Now a rough hand was unbuckling his belt and jerking his pants down. *Oh, no. Oh, God, no!*

"You fuck wit my guy who's up here keepin' a low profile and you, you fuckin' hick, shoot at his house!" His voice rose in rage with each word. "I'm cuttin' your fuckin' dick off, you little weasel!"

Now Buck was screaming like a girl. Pleading, whining, begging. Suddenly, nothing was happening. Buck could hear voices murmuring. The knife was now pressed on his bare belly.

"My kindhearted partner dinks I should give you one more chance."

"Yes, please," Buck broke in.

"If I were to do dis ding, against my better judgment, do you know what is required from you?"

"Yeah, help you in any way I can."

"Help us in any way he can," the mocking voice was talking to someone else.

"No, no, no!" The knife pressed against Buck's belly.

"We do not require de services of a dickhead from Podunk! Capisce?"

"Whatever you need."

"What I need is for you to live your Podunk life in your Podunk town and stay the fuck out of our way. If I ever even hear a word about you again, I swear to God I come up here and skin you alive!"

The knife dragged across Buck's belly.

"You got that, dickhead?"

"I'll be good! I'll stay away. You got it!"

"I still dink we should oughta cut his dick off," the voice was talking to the silent partner. "No? I dink it's a mistake," the voice warned.

"Please," Buck groveled.

"Okay. One last item. What happened to the rifle?"

Shit, they know about the search. If he named Rashid, Rashid would blab about the guns, the ATV and everything else he'd fenced there. He was thinking fast. The knife was back on him. "Eddie, in Newport."

Long silence.

"Who da fuck is Eddie in Newport?"

"Eddie. The pawn shop!" These guys weren't from around here.

There was some rustling and a "snap." Buck fell to the

ground and hit his face again. He screamed out.

Now something was pulling at his wrists and another "snap." His hands were free. *Thank God the worst is over.*

"Do <u>not</u> move a muscle!" the voice commanded. "Not an inch. And keep your mouth shut!"

More rustling. Then silence. In a few minutes he heard a car start, then pull away. Then more silence.

How long had Buck laid still? Five minutes? Half an hour? He wasn't sure, but his body ached and he needed to move. He chanced it, dragging his hands up to his neck, he pulled the bag off his head. Between the moon, the first light of dawn and his pupils being dilated from being in the bag, he could see quite well. He looked around cautiously. By God, he was in his own front yard. He looked around on the ground. His own shovel had been the bar under his arms and his own block and tackle was set up in the hickory tree above him. He felt his neck. A hunk of dried blood was crusted on him. He looked at his belly. Scratched was all.

Buck made it to his feet and pulled his pants up. He didn't have anything to cut the big cable tie around his ankles so he bunny-hopped to his front door and into the house.

Matt and Detto were laughing out of control. Matt almost drove the Monte Carlo off the road as tears filled his eyes.

"Shit, you want Gigi to super glue my dick to my leg? Stay on the road. Take it easy."

"Dis, dat, dink!" Matt was still laughing uncontrollably. "That was the worst goomba shit I ever heard!"

"Yeah, dickweed, like you would know." Detto started laughing all over again. "But let's face it, if you need your shoes shined or your ass wiped, he's your guy!" Laughter. "Shit, I gotta get <u>me</u> one of those!"

"Yeah, yeah, let's go get a couple hours of shuteye. Then you better disappear for a while."

"You gonna talk to the sheriff about Eddie?"

"Yeah, I'll find a way to get word to him." Matt smiled. Sam Hood might be the right guy.

"And who the fuck is Clyde? I think Clyde might be scarier than us," Detto chuckled.

"I doubt it."

"So, who is he?"

"I have no idea." Matt shot Vito a serious look. "But I'll find out."

Chapter 31

Sam Hood pointed his green truck up Matt Striker's driveway and immediately his trained eyes were attracted to a brushy point that stuck out into the field beyond Matt's house. He could make out one, maybe two figures, dressed in camo sitting behind some apparatus. A rifle on a bipod? No, something else. The truck got closer and closer. It was a camera on a tripod. A big camera. Sam pulled up by the house and remained in the truck.

Matt stood and gave the game warden a wave. Then a smaller man, no it was a boy, stood and looked toward the house. They spoke to each other then started across the field.

"Well, hey, Matt, didn't mean to interrupt anything." The warden smiled and shot a quizzical look toward the boy.

"Hey, Sam." The two men shook hands.

"Who's your partner?" Sam asked.

Nick beamed at the notion.

"Sam Hood, like you to meet Nick Halliard."

Sam and the boy shook hands.

"Well, sure, Kate Halliard's boy. Haven't seen you in ages. You're practically all grown up."

"Nice to see ya, Mr. Hood."

"You fellas out on maneuvers?" Sam nodded toward the field.

"Setting up an ambush," Nick piped up.

"That so?" the warden answered but looked at Matt.

"Predator set up. We're gonna try to call something in and take a few pictures."

"I'm signed up for Hunter's Safety."

The warden placed his hand on Nick's shoulder. "Well, that's a fine thing, Nick. You pay close attention. This is serious business, hunting. The warden had a grim look on his face.

"Yes, sir, I understand. Mr. Striker's been teaching me."

"Has he now?" Sam looked at Matt.

But Matt was looking beyond the warden at a car coming up the drive. Sam turned and looked also. Nick groaned.

As Kate came up the drive toward Matt's house, she could see Nick bracketed between two men, engaged in conversation. Nick was with two responsible men, interacting with them. Kate had a wave of warmth and thought for a moment she might get choked up. She shook it off. It wouldn't do for Mommy to arrive at this manly gathering blubbering, wearing her emotions on her sleeve, her face, her entire body. She sucked it up.

"Is this an all-men's meeting or can a lady intrude?"

"By all means, Ms. Halliard. Nick here was just telling me about his upcoming plans."

"And which of his many plans was he sharing?" Kate played along. She walked up and gave Matt a peck on the cheek. Sam Hood felt a little awkward, but voyeuristic at the same time. "Seems your young man here is accepting the responsibility that goes with Hunter's Safety. It's a big step."

Kate was glad, if somewhat surprised, that Matt and now Sam Hood were taking this "Hunter's Safety" thing with such gravity. It was a good lesson for Nick, and she had to admit, some comfort to her as well. She casually mussed up Nick's hair which she could see embarrassed the boy.

"It's nice to see him in the company of two good role models."

"That's awful generous of you, ma'am, but Matt's carrying the wood here. I just stopped by." Sam was the kind of man who had trouble taking credit for things he had done, let alone things he hadn't.

"Still, Mr. Hood, it's nice to see you here."

"Unless you're here to write me a ticket," Matt joked. The warden tipped his hat and announced that he'd better leave "you good folks alone," and started to move toward his truck only to have Kate grab his sleeve.

"No, you don't. I didn't fall off the turnip truck

yesterday. You stopped by for a reason and I'm here to pick up Nick and get going." She looked at Nick. "Let's hit the road, Sport, we're picking up Connie in ten minutes. Gotta go!" She scampered toward her Subaru.

"You did good today," Matt said by way of praising the boy as he walked him to the car. "We'll keep working on it. Got some ideas for us."

"Can I bring Rami?" the boy blurted.

Matt was caught off base. Rami Saeed was the son of Shuri and Rashid al Saeed who ran the convenience store out by the highway. Matt knew the two boys were friends and should have expected that this might come up. When he thought about it, Nick was probably gushing to Rami about every "adventure" Nick and Matt were experiencing as Matt taught the boy the ways of the out-of-doors. It was probably hard for both boys to have one left out of such doings of gravitas. They were both "coming of age" after all. How could best friends have one foot in the new world of manhood and leave the other in the realm of boys?

Kate had gotten into the car, but the window was down. She heard the question and shot a look and tilt of the head at Matt that said, "I don't know what to do with this one."

Matt turned Nick around and looked at the boy eye to eye.

"Nick, I don't know Rami. I need to ask you about him. This business..." Matt thumbed over his shoulder to where they had been set up in the brushy point, "...is serious stuff. Do you think Rami is ready for this?"

Nick put his head down to study both rocks on the ground and the question. In a moment he looked Matt in the eye.

"Yes, sir, I think he's ready. We could watch him and help him get caught up." It was obvious that Nick now saw himself as a relative expert compared to Rami.

"I like the way you thought about that before you answered, Nick. That was very grown-up. You bring Rami out, if it's okay with his parents."

Matt looked over at Kate who nodded discreetly back to Matt to show that she understood her role in this. "We'll try him out."

"Thanks, Mr. Striker. He'll do good, I promise!" Nick scrambled to the car door on the other side and hopped in. He was beaming.

Kate started to put the car in reverse to turn around, but hesitated and stuck her hand out the window, pointing at Matt and curving her finger in the typical "come here" gesture. She kept it going until Matt had his hands on the roof of the Subaru and his face down in the window. She kissed the big man on the lips and whispered, "You're a good man, Matt Striker."

Matt walked up the drive toward Sam Hood who started talking before he got to him.

"Looks like you're gettin' in with both feet." Sam nodded toward the Subaru that was just pulling off the long drive onto the paved road. Matt looked around and stood watching the car disappear down the road before turning back to the warden.

"You didn't come out here to talk about that." In spite of throwing up a wall, Matt smiled at Hood good-naturedly.

"Nope. Can we sit on the porch a few minutes?"

"Let's do it." Matt held out his hand as an invitation. "Can I get you something cold?"

"On duty. Glass of water would be appreciated."

When both men were settled in Adirondack-style chairs with their ice waters sitting on the big flat arms, the warden started with a seemingly casual statement.

"Saw ole Buck LaDue in town yesterday."

Matt was immediately wary but didn't show it in his countenance. It had been a week since he and Detto had been out on "night tactics."

"Did you?" was all Matt offered.

"Had tape across 'is nose, two black eyes and a lump on his forehead. Looked like he'd tangled with a bear." Hood was smiling now. "Had a pretty tall tale to go with the look, too!"

"Do tell."

"Oh, yeah, he had quite a whopper going, at least according to the boys down at Wendell's store. Course those old coots have been known to embellish a story a bit.

But Gidding himself was telling this one and he's pretty steady."

"Yeah, Wendell's all right." Matt still exerted caution.

"Well, according to them, we got the mob here in the Kingdom." Hood was chuckling.

"The mob, you say?"

"Yeah, right here. And old Buck, he's got an 'understanding' with them. Says he knows what's what and he's not in <u>with</u> them, but on the right side of them. Says he's got their respect and says he knows where to keep his nose in and out."

"The broken nose?" Now Matt smiled.

"Yeah, that bent broken mess on his face. Anyway, says the mob's got people up here and now he knows whose ass to keep in line and whose to let slide."

"He giving out names?"

"Nope. Says he's got their confidence. And he laid on a little warning that he's got their backing if it comes to it. What do you make of all that?" Hood turned his eyes from the field in front of them to Matt's eyes.

"I'd say that is a whopper and a half."

Sam Hood studied Matt like a man trying to see something on the streambed when the water was rushing over it.

"Thought you'd find it interesting." After a pause, added, "I imagine you're not too concerned about him being backed by the mob." He was still smiling. He wasn't sure what happened to Buck but he was "odds-on" that Matt already knew all about it.

"Say why his nose was broken?" Matt probed.

"Initiation. Said the boys wanted him to respect their rights up here. Says it was no big deal and now they're all square. Says they got nothin' to fear from him."

"From him?" Matt was really amused now.

"What he said." Hood insisted with mutual amusement. "Well, anyway, thought I'd share that little tidbit with you. Better get back in the saddle."

The warden put his empty glass back down on the arm of the chair and the ice rattled. He started to rise but was stopped by Matt holding up a hand.

"Can you sit for another minute or two?" Matt asked Hood. The warden slumped back down in the chair. "Sure, what's on your mind?"

"Just wondered if you knew anybody named Clyde around here?"

Now the warden was really studying Striker.

"Clyde Prichard. Dairy farmer down toward Burke," the warden answered.

"Any trouble with him?"

"Not really. Sometimes takes a deer claiming crop damage. Maybe it was, maybe not. Hard to say for sure."

"That's it? Nothing else?"

"No, he's a pretty good old 'chuck. Everybody seems to like him all right."

"Any other Clydes?" Hood thought for a minute before answering, then got a very wary look on his face. It was a look that had pieces falling into place in an unpleasant way.

"There's Clyde Gash, of course, up at the compound. You don't mean him do you?" The "him" sounded like trouble.

"Don't know the man." *Compound. What the hell is the compound?*

"Bunch of survivalist paranoid types. Clyde Gash is the leader. They even call him the Commander. They're always up on their place shooting weapons and playing Army. Shit like that."

"Ever have any trouble with them?" Matt was totally tuned in now.

"Little bit. State went up there and raided the place few years back for alleged child abuse. Kids weren't in school, rumors of incest, arranged marriages, bigamy, you know the drill." Matt nodded and Hood continued. "Most of it was thrown out in court. Gash claimed they were home schooling. Couldn't prove the other charges. Pled down on a couple gun charges. Had some full-autos, machine guns, without the permit. Feds looked at it, slapped him on the wrist. Kids eventually all went back."

"They pretty much stay to themselves. Come into town in small groups for supplies. Drive full camo trucks. Seem to stand guard over their women when they come into town."

"What's the 'compound'?" Matt's curiosity grew.

"They got themselves about a thousand acres cheap from the paper companies when they'd logged it out and were strapped for cash. Like a lot of industries, hurt by foreign imports. Anyway, Gash comes up here and starts buying it up and brings a slew of followers with him. Like-minded nut jobs come and go from there pretty regular. Tags from all over. West Virginia, Carolinas, Georgia, Arkansas, Kentucky, like that."

"They seem dangerous to you?"

"Like a copperhead. If you don't step on it, it's no problem. After the big raid, Clyde was bellowing that lawmen wouldn't barge in so easy next time. The whole thousand acres has a six-foot fence topped with razor wire. There are a few gates in the hinter areas where they go in and out to poach what they need. Guards at the gate."

Matt looked at the warden in surprise.

"Hey, I carry a 9mm Glock and <u>maybe</u> a hunting rifle or shotgun. There's dozens of those wack-jobs up there with ARs. I work alone. And I <u>don't</u> make it a habit of working close to there." The warden was unashamed. "I got a job to do, but I got a family as well. I'm not steppin' on that snake!" The warden shook his head and continued. "Besides the troopers, Sheriff Drew and even I have passed the pertinent information on to the feds. And as far as I can tell, Clyde's still right there." Hood looked Matt in the eye as if to say, "It's up to you guys."

"Anyway, what got you on to Clyde Gash?"

"Assault rifles, you say?" Matt ignored the warden's question.

"Assault rifles. Maybe still got full-autos up there, explosives, RPGs, who knows what?" Then a look of recognition came over Hood's face. "Any connection between those guys and Buck LaDue?" the warden asked Matt.

"Don't know." Matt was looking out over the field. His wheels were turning.

Chapter 32

Omar Aziz loved Burlington, Vermont, but not in the ways one might expect. It wasn't the quaint beauty of the downtown with its restored, century-old brick buildings and closed-off, pedestrian-only brick and stone streets. It wasn't that it was a college town with both the University of Vermont and Champlain College and all the vitality that those institutions brought to the community. It wasn't the stunning waterfront, the many outdoor sports opportunities of the towns or the arts. Nor was it the majestic views of the sun setting across Lake Champlain, turning the Adirondack Mountains more shades of purple and blue than could be imagined. It wasn't any of those things. It was that Aziz could operate his little cell with impunity.

Once the Abenaki Indians were driven from the area in the seventeen hundreds, the colony turned country turned state of Vermont was settled by and large by hearty Anglo and Franco pioneers and business people. Virtually all those, even in modern times, who stake a claim as a "real Vermonter" had such roots. It wasn't until the "hippie" invasion of the late sixties and early seventies that things in Vermont changed much. But in a little over forty years the change was dramatic. The soul and political fabric of Vermont went from stoic "leave me alone; I'll take care of myself" to a full-fledged progressive social experiment, so broad in its application as to be headshakingly ambiguous.

The state pushed a leftist agenda of wealth redistribution and anti-corporate policies, while at the same time relied on some of the biggest of the blue chips, like IBM as employers of its people. It held high visions of health care for all (though they pointed less and less to neighbor Canada as the example) while they preserved some of the most unrestrictive gun laws in the country. Not only was Vermont an "open carry" state, they honored the timeless tradition of "rifle" season for <u>fish</u>.

Where else on earth could a trust-fund hippie drive his micro bus with his weapon laying on the seat, pull up to the back waters, shoot a Northern Pike, take it home, cook it over a campfire and sing Kumbaya? Add a little homegrown weed to the equation and you reached rainbow nirvana.

But there was one thing missing in the grand state of Vermont and Aziz took full advantage of it. The dichotomy of Vermont was that they held diversity on high, but sadly had virtually none of it. The black population of Vermont was less than one percent. While Latinos ranged far and wide in the rest of the country, few made it to the Green Mountain state. And Muslims were as rare as diamonds on the hands of women wearing rag wool socks and Birkenstocks.

And so, when Omar Aziz chose Burlington, Vermont, for the location of his cell, it served a symbiotic need. Both the community and Aziz perceived benefits. Educators, intellectuals and elected leaders had one more example of diversity to display, and Aziz had an environment to work in that was relatively free from scrutiny. Not that he was doing much but awaiting orders. But at least he didn't have to fear a slip of the tongue, that he might if he were in, say, Peoria. In fact, he could be invited to seminars and discussion groups by local intellectuals and freely refer to Western Imperialism and its many threats to Islam. He could speak one-sidedly of the plight of the Palestinians and get thoughtful nods in response. And could even refer to the desperate need of Middle Eastern Muslims to take up arms to protect their rich natural resources and way of life without sounding a single alarm.

As far as Aziz was concerned, he could not only exist among those dunderheads, he could be elevated among them as he plotted their godless demise. He was particularly amused by the irony that, in the name of diversity, they would accommodate his Wahhabist goal of no diversity. In the end, though not in his lifetime, the world would all be Muslim. Praise be to Allah. Allah Akbar.

And now, as fall approached, Omar Aziz, a former Saudi peasant, greatness was coming to him. He needed to acquire a boat. A boat that could easily make the trip from Lake Champlain, down through the thirteen locks into the Hudson River and on down to New York City itself. Aziz throbbed with excitement. He was not privy to the grand plan but he sensed that it would make 9/11 look like child's play.

Rashid al Saeed was bouncing off the walls. He was able to report to his brother-in-law Abu bin Seidu that all things were ready. But he could not stop the head-throbbing stress. He desperately hoped that nothing else would be asked of him.

On the home front, the tension between him and Shuriana was easing. She was becoming less watchful of him and he found that he could be somewhat more relaxed and natural in her presence. The store was running well, business was getting better and better and even Buck LaDue was a little less aggravating.

In fact, it was LaDue that was easing his mind about the time his son Rami was spending with his friend Nick Halliard and the man called Striker.

When Rashid first heard from Buck that Rami was receiving some sort of lessons from this Matt Striker, he was incensed and railed at Shuriana for allowing such an irresponsible act. But then he learned that the man was teaching the boys, Rami and Nick, to use firearms, and Rashid began to find wisdom in it. Maybe even the will of Allah. Rashid knew that he was prohibited, as a non-citizen, from touching a firearm in the United States -- though he knew that the restriction was regularly ignored by some immigrants -- and here was this American teaching the skills to his son. What was more, Buck was telling him tales of organized crime that LaDue speculated would help them both. Maybe Stricker wasn't all that pure; maybe he could be compromised if need be.

Rashid liked an environment that was driven by price more than principle. He knew Buck was of that ilk, even if he was abjectly offensive, and it sounded like this Striker could be cut from the same cloth.

Rashid was being drawn toward the epicenter of something terribly big and he didn't need to be under the scrutiny of a do-good citizen who was operating close to his family. After the information that was spewed through LaDue's braggadocio, Rashid was at ease with the presence of Striker. He would be no problem, he reasoned.

For Shuriana's part, she was relieved that Rashid was reentering the realm of "normal," but deep suspicions lingered. She wasn't stupid and she was acutely aware that behavior that was winked at in her country, and in fact revered in the Peshawar, represented serious crimes here. She prayed to Allah that Rashid would not bring their world crashing down upon them. If they just stayed on the straight and narrow, didn't overreach and served Allah, life would be good. Rami would grow up well. He would be educated, civilized and successful. And as such, could truly serve their Muslim faith.

But Shuriana could only nudge Rashid in subtle ways. To do otherwise would be to go against deep traditions and risk retributions and backlash. She was a practiced master of hints, innuendo, and provocative, rhetorical questions. Shuri would never totally control Rashid, nor would she be able to keep him away from the lecherous Buck LaDue.

Life was a delicate balance.

Matt Striker hovered over the shoulder of the shooter, whispering instructions. "Move your aim slowly to the left. I think I see something on the edge of the woods." As he watched the boys his thoughts went to the dark side. *The last one I killed was not much older than these boys.* He had taken everything she had.

"Okay, to the left," returned Nick Halliard.

"I see him!" hissed the excited whisper of Rami al Saeed as he moved his Leupold spotting scope to the target area.

"Got him," Nick said softly, his finger feeling for the trigger.

Matt slowly reached over Nick and dialed up the zoom lens for slightly more power. "Better?" he asked. He shook the dark thoughts away.

"Yeah, I see him now. Here he comes."

First a nose, then eyes, then the full head appeared through the brushy edge of the field and woods.

Matt slowly placed the call between his teeth and blew gently, making a mournful squealing noise.

Across the field the big coyote stepped halfway into the field and halted, looking warily left and right.

"Now?" whispered Nick anxiously.

"Not yet," Matt said as he slowly tipped his head to the right and, covering the predator call with his cupped hand, gave the instrument a vigorous blow. The urgent squeal, much louder this time, seemed even to Nick and Rami to be originating off to their right.

The coyote responded immediately, looking on to a point of trees and brush to the left of the shooters. He took two full steps into the field and paralleled the brush line, exposing the right side of his body in full.

"Now," whispered Matt.

"Okay, here goes," said Nick as he touched the trigger with his sweaty, shaking finger.

Click, whir, click, whir, click, whir. The camera softly spoke.

"I got him," Nick said a little too loudly.

The coyote jumped back into the brush and was gone in an instant.

"Wooo, we got 'em." The two boys hooted as they jumped up from the bench. "That was sooo cool!"

Matt slapped the boys on the back, fueling their

excitement. "Well done, guys! You did it just right!"

"You called him right to us!" exclaimed Rami.

"Yeah, if we had just sat here and not moved, he might have come right over to us!" Nick speculated.

"I don't know, boys. Those dogs are pretty smart critters. I think you got about all you could with this set up." He pointed to the picnic table pushed up to the railing of the deck on his house. "It would take far better camouflage to get him in much closer."

The boys nodded their heads in serious agreement, trying to shift their boyish excitement to a manly gravity.

Returning the serious look, Matt noticed that both boys were shaking from the cold and the adrenalin spike. "Who's up for hot chocolate?" he said.

"Me!" came the harmonious reply, the boys raising their hands in the air like they were in school.

As Matt herded the boys inside, he was thinking how strange — and wonderful -- this all was. Then he saw the spray of blood and brains from the girl's head again in his mind.

"Detto."

"Is this the lady of the house?"

When Vito Debenedetto's phone rang, he was at his home in Brooklyn. He and Gigi had thought of moving over to Queens or even out to the 'burbs on Long Island, but never got serious about it. Brooklyn was home; virtually all of their two big families were there. Gigi's parents, siblings, cousins, aunts, uncles as well as Vito's, were almost all within walking distance.

They did have a little two-bedroom, one bath cottage all the way out at Greenport on Long Island. It was a couple of blocks off the water and had been passed down through the family. They and their siblings were constantly renovating the old lapboard frame building, but it was a great retreat all the same.

Vito recognized the voice of the caller.

"Kemo Sabe, how's it hangin'?"

"Everything's cool here, my man. How about there? Gigi and the kids okay?"

"Kids are drivin' me nuts. I wish school would start or that Gigi would take 'em out to the island."

"You guys getting out there much this year?"

"Some. I'm tryin' to avoid it. Gigi wants to repaint the kitchen -- again. If I keep puttin' it off, maybe her brother will do it. His turn anyway."

Matt listened patiently to his friend's family dynamics. He was both relieved and yet felt a void. His own family was too small to fight with. With Detto, it was always something. As much as he bitched about it, Matt knew his friend wouldn't trade it for the world. Matt could only imagine what it was like. He finally stepped in to change the subject.

"Can we talk shop a minute?"

"Shoot."

"Remember that guy Clyde we were wondering about? Guy's name is Clyde Gash. Survivalist type as into all kinds of interesting armament." Matt let that sink in a moment. "And his compound is up here in the Kingdom. Not twenty miles from where I'm sitting!"

"Where are you sitting and is anyone sitting on you?"

"I'm at home <u>alone</u>, dickweed!"

"Yeah, that's what you say. Tell the lovely Ms. Halliard I send my regards."

"She'll melt at the words. Now, we were talking about Clyde Gash, and while you may not have dementia, I'm wondering about attention deficit disorder."

"Spell the last name." Detto was done playing around. Matt spelled out G-A-S-H.

"Like 'cash' with a G."

"Let me check it out."

Chapter 33

"Hold it right there, Clyde. I'm not takin' a thumpin' today."

Buck had been counting his cash in his truck when he saw the camo-colored pickup pull in behind him. He was debating himself about paying his sister back. The eight hundred bucks wouldn't cut into his current stash painfully. But eight hundred bucks was eight hundred bucks. The problem he knew was that if he didn't pay her while he could, she'd be done with him, and Christ knew he might have to tap into her again at some future low point. Finally, he figured it was like paying for insurance. If you didn't pay for it, you couldn't file a claim, legitimate or otherwise. He'd pay the hag back and keep his options open.

When Buck looked in his mirror he immediately jumped out of the truck. Clyde was getting out of the driver's side, Ray and the other goon he'd seen at the compound were coming out of the passenger side. Buck was holding his hands up, palms out, looking around the streets and licking his lips. The street was lively with shoppers and loggers coming in from the workday.

"It's a new ballgame now. I got backing!"

Clyde stopped short. "Didn't come to thump anybody,

Buck. What you mean 'backing'?"

"I mean I'm connected now and I ain't takin' any shit from you nor your ass kissers." Buck pointed to Ray and the other goon.

"We just come into town to supply-up is all. Only I figured if I seen you I'd make sure you still know what's what. You square with the law now?"

"Shit, old man, that was over before it started. Law ain't nothin' 'round here. I'm tied in with the real power."

Clyde was glancing around the street. Lot of people, some starting to watch them. "Well, that's real fine, Buck. You sayin' you got religion? That what this real power is?"

Buck snorted. "Goddamn, Clyde, you just ain't tuned in to what's goin' on 'round here. There's bigger play here. And I'm untouchable now, by God."

Now Clyde was totally baffled by this blowhard. "Buck, I don't know what fuckin' planet you're on or could care less, but what I told you about the law still stands. We understand each other?" Clyde was sporting a menacing look. He was tired of this riddle. His patience was stretched further by what Buck did next.

"I told you!" Buck was jamming his finger in the air at Clyde and his boys alternately. "Ya ain't got shit to worry about with the law. That's done with! And as long as you and yours do what ya do up at the compound, you'll be all right. But if you decide to operate here around town, you better be checkin' in with <u>me</u> first!" Buck reared his head back to look down his nose and enhance his finger poking, in case there was any doubt about how full of himself he was.

Clyde looked at his boys and gave them a nod toward the truck. Then he looked at the lunatic in front of him and shook his head, mystified.

When Clyde got in the truck, he looked across the seat to his passengers. "Either of you nimrods got a clue what that fuckin' frog was talkin' about?" Clyde didn't like to be confused. He liked a black and white world where <u>he</u> was in control. The two men shook their bewildered heads. "Well, I'll tell you what. We're gonna go back and you two are gonna get another vehicle and keep an eye on that numbskull for a few days. We're gonna figure this bullshit out! Think you can handle that, or do we need to call in Dick fuckin' Tracy?"

Neither man was in the mood to challenge the fully enraged Clyde. Ray was hoping he wouldn't screw it up and incur the "Wrath of Clyde." The man called Willie hoped he could do it without looking as good at it as he was. They pulled over to Wendell's store down the street, got out and split up.

"I'll be in Mr. Gidding's store," Nick announced to his mother and Matt Striker. The two adults were obviously distracted by something down the street that he could care less about. He wanted to go into Wendell's store and look at guns and hunting equipment. Kate gave her son a distracted wave of assent.

"Some of Buck's cohorts?" Matt asked Kate without taking his eyes off the men standing in the street.

"I don't know. That looks like some of that bunch up at what's it called, 'The Compound.'"

Matt snapped around to look at Kate. "The Compound?"

"Yeah, bunch of survivalists or something live out about twenty-five miles. Middle of nowhere. I've tried to send visiting nurses from our program out to see some of the women, but they were turned away. At gunpoint. Thought I'd never hear the end of that fiasco. Nearly lost a good nurse. Scared her to death!"

"Know any of those characters?" Matt asked neutrally.

"No, I don't think so. But from what I've heard around town, I'd bet the big one in the overalls and the Dixie tee shirt would be Clyde Gash. He runs things up there. Whatever that means." Kate shivered.

"Well, here they come."

The camo truck had pulled away from Buck LaDue and was coming toward them. Kate instinctively started looking around for Nick, then remembered he was in the store. She started that way and tugged on Matt's arm.

"Let's go see what this little monster you've created is into," she said good-naturedly.

Matt walked with her up the store steps but kept his

eyes on the truck and its passengers.

Once inside, Kate scanned the busy store and spotted Nick way down in the back. Wendell was showing the boy a rifle. *Great.* She could see that the storekeeper was holding the gun away from Nick, not letting him handle it at least. She and Matt headed that way.

"Well, young man, I've got some customers to attend to." A couple of loggers were headed for the register, arms full of coffee, pop tarts and Little Debbie's cakes. "I'll get back here as soon as I can..." Wendell looked and saw Kate and Matt heading his way, "...or you can ask Mr. Striker any questions you might have. Yep, imagine he knows more than me anyway."

Mr. Gidding hustled past Kate and Matt and exchanged hellos.

"Hey, Sport, what you find?" Matt asked Nick.

Mr. Gidding showed me a .243. Said it'd be good for someone my size!" Nick was bubbling over.

Matt looked over his shoulder, then back to Nick. "I'd say Mr. Gidding is pretty sharp. A .243, a .284, or even a 7-08 would work well for a fellah your size. What make of rifle did Mr. Gidding show you?"

Nick looked uncertain. "A Browning?" he ventured.

"Was it called a Micro Medallion?" Matt named the maker's small frame rifle.

"Yeah, that's it!" Nick was proud of his guess.

"Nice rifle." Matt held his hand to his chin and looked

to be silently figuring. "'Bout a thousand dollars when you top it with a decent scope."

Nick's eyes bulged out. "A thousand <u>dollars</u>?" He glanced at his mother and caught a look that he'd grown to know as "Not a chance."

Matt caught the boy's look of disappointment. "Don't worry; I have a Browning 7-08 BLR lever action that you can try out." He looked at Kate. "If it's okay with your mom."

"Oh, sure, I get to be the witch," she said under her breath, then louder, "We'll see." Nick hated "We'll see," but he saw Matt wink at him.

"Let's see if there's a hunter orange hat your size in here." Matt turned back toward the store in time to see one of the men who'd been with Clyde Gash walk through and into a hallway in the back. There was something about the countenance of the man that triggered a thought in Matt's mind.

They went through the hats until they found one that was polar fleece and had earflaps that folded down from the inside.

"This one looks warm and it fits you pretty good."

"Yeah, feels pretty good." The boy was tugging at the bill on the hat working it back and forth on his head.

"Maybe we could find a scarf to go with it." Kate knew she'd said something wrong when Matt and Nick shot her the same "Say what?" look. "Well, I don't know what you men wear out there!" she defended herself. The "you men" was all Nick needed to cut his mom some slack, but Matt had to choke back a snicker. She punched the big man in the arm. Hard.

Matt held his hand over his bicep and held up the hand of the arm under attack. "Cease fire! I surrender."

"I gotta go," Nick announced and headed toward the same hall in the back of the store that Clyde's man had gone to. Kate hadn't seen him, and Matt wasn't too worried.

"I have to tell you, Matt, this thing with Nick and hunting and guns…I don't know." She looked off into space.

Matt touched her shoulder. "Give him and me a chance on this, Kate. I know where you're at. We're moving slow and careful. I'm not going to let any harm come to him."

"Oh, I know that." She turned and placed a hand on Matt's chest and looked down. "I trust you and I know this is right for him—to be around you to experience the presence of a good man." Now she looked into Matt's eyes. "I just need to…"

"What the hell's he doin', passin' an elephant?" Clyde Gash bellowed. He and his nephew Ray had walked into Wendell's store and managed to turn everyone's head toward him and Ray. Clyde had a copy of *Gun News* under his arm and Ray had a big bottle of Dr. Pepper in one hand. Clyde fanned his vicious expression from left to right.

"Yuns lookin' at? Never seen a pure-blooded white man in here?" Clyde chuckled at his own joke.

Everyone in the place looked away. Everyone except the big man in the back talking to the purty little thing next to him.

Clyde fixed a hard gaze on Matt Striker that said, "I don't take shit from no one!" He got a scorching look back from Striker that said, "Stay out of my way, fat ass!"

Inside the locked restroom, the man known as Willie Jones felt behind the toilet tank until he found a plastic bag taped to the back of it. He pulled out a piece of paper, read a short message, then took a stub of pencil out of his jacket pocket and wrote a reply. Then the doorknob rattled. He shot a glance at the door. Someone was trying to get in. He hustled the plastic bag back into place and re-taped it to the back of the tank, flushed the toilet.

When Willie Jones walked out of the restroom, a teenager blew by him in a rush that knocked him to the side. He wanted to tell the whip to slow down when he heard Clyde Gash bellowing in the store. He forgot the boy and stepped out.

"Christ Almighty, you shit a brick in there? Come on, boy, we got business to tend to!" Gash shouted.

Willie Jones double-timed it through the store and out the door behind Clyde Gash and the other bonehead with him.

"Charming!" Kate said, talking to no one and everyone.

Matt nodded affirmation and moved to the front window. The threesome was huddled up and pointing down the street. Pointing at Buck LaDue's truck. Matt strained in vain to hear any words spoken. There was something about the character that went into the restroom that had him thinking. Then from the corner of his eye he saw a stranger on the sidewalk coming from the opposite direction.

The stranger bounded up the steps of the store without so much as a glance toward the huddled mass of Gash and Company. The man walked into the store and headed straight for the restroom. As he got past Matt, the letters I.C.E. were easy to read on the back of his dark blue parka. Immigration Customs Enforcement. Federal lawman.

Matt had it figured out: dead drop.

Chapter 34

"The Buck is back!" he slapped the steering wheel of the old Chevy pickup.

Buck LaDue was oblivious to the fact that this would be his last day. In fact, Buck was full of hope this crisp Vermont morning. Who would not be an optimist driving up this deserted highway in the midst of the explosion of colors referred to in the travel guides as "peak foliage?" Buck had never actually read a travel guide himself.

"Yeah, baby, connected and back on top!" He spoke his delusions to no one as he ginned up his warped sense of invincibility. He might be a woodchuck but, by Jesus, he was a crafty one.

As he drove up the highway he smiled as he pondered his situation. The faded old Chevy truck was running pretty well, although she smoked a bit. *Rings are going bad.* He would throw in a can of gunk with the oil—whenever he got around to changing the oil. *That'll hold 'er through the winter.*

Once he had solved the truck maintenance issues, he got back to his current state of affairs. He glanced over at the old green and chrome thermos sitting on the worn seat of the truck. Two unopened cans of Rolling Rock accompanied it. They weren't likely to be unopened long. A half dozen empty cans rolled around on the floor.

His trusty old Savage 300 lever action rifle hung in the rack along the back glass of the pick-up. He loved that old gun—and the long history of giant deer and fierce bears that had been taken with it. Much of that history he had invented himself. All the same, it had been handed down from his daddy before he passed on and he regarded it with a certain reverence. Usually his nostalgia would evaporate into recollections of being slapped around by the drunken old fool. But the old bastard was gone now and the rifle was his. He figured he'd earned it.

As he glanced in the rearview mirror, he caught the reflection of the new camo-colored ATV in the bed of the truck. He smiled as he thought of how clever he had been when he stole it. Hell, it had been simple. He just drove over to Burlington and drove around the parking lot of the shopping mall looking for a pick-up truck with an ATV in the bed. It was Fall and this was Vermont. There were several to choose from, including a truck with a big, burly new ATV in the bed.

He simply backed up to the other truck, opened both his tailgate and the one on the other truck and rolled the ATV into his own truck. Slicker than goose shit. It was even easier than when he stole the one for Rashid.

Now, here he was two weeks later on this cold, clear morning headed up to the remotest section of the north woods of Vermont.

"The Northeast Kingdom, by Jesus, life is good." With any luck, he would poach the biggest deer of his life and finally live up to his name. All the stars were lining up. Nothing could go wrong this time, he figured. Deer season was only a few days off. If he took the deer today, he could hide it until the first day of the season and then go over to the check-in at Gidding's store. "That would get things stirred up down at Wendell's," he murmured. "Why, there'll be backslappin' and storytelling for hours!"

He had first spotted the giant deer ten days ago in a thick patch of fir and spruce about a mile east of Gore Mountain. The area had been an old burnover, probably lightning induced, and was rife with reachable food and dense cover. Remote and tough to access, it was perfect; a veritable deer paradise. He had now seen the big bruiser twice. The monster was at least 300 pounds with antlers as thick at the base as Buck's own wrists.

Good Christ, if he actually got this deer he could be as famous as the Bennateau brothers over at Newport. There would be interviews for newspapers all over the state; he might even get on TV. Buck fancied himself the talk of the Kingdom, subject to admiration and jealousy in every burg from St. Johnsbury to the Canadian border. Maybe even Kate Halliard would look at him with a new respect! *Probably not — got to be realistic. Forget that bitch!*

He turned the truck up a desolate road. The pavement

gave way to gravel as he headed toward the mountain. Eastbound now, the morning sun turned the smoke and dirt of the windshield to a blinding glare. He popped his first Rolling Rock and took a long pull from the can.

Now Buck picked his way along the alternately shaded and sunbathed secondary road. Not wanting to miss the next turn, he intently watched ahead for an old logging path going off from the road. This required close scrutiny as the north woods were full of logging roads. When he spotted a turnout in the washboard road, he stopped, put the truck in neutral, reached over and yanked the four-wheel drive lever into place. Setting the brake, he slid out of the truck as he reached in the pocket of his worn, green plaid wool jacket and found an unopened pack of Marlboros. He turned his head up, enjoyed the earthy smells of the outdoors and the faint odor of a wood stove fire that had drifted in from miles to the north. He unconsciously tapped the pack of cigarettes against the fender of the Chevy in an age-old ritual. It was like spitting in the urinal when he took a piss. There was no real reason for it, but it was a practiced habit nonetheless. Peeling the wrapper from the pack, Buck threw the cellophane to the ground without a thought. Mechanically, he tapped out a single smoke, grabbed it with his lips while spinning the wheel of his old silver Zippo lighter. Absently, he ran his thumb over the engraving on the lighter. He lit the cigarette and snapped the Zippo shut. He took a cursory look around as he enjoyed the smoke.

There was an overgrown clearing across the road that had been part of a hardscrabble farm now long since abandoned. A dilapidated barn, faded to an ashen hue, sagged in the overgrown meadow, defying gravity as it somehow managed to support a ragged rusted tin roof. Rays of the sun were working their way down across the roof, leaving a hard line between the dirty white of the shaded untouched frost on the lower section of the metal roof and the illuminated upper section, which was black and steaming in the sun's light. The cold smoke rose some several feet above the roof before drifting off to the south and disappearing into thin air.

Looks like it might warm up a bit. The ground is frosted firm now, but it might get greasy later.

The deeper he got into the wilderness, the more euphoric he became. Ahead he spied his landmark, two paper white birches growing side by side not eight feet from the road. The one on the right had been bowed over by some past ice storm, while the other oddly stood ramrod straight. There was a wide tire-tall earthen berm to the right of the trees.

It hardly looked like a trail at all. But Buck muscled the old half-ton up over the mound using the truck's creeper gear. Inching on up the trail, the truck clawed, scraped and bumped through the brush. At five foot nine, Buck wasn't tall enough to see every obstacle over the hood of the truck as he moved along uphill. At one point the truck lurched and slammed down hard on a rock with a teeth-rattling jar. Pulling up to a flat table, he stopped and got out to take a close look under the truck to see if the oil pan had survived the thump. As he knelt down and bent over, the Zippo slipped from the top pocket of the old Johnson wool jacket and quietly landed on the ground. Satisfied with the condition of the pan, he climbed back in and continued on. By minor miracle the back tire of the truck missed grinding the lighter into the dirt.

Another mile down the trail he came to a small clearing barely bigger than the truck. It was flat, open and provided the perfect place to unload _his_ new ATV.

After the Chevy stopped, Buck folded down the tailgate and slid out two metal ramps. He climbed aboard the machine, started it and backed it out of the truck. Jumping off, Buck opened the truck door and grabbed the old coffee thermos, the unopened Rolling Rock and his Savage rifle. He packed the beverages away in a plastic trunk mounted on the rear of the ATV and set his rifle across the back on a built-in rifle rack.

This is a pretty slick rig. Wonder what it cost?

He slipped his compass out of the pocket of his wool Cadet pants and took a quick look. The plan was set in his mind. He would circle the mountain, taking the trails leading south and east for another two miles then park the ATV and travel on foot due north into the wind and parallel to the VAST trail. The trail would be deserted during this season and like all cleared but unused trails, it would likely be an undisturbed big game highway this time of year. Coming in from downwind, Buck could quietly slip down the mountain to his right from time to time and observe the trail for his prize deer. All the while, stealthily working his way north to the thick cover where he had discovered the monster buck earlier.

Consumed with the plan, Buck rode along on the ATV and sooner than he realized, was in the brushy area where he intended to hide the ATV.

Don't want no one to steal it!

He smiled at his own joke.

He opened the plastic trunk and briefly debated whether to drink the coffee or the beer. The beer was pretty good, but he might need something cold by the time he got back. He drank the coffee. He took the beer from the trunk and laid it in a pile of maple leaves in the shade under the ATV.

Checking the compass one more time, he pulled off his rifle and started side-hilling to the north. An old game trail made the footing for his worn gum rubber and leather hunting boots easy going. The sun, where it broke through the canopy of brilliant maple and deep green spruce and fir, was thawing the top coat of the ground making it slippery. He'd keep a close watch for such places as he wanted to be as stealthy as possible.

He reached up to the brim of his greasy old hunter-orange cap and pushed the bill back so he could see better. From here the big deer, *his big deer*, could show itself for a quick shot from the Savage. He worked the lever action, jacked up a shell and set the safety.

Don't want to slip in the grease and shoot my damn foot off.

Where the rifle sling met the front swivel on the forestock, he had tied on a short piece of red yarn to serve as a "telltale." He held the rifle out horizontally in front of him and looked at the yarn. It swung back toward him, pushed by a breeze so slight he could not perceive it on his face.

Still coming from the north.

He eased on into the wind, now on high alert. After covering about a hundred yards, he suddenly jerked to a stop as his peripheral vision caught the motion of a great horned owl swooping down the mountain and across his trail not twenty-five feet in front of him. He jumped back as the big owl hit a snowshoe hare off to the right of the trail. For an instant, feathers and fur flew everywhere and then the giant bird continued on down the slope with the squealing hare in its talons. It was all so fast he couldn't immediately register what had happened. His heart was thumping and he absently drew the sleeve of his jacket across the beads of sweat above his lip.

Good Christ, never seen that before, was all his rattled mind could put together.

He stiffly walked over to where the owl and snowshoe collided and with a trembling hand picked up pieces of fur and a feather, as if to convince himself that his eyes were not playing tricks on him. "Damn," he muttered.

As his heartbeat started back toward normal, it occurred to him to get moving again. After another hundred yards, through the thick forest, he stopped and tied a small orange ribbon to a tree branch to help him with his return to the ATV. He hoped he'd have to go fetch it to haul his deer back to a good hanging spot.

As he moved on away from the marker, he tried to concentrate on the shapes in the woods in front of him. Most things in the woods were lateral, up and down. What he was looking for were horizontal shapes, like the belly or back of a deer, or a twitch of white from its tail—maybe even the glint of sunlight off of antlers. He eased on to the north.

He had just stopped to step over a fallen log when he thought he heard a very faint, faraway sound. *What the Sam hell?* He was starting to get agitated. Just as he was about to puzzle through the sound, it faded away. If it was what he thought it was, it meant that his day was shot. There'd be no point in continuing on. He stood stock-still, cocked his head and strained to hear.

Voices? Nothing. He stood so still that soon he was aware of his breathing. He could hear his coat rub the rifle, now slung over his shoulder, with each inhale and exhale.

A foreboding began to creep through the small cracks of his high hopes and plans for the day. But he stood there silently listening. Inside he was building up a brew of anger and little dose of fear.

Who the hell would be way out here?

If it was voices, that meant that it was more than one person. The only good way over to this side of the mountain was the way he had come. He hadn't seen any truck tracks. No fresh snapped twigs or any other sign of intruders. If they had come from the north, they would have to have started into the woods last night — and traveled all night to be here. He stood still, straining to hear. Nothing.

Waiting longer, he still heard nothing. He began to entertain the notion that everything was okay, that there weren't some "flatland yahoos" coming in from the north, with the wind on their backs, stinking up the woods with human scent and driving *his* big deer miles away.

Stiffness was setting in from standing still so long. Time to move on. As he carefully moved forward, he debated himself.

Move on to the deer haven he had found days before or drop down the mountain and check the VAST trail?

VAST stood for Vermont Area Snow Travelers. VAST was as much a phenomenon as a group of like-minded people. The accomplishments of VAST were mind-boggling in scope and nearly as impressive as the ancient Roman's aqueduct system. Instead of moving water, VAST concentrated on moving snowmobiles, or "sleds" as they are known, and not just moving the sleds short distances, but rather moving them along a super highway system that went for hundreds and hundreds of miles through farmlands, along roads, across frozen lakes and ponds, and through large tracts of wilderness. There were primary trails, secondary trails and access spurs forming a network that blanketed the entire state of Vermont. They then connected to trails in adjoining states and Canada.

Trails were built and maintained by hundreds of volunteers from all walks of life, woodchucks to professionals. The entire marvel accented by the fact that very nearly all of the trail system lay on private land and virtually no government assistance went into its making. Thus, the system was regarded with a sense of reverence by all that knew it, nowhere more solemnly than by all, prince to pauper, who resided in the Kingdom. Any blasphemy that was visited upon the VAST system was spoken of with contempt.

Hearing no other strange sounds, Buck dropped down toward the trail. Not knowing precisely where he would intersect the trail, he simply moved downhill and to the east.

Buck was frozen in place. He stood stock-still locked on to the sight _and_ sounds below him.

His worst fears materialized before his eyes. There were men down on the trail and he could hear the cadence of bickering. Straining hard to hear, he couldn't make out the words. Carefully, he eased to his right to see better through the light underbrush. A tire, parts of an engine, a roll bar, something on top of the roll bar he couldn't make out.

By Jesus, the dumb bastards have an ATV on the VAST trail.

Hot blood rushed up his neck onto his face, turning both crimson.

ATVs were strictly forbidden on the VAST trails, though there was little to prevent them other than the wrath of the masses who would, any one of them, not hesitate to dress down a violator -- preferably in public.

The potential damage done to a sled trail could be horrific. Big fat tires grinding away in soft, yet to be frosted soil would create huge ruts of destruction. Bad anywhere, worst of all in the many cedar bogs along the trail. The offense was so low that not even a deer-poaching thief and small-time fence like Buck would stoop to it. Not in broad daylight.

He stiffened with his surging anger. Not just because of the ATV offense, but because these flatland idiots surely had spooked his giant deer away and stripped him of the fame and fortune he thought he so richly deserved.

Moving a bit more to his right to better witness the atrocity before him, he carelessly stepped down on an old dry, brittle tree branch, just as the bickering below him came to a lull. SNAP!

Buck stood rigid in the thin cover. The crack of the tree branch, he knew, could be heard by anyone within a hundred yards. He figured the interlopers to be about thirty yards downhill from him.

THWACK! The first bullet hit the walnut stock of his beloved Savage 99 as he had cradled it through his arm. The impact blew splinters from the shattering hardwood, spinning Buck and knocking him to the ground. Instinctively, pointing the Savage downhill and throwing off the safety, he yelled, "There's a man up here, ya dumb sons a bitches!" *Just like flatlanders to shoot at shadows*, he groused to himself.

The ground around Buck erupted in splinters, twigs flying and a deafening barrage of gunfire.

Buck looked down at the blood pouring from his side and started running.

Chapter 35

While the boys were warming up with their hot chocolate, Matt dug into a drawer and pulled out two battered old automatic thirty-five millimeter cameras and handed one each to the boys.

"Batteries are up, film is in them."

Both boys handled the prizes with reverence.

"What should we take pictures of?" Nick asked.

"Yes, we do not have the big lens." Rami was pointing out the obvious difference between the little cameras and Matt's big Nikon with the high speed telephoto lens.

"Anything! Everything! And good pictures don't always require a big lens. In fact, <u>most</u> don't." Matt pointed to his own walls.

The boys nodded in understanding.

But as thrilled as Nick and Rami were, there was a burning question on both their minds and they were independently puzzling over how to bring it up. They didn't have to.

"And for every truly exceptional shot you get, we take an hour of practice with the rifles," Matt announced to their delight. "First, the twenty-two, then we'll use the seven oh eight. But the photo has to be <u>good</u>. Good composition, good subject matter. Think you can do that?"

"You bet," "Yes, sir," their replies were spoken over each other.

"Okay, here's what you have to remember. Each camera has a 36-shot roll in it, and you'll be <u>lucky</u> to have one or two good ones. That's how photography is."

"We'll have lots of good ones," Nick boasted like the teenager he was.

"I like confidence. Let's see if you have the discipline to go with it."

After the boys left, Matt's cell phone vibrated in his pocket.

"Detto, speak to me."

"What kinda freakin' wilderness paradise you got up there? That Clyde Gash is on the ATF radar screen," Detto said.

"No shit?"

"I shit you not. In fact, we got a guy on the inside."

"At the compound?"

"Unlike you U.S. Marshall turds, we ATF guys are all over it!"

"What ya got?"

"Definitely serious weapon charges, conspiracy, and get this, maybe attempted murder is simmering."

"Know the target?" Matt asked, his mind racing.

"Not yet. Our guy's working with a dead drop in, get this, Big Larch. We got an ICE guy leaving and picking up messages in town there." Immigration Customs Enforcement was part of the U.S.-Canada border operation. Some of the agents lived in and around Big Larch, the border being only twenty-five miles away. ICE agents were a common sight in the Kingdom, particularly on the highways north of town.

"Tell me about the guy on the inside."

"Don't know him myself. Ex-ranger, cracker from down south. They say he's good. Real good."

"So when's the bust?"

Chapter 36

"Any of you jaybirds seen LaDue around here of late?" Sheriff Drew had walked into Wendell Gidding's store. A fire was burning in the old stove on this crisp October morning. The old boys, Cecil and Howard, were in their regular spot hunched over a checkerboard. Wendell was up at a shelf pulling down some ammunition that the warden, Sam Hood, had stopped in for. Everyone turned their heads toward the sheriff.

"Mornin', Sheriff." Wendell acknowledged the rare visit from Drew. "What's that about LaDue?"

"Seen him?"

"Not for...." Wendell looked at Cecil and Howard for help. One said last Tuesday, the other said last Thursday. "Musta been Wednesday or so." Wendell smiled.

"You gonna pick him up?" Sam Hood knew better than to ask that in front of the heart and soul of the town rumor mill, but it slipped out.

"Nothin' like that. His sister down at White River Junction says he was supposed to be down at her place a few days ago. Says he was goin' down to pay her back some money he owed her. Said he hasn't been answering the phone." Drew looked around at the bland faces a moment.

"Call me if you see the weasel."

"Hell, I can't find him. Don't want to find him." Warden Sam Hood stewed.

Troopers were looking along the interstate between the Kingdom and White River Junction for any sign of a vehicle going off the road. The sheriff's deputies were looking along the secondary roads and the rumors were flying. Some said he went to Canada to hunt. Some had him over in Maine. Others said he was holed up with some ne'er-do-well watching all the fuss and laughing his fool ass off. Some even speculated he'd been rubbed out by the mob.

As the sheriff predicted, Warden Sam Hood got roped into the search. A task force had been set up between the state police, the sheriff's office and fish and wildlife officers.

Hood got a call from his superior down in Waterbury announcing that he would be their representative and that he was to render "all assistance" to Sheriff Dick Drew.

Great. Hunting season just around the corner and I'll be out chasing a jerk I'd hoped would <u>never</u> come back.

The warden was processing all this when he went past the Blueberries-in-Thyme Restaurant.

Matt, Kate and Detto sat in the booth next to the front window eating lunch and conversing.

"So, Vito, what brings you back up this way?" Kate was asking.

Vito looked sidelong at Matt before responding. As it turned out, he didn't have to make up an answer on the spot. Someone was tapping on the glass right beside where they sat. The guy in a green khaki uniform motioned to Matt.

"Excuse me just a minute, folks." Matt got up and went outside on the sidewalk to talk with Warden Sam Hood.

Just then, Vito's cell phone rang. He got a pained expression on his face and spoke to Kate. "Geez, I'm really sorry." He got up to take the phone outside.

When Detto got outside, Matt and the other guy were left so he went right.

"You heard about Buck LaDue, I guess." Hood spoke to Matt, who nodded affirmatively. "Well, I'm officially part of the search now. So before I start running my ass all over the backwoods of the Kingdom, I got one off-the-record question for you."

"Fire away," Matt invited.

Before he began, the warden looked around him to see if anyone was in earshot. "Tell me straight up, Striker, you know anything about this?"

Matt held his palms up. "Give me some credit here, Sam. If I'd taken that knot-head out, it would have been way back; it would have looked like an accident, and I wouldn't have been within a hundred miles of here when it happened, and I'd have no less than a dozen people swearing to it!" Matt was irritated, and he saw that Kate was sitting alone now. He started back inside.

"Hey, I had to hear it from you, Matt. No offense."

Matt turned back with a softer look. "None taken." He grabbed the door handle.

"Kemo Sabe!"

Now what?

Detto, who he mistakenly trusted to stay and charm Kate, was yelling for him down the sidewalk the other way.

Matt stuck his head into the restaurant for a moment and said something to Kate, then walked toward Detto. Hood was well down the sidewalk the other direction.

"This is a quiet little town. Why does it feel like Grand Central Station?" Matt asked his pal.

"Hey, I got a call from down at ATF. Seems our guy inside the compound is overdue at his dead drop here in town."

Chapter 37

Magog Gadue was confused. As he lay on his belly looking down over a rocky cliff to the scene below, he tried in vain to make sense of it.

There were two funny men below him. At least they talked funny. Some kind of gibberish that he could not understand. Not that he understood much of any language, but this one left him with his big moon-shaped face screwed up, deep in thought. They even looked funny somehow. Different.

He wanted to conclude that they had come from a hole in the ground. When he was very small he had heard that such things happened from time to time. But even his simple mind could not reconcile the ATV the men had been riding. He knew about ATVs. He found one parked in the woods over a year ago and had taken it. He wasn't sure why he took it. It was noisy in the woods and it used gasoline which he normally had none of. So he parked it in a dense brushy draw and left it to rust. Maybe he would think of some use for it later.

But this was a very different ATV. It had two seats side by side. The riders didn't straddle the motor, and there was a rack on top with some kind of long tubes. Magog had never seen anything like it.

And now things were really getting strange because the two funny men had gotten out of the strange ATV and had proceeded to open up a hail of gunfire directed at a big bull moose not fifty yards up the trail. He had never witnessed such a waste of ammunition nor heard such a barrage of firing. He didn't understand at all.

As if things couldn't possibly get stranger, the men got back in the ATV and proceeded down the trail driving right past the big bull, not taking any meat or even the impressive horns.

The entire scene defied every ounce of logic that Magog possessed.

Bewitched, he decided to follow. He would come back for the moose later.

Chapter 38

Omar Aziz couldn't believe his ears. Time-share ownership of a <u>boat</u>?

The terrorist was standing on the dock at the Burlington waterfront looking at a late model thirty-two foot, twin V-8, fly bridge Carver cabin cruiser. The cabin was heated and had a second helm. There was a galley, sleeping for six and two heads. It even had a thumping sound system.

Ernie Norris, part-time Burlington city council member and full-time craft shop owner, was explaining the details to Aziz.

"So, for five thousand dollars you can own the month of October every year. We put the boat away for winter storage after the first week of November. You would actually use it right up 'til that point, no extra charge. Course, there is a one thousand dollar a year maintenance and dockage fee for each month of rental."

Aziz nodded his understanding. Inside he was jubilant.

These stupid infidels are victims of their own design. This boat, the one that will deliver the deadly payload to New York, is being provided by the western pigs for next to nothing —because they have figured out yet another scheme of godless consumption.

"So for six thousand dollars, it's yours for the next

month, and one thousand dollars makes it yours for October next year." Ernie smiled at the Arab.

Aziz knew he would buy in. He also knew there would be no "next October."

"How fast does it run?" Aziz asked.

"She'll cruise at twenty-eight knots."

A nautical mile was a bit more than a statute mile. A boat cruising at twenty-eight knots was cruising at just over thirty miles per hour. Very fast for a big cruiser. Aziz was delighted.

He bought in.

As instructed, Ray Gash and Willie Jones tailed Buck LaDue's truck and trailer up toward Gore Mountain. They were tempted to follow him up the dirt track that led into the wilderness but finally thought better of it. They didn't want to blow the surveillance by rounding a curve in the brush and finding Buck right in front of them. Buck would spot them for sure. Besides, it looked like one way in and one way out. They went back down to the highway and waited for LaDue to come down.

Ray rolled his window down, lit a cigarette and Willie cracked open a thermos of coffee. They chatted a bit, speculating on what Buck was up to and then settled down for a wait.

"He had an ATV in the truck." Ray stated the obvious.

"When did he buy that?" Willie was mildly curious.

"When did he steal it more likely," Ray snorted.

"Yeah, probably," Willie allowed. "Makes it less likely he was talking to the law up there."

"Maybe it was a gift," Ray said, sitting up straight. "Yeah, a gift from his new partners he was blowing off about." Now Ray was excited by the brilliance of his speculation.

"So where is he now?" Willie said calmly, adding, "He's probably doing a little out of season hunting is all."

Ray slumped back down in his seat a bit. The image of him telling Clyde about Buck doing next to nothing wasn't very attractive.

Willie was probably right. Ray had observed that Willie was right most of the time he'd known him.

"So I guess we got two things to tell Clyde," Jones announced. "One is he's tending his criminal enterprise, running around with stolen ATVs, so he ain't lickin' up to the law, and two, he roams out to lonely places, so if we want to take him, it won't be all that hard --if we can find him." Jones looked over at Gash's nephew. "He's your uncle. Why don't you tell him?"

"Okay, I'll do that." This was like a gift from above. He could be the sly dog explaining the situation to his uncle. He knew he'd rise a few rungs on the ladder around the compound with recon information like that. Then Ray looked suspiciously at Willie.

"How come you don't tell him?"

"Ain't my uncle."

"Hey, Detto what's up?"

Matt, Kate and Nick were at Kate's house when Matt's cell phone rang and vibrated. He had excused himself and stepped out on the porch.

Brutus followed Matt out and sat next to the big man when he sat on the porch swing. Matt absently petted his head as he spoke into the phone.

"How'd ya figure it out?" Detto asked.

"Figure what out?"

"The dead drop? That was it. We got it."

"Just put the pieces together at the time. So, what you got?" Matt asked his friend. It had been a week — he'd almost forgotten.

"The target is none other than Buck LaDue."

"Weapons for sure. Maybe trafficking in weapons, explosives, conspiracy to commit murder. Looks real good now."

"So what's the plan?" Matt knew what was coming.

"Take 'em."

"When?"

"Soon as we can lure him out. We'll take him outside then hit the compound when there's no leader. From what we've heard, the rest of the crew's a bunch of dimwits."

"Dimwits with a lot of firepower," Matt corrected.

When Sam Hood went into Wendell Gidding's store a week after Clyde Gash and Matt Striker had been there, he had no idea of the mess he was walking into.

Wendell Gidding liked Magog Gadue. Or felt a little sorry for him maybe. Out there alone all the time, living a life of subsistence. No family. No friends. No permanent shelter from the godawful, unforgiving elements of the Kingdom. He knew that among the pelts brought in by the trapper he also brought in prizes from out-of-season game. Poached game. Like deer hides in September. But Wendell turned a blind eye, bought the goods or more often traded for flour, cornmeal, sugar, traps, ammo and whatnot. But this time Wendell was nervous.

Magog came into the store looking like a real by-God mountain man. He was covered in animal skins, fringe, boots with the fur turned out, rawhide laced in his long hair. And carrying a huge set of moose antlers. Everyone knew moose season wasn't for two weeks yet and they likewise knew it was reserved for the fortunate few who were drawn for the hunt by lottery. And here was Magog walking in, in broad daylight, carrying the big antlers.

"Geezem-crow, Gadue, you're gonna get us <u>both</u> arrested!" Wendell wrestled the big rack from Magog and laid it on the floor behind the counter.

"Sell to you. How much?"

"Shit, Gadue, I can't buy them things. Couldn't you

wait a few weeks for the season to come in?"

Magog Gadue looked a little confused. He couldn't get his simple mind around this season business. Besides, he hadn't shot the moose, just cut the antlers off a dead one. The one the funny men shot. What could be wrong with that?

"I find them. Everything okay. You buy them."

Wendell looked skeptically at the horns attached to part of the skull that was sawed away from the carcass. There were still bits of brain matter on the inside of the skull. Wendell knew that people often found antlers naturally shed by deer and moose. These were no sheds.

"Can't do it, Magog. We'll both be in trouble. You gotta get these out of here. Bring them back in a few weeks maybe. Then we can make up a good story for you."

"Not sell them. Trade. I trade for...." The halfwit started looking around the store. Then Sam Hood, the game warden, walked in.

Magog Gadue snapped his head back toward Wendell and his face turned beet-red. He stayed in that position and closed his eyes, hoping against hope that the bad man would go away.

"Hey there, Wendell," Sam greeted the storekeeper who was moving away from Gadue. He looked like the cat that ate the canary. Hood also noticed the two old men, Cecil and Howard, look away when his gaze swung their way. They went back to checkers. Or pretended to.

Magog fumbled something silver out of his pocket and started to absently play with it. Snap. Snap. Snap.

"What you two up to?"

Sam knew Wendell Gidding to be a well-meaning, honest man. It was his experience that when such men got caught in a compromise, they wore it all over them. The way Wendell looked at this very moment. The warden moved in for a closer look at what was going on. He sidled up to Magog, who was nearly shaking, and looked over the counter, spotting the moose antlers. Then he looked at Wendell like a disappointed parent looks at their kid sucking on their first cigarette.

"It's not what it looks like, Sam," Wendell said lamely.

"Oh, well then, Mr. Gidding, what exactly is it?" Hood said sternly.

Gadue, standing on the other side of the warden, took the opportunity to start to slip away while Hood spoke to Wendell. Without even looking at him, the warden's hand shot out and grabbed Magog's arm firmly.

"No you don't son. You stay put where you are. Now Mr. Gidding, you were saying...."

Sam was obviously using "Mr. Gidding" instead of "Wendell" as a distancing technique. It wasn't lost on the storekeeper. As Wendell started telling the brief story, Magog got the silver object from his pocket again and handled it nervously. Snap. Snap.

"....said he found it up on Gore Mountain." Wendell

was near the end of the story.

Snap. Snap.

The warden turned to Magog Gadue. Snap. Snap.

"Goddamit, quit playin' with that!" Hood snatched a silver lighter out of Gadue's hand. At first he didn't look at it.

"Found it?" the warden asked the dimwitted mountain man.

"Found it!" Magog shook his head emphatically.

"You didn't shoot it?" Hood's tone was mocking.

"The funny men shoot it."

"That's what he's been saying," Wendell jumped in.

"Funny men? Funny like how?" Sam decided to play along.

"Talk funny," Magog explained.

"Talked funny." Hood was getting exasperated. "Mr. Gidding, set them antlers up here on the counter where I can see them."

The storeowner walked over and complied. The first thing that was evident was the sheer size of them. It made the warden steam that a majestic bull had been poached in his jurisdiction. He examined the rack more closely. Fresh. Still had flesh hanging from the skull. *What the hell was this?* He ran his hand over a mud patch that broke off revealing a neat little hole in the skull. A twenty-two caliber hole. No bigger than twenty-five caliber, that's for sure. Something was wrong here. Sam Hood had been playing cat and mouse with Magog Gadue for years. He knew the man was mentally limited, that he had no regard for hunting seasons. Probably didn't understand them. He knew he was living out there on a state of subsistence. And he knew Magog carried a lever action thirty-thirty, mostly. If Magog Gadue was going to take a moose, it would likely be a tender young cow, not a tough old bull. And he'd surely shoot it with the thirty caliber rifle.

Hood took his hands off the moose antlers and absently picked up the silver lighter he'd taken away from Gadue and started turning it in his hand thinking.

Found. Funny men. What the hell?

Then he glanced down at the lighter and noticed it was engraved. He thumbed away some dirt on the side until he could read it clearly.

"Well I'll be damned."

The engraving read "BUCK".

Within a few minutes, Sam had run the old coots out of the store and had Wendell and Magog sitting at the checker table. The "closed" sign was in the window and two phone calls were made.

Matt's irritation melted away as soon as he heard what the warden had to say.

"You call the sheriff?"

"He's on his way," Hood responded. "Can you come

on down?"

"Why me?"

"'Cause when we get into the woods up there, we'll need good eyes, good instincts."

Matt looked into Kate's house. He could see Nick and Kate in the kitchen getting a quick meal collected. "You mean now?"

"Now."

"Okay." Matt hung up and went into Kate's house, Brutus in tow. He delivered the news.

Kate and Nick were visibly disappointed. "Right now?"

"Yeah, they want me down there at Gidding's. You know anything about this Magog character?"

"He scalps people when he catches them in the woods," Nick said. Obviously the kids in the area had their own wild stories about the mountain man.

Kate shot Nick a hard look. "That's nonsense, Nick Halliard, and you know it. Now let us talk a minute."

Nick was both offended and ashamed at himself. He'd acted like a dumb kid, and now he was excluded from the adult conversation.

"He's mentally incompetent by most standards. Has the mind of a twelve-year-old. People guess him to be in his late thirties. Parents lived up in the wildest part of the Kingdom. Subsistence. Mostly trapping. Parents stopped appearing in town years ago they say. Probably died up there; who knows how. Magog comes into town once a month or so. I've seen him a couple times myself. Right out of *Jeremiah Johnson* if you ask me. I feel sorry for him. Up there all alone, comes to town and people look at him like he's a freak. He speaks a little, but it's obvious that he's not getting much practice up in the mountains. Unless he talks to the animals." Kate had a wistful tone. It was obvious that she felt for the man's isolation. Maybe she was thinking of her own isolation. Then she snapped back. "He's harmless, Matt. Go easy."

As Matt strode over to the table, he could see a topographic map laid out on the table. The mountain man sat uncomfortably on a chair, fidgeting and looking around nervously. The arrival of the big man didn't help his anxiety. Matt could see the effect and was careful not to close in on the man.

"Magog here was just helping us figure out where he found ole Buck's lighter." Drew used a good-natured tone obviously trying to put the mountain man at ease.

"That's right," the warden looked at the man dressed in skins. "There are some 'funny men' up in the woods who shot a moose and might have something to do with Buck going missing." Hood's tone was totally condescending. Magog was suspicious. He was acclimated to the warden's stern lectures, and the softer side was something new altogether. "He was just about to show us on the map here where he found Buck's lighter and where the 'funny men' were."

After a few minutes of looking at the map and trying to get input from Magog Gadue, the warden and the sheriff were both clearly frustrated. It was clear that the mountain man had probably never seen a map of his own backyard.

"Well shit!" Hood gave up. Then he looked at the mountain man. "You'll just have to take us there. You can do <u>that</u>, can't you?"

Magog shook his head affirmatively. "Too late to go up there today. Be dark in a few hours," the sheriff said. "First thing in the morning."

Sergeant Munson nodded agreement.

"What you gonna do with him?" Matt asked about the mountain man.

"I can take him down and put him in a cell for the night."

Magog looked wild-eyed at the people around him. He just wanted to go back to the woods and be left alone. "No. Shit, I'll take him home with me. We're not locking him up," the warden said with finality.

Magog looked relieved. The devil you know....

"Hell, I knew you weren't the hard-ass you make out to be." The sheriff smiled at the stern-looking warden.

"Let's get to work here." Hood bent over the map. "Striker, get on in here and look at this map with us so we don't go up there and step on our own dicks."

When Matt got outside, he flipped on his phone and hit the speed dial. "Kemo Sabe, speak to me."

"You aren't going to believe <u>this</u> shit." Matt told Debenedetto the whole story "This is getting a little weird," Matt understated.

"Yeah, and it gets more weird. You got Clyde Gash saying he's going to take LaDue out and I got a call from the ATF lab an hour ago. Remember the marks on the shell casing?"

"Yeah." Matt had nearly forgotten about the casing he'd picked up when his house got shot up.

"Did I tell you there was something strange about the extractor marks?" Detto was gloating. "Well get this. They weren't AR, they weren't Ruger, they were Kalashnikov!"

"Bullshit, they were .223. Kalashnikov doesn't make a .223."

"What did I just tell you, hardhead? They were Kalashnikov!"

Matt's head was swimming. He stopped and thought it through. Finally it hit him. "Conversion?"

"Bingo."

Someone had rebuilt a Kalashnikov rifle to accept NATO or Remington .223 caliber cartridges. But the extractor marks remained the same as any other Kalashnikov.

"Well, that ought to narrow things down a bit," Matt reasoned.

"Maybe something will turn up when we take Gash and the compound."

"When is that?" Matt asked.

"Day after tomorrow. Just about everyone's in the vicinity now. The meeting's tomorrow night. Your place."

Chapter 39

Shuri was terrified.

Her brother Abu bin Seidu and Kahem Raziq Khan had been in their home for several days now. She remembered Khan from her childhood. He was a savage. He being in her home, here in America, was surreal. Something very bad was happening. The house was filled with whispers, tension and looks of disdain. She nearly pushed Rami out of the house to go play with his friend Nick Halliard at every opportunity. She wanted him safe. The men were hanging around the store and the warehouse, talking on their cell phones. At home, they sent and received messages from her husband Rashid's computer.

In just a few days, the world had gone crazy. Rashid was a mess, Rami was mystified by the presence of the uncle he barely remembered, and the frightening man with him. Shuri was caught between abject fear and trying to make things seem normal in the vain hope that maybe they could be. But she knew she was deluding herself.

Where could I go? What could I do? Could my little family be butchered in their sleep?

Thankfully, when the boys, Nick and Rami, were

together, they were fully distracted. They had gotten their hands on cameras and were running around town snapping shots at everything. It had something to do with the big man Kate Halliard was seeing. Shuri was thankful for the distraction. Maybe it would help keep Rami out of harm's way.

She shivered.

Kate had taken the news from Matt pretty well.

"So I'm going to be tied up for a couple of days it looks like."

Kate moved in close to him. "I want you to be careful." Then she looked down.

Matt wasn't used to this kind of concern. In his world the next two days were a piece of cake. What was there to worry about? He put a finger under Kate's chin and lifted her head to see his smile.

"Kate, this is duck soup. Really! Besides, I'm just the water boy on these teams."

Kate nodded her head then changed the subject. She didn't want to look like a wimpy female. "The boys think they're coming to your house on Sunday."

Matt thought a second and nodded his head. "Yeah, that's on."

Kate smiled. "They've been taking pictures of <u>everything</u>!"

"They've only got thirty-six shots a piece," Matt said.

Kate looked sheepish. "I am right, aren't I?"

"Well, not exactly."

"You gave them more film, didn't you?"

"Two rolls. Each."

"Two rolls of twenty-four each?"

"Thirty-six," Kate confessed.

"You're killin' me here!" Matt shook his head in mock pain. Then added hopefully, "Any shots of you in the shower?"

Kate slapped him on the shoulder. Hard. "You're bad, Striker!"

"We'll see about that." He leaned in and kissed her softly on the lips. She moaned.

"No fair."

Matt picked her up and carried her into her bedroom. For the next hour, the world went away.

Connie held her stare.

She had gone into the convenience store to pay for the gas she'd pumped into her old Volvo wagon; she was immediately struck by the mood of the place. Shuri was fidgety, Rashid was fumbling with a stubborn cash register tape and two men with dark complexions stood in the back whispering to each other. When she looked at the men she stared directly at them.

Connie Cutter was a progressive, liberated woman. She looked eyeball to eyeball with anyone. If they didn't like it, then fuck them.

But this time the look that was returned from the two men gave her a chill. Were they there to rob the place? She eased up to Shuri and handed her a twenty.

"You okay here?"

Shuri gave Connie a stiff smile. "Everything's fine. My brother came for a visit. He'll be gone soon." The last part sounded like a hope more than an explanation.

"Oh, well, that's nice," Connie said flatly. She didn't go for that Middle Eastern subservient woman crap. She wished she could go over and kick the two men in the balls. But life wasn't perfect. She took her change and walked out.

Something is wrong in there.

Chapter 40

When Matt, Sam and Magog spilled out of the truck, they were two hundred yards up a logging road off the highway north of town. They were less than fifteen miles from the Canadian border. Magog moved up the trail ahead of the lawmen.

"Everything go okay at your house last night?"

"He slept on the floor. We put him in a guest room, but he wouldn't use the bed. Slept on the floor right below the window. Thought my wife was gonna kill me. She said he stunk. Kids thought it was kinda cool, but then said something about being scalped. It was quite a night."

"Sounds like it. Why didn't you just let the sheriff take him?"

Hood pointed ahead at the half-wild man who was moving through the woods like he owned every square inch of it. "Wouldn't have been right."

"I guess," Matt concurred.

The hike to the spot where Magog had found the lighter was easy. They never left the two-track trail. The imprint of the lighter was still stamped in the mud. Tire tracks ran by it. They followed the trail on to where Buck LaDue's truck was parked. It sat still and alone in the woods. Inert.

Hood signaled Magog to stop, and he and Striker approached the truck cautiously. Matt had his hand on a Glock 19 on his hip. The truck was empty. Hood took a GPS out of his pocket, entered a waypoint and took note of the latitude and longitude. He got on a radio.

"We got Buck's truck, Sheriff."

"Anything else?" the radio crackled.

"Empty beer can and ATV tracks."

"Okay. Give me the location of the truck. I'll get a team to come in behind you. We're making our way up from the southeast. Slow going on the machines. Muddy. ATV tracks down here too. We're probably two hours out at this rate. Maybe more. You fellas keep going. I'll put Sergeant Munson's team behind you."

"Roger that." Hood clipped the radio back on his belt.

"Let's see where this ATV went."

"Forget the moose?" Striker asked the warden.

"For now, yeah."

"Good move."

It was an hour of hard hiking before they came upon the ATV. It was in the brush half-hidden. They approached with the same caution that they used for the truck.

Hood was back on the radio talking to the sheriff, giving him the location of the ATV.

"You hear that, Munson?" Drew was asking his sergeant who was monitoring the same frequency.

"Affirmative," the reply crackled.

"Tape off the truck then go on to the ATV," the sheriff instructed Munson.

"You think you can track him from the ATV?" the sheriff asked the warden.

Hood looked at Magog Gadue. "You know which way?"

The mountain man looked around on the ground then shook his head.

"Yeah, we'll keep on here," Hood told the sheriff.

For the next hour, Matt, Hood and Gadue in the lead followed a thin game trail around a large mountain that loomed to their left.

"Gore Mountain," Hood pointed out for Matt's benefit.

Matt looked up and nodded as they pressed on.

Suddenly, Magog dropped downhill off the trail. Hood and Matt looked at each other. Whatever he saw, they missed. After about ten minutes of slip-sliding downhill, they came to a shelf that had a view of the valley floor below them. They could make out a trail of some sort.

"VAST trail," Hood said.

"Like snowmobile trails?" Matt asked. He knew of the trail system but had never ridden them.

"That's it. They're off limits to anything but snow machines and foot traffic," the warden instructed. He looked back to see Magog pointing toward the ground.

"Well sonofabitch." Hood dropped to one knee and picked something up for Striker to see.

"Splinter of rifle stock," Matt observed.

"That's what I'm thinking."

Matt started looking around. Saplings all around them were splintered and bent over. Bark was chipped from the trees. He pointed out his observations to Hood — as the hair went up on his neck.

"Firefight," he said softly.

"What? What are you talking about?" The warden was clouded over.

"Look around, Sam. This was a firefight. Fifty, maybe a hundred rounds poured in right here." Matt dropped to his knees and got his face down to the leaves around him. In less than a minute he announced, "I got blood here."

Sam Hood went over by Striker, trying to be careful not to disturb anything. Then he jumped back on his radio to the sheriff. When he got off the radio, he looked around him. Striker was staring down toward the VAST trail. Magog was gone.

"Fuck, fuck, fuck!" The warden got to his feet and did a three-sixty. He was gone all right.

"Doesn't matter," Matt said flatly.

"What do you mean, it doesn't matter?" Hood shot Matt an angry look.

"We don't need him. I can figure this out from here. I've done this before," Matt said calmly.

"But the moose," the warden started when Matt waved him off.

"Doesn't matter now. Besides, we'll probably find that

too." Matt started downhill. "Tape that area off." He turned back. "You got some timber cruising tape in your bag?" The warden nodded yes. "Tape it off. Stay here 'til I come back up!" Matt was taking charge now, giving orders. It was a smooth transition. The dynamics had changed. In a few minutes he was calling the warden.

"Come on down, Sam. Have a look."

The warden made his way down to the relative flatness of the trail below. Matt threw something and the warden caught it.

"Look at that."

"Shouldn't we leave these where they are?"

"Doesn't matter. They're everywhere." Matt waved his hand around.

"Two twenty three."

Silence.

"Like the moose."

Silence.

"Like my house."

Hood looked up at Striker. "What the fuck is going on here, Matt?" The question wasn't "official," it was man to man.

"Don't know." Matt started down the trail. "Don't know. Get on the radio, give them this location and we'll follow the progress of the fight. See where it goes."

Matt eased down the trail looking closely at the ground, at the vegetation, up the hill to his right. Hood did as he was told then caught up.

"Here we go," Matt started to angle up the hillside. About twenty yards up he stopped.

"LaDue was hit over there," he said, pointing up and to the right. "Then he started to side-hill this way, staying level, maybe going uphill a bit if he was able. Shooters are coming up the trail chasing, firing. Maybe Buck shoots back a couple of times. We'll look for his shell casings later."

"Shooters? More than one?" the warden asked.

"Two. Got to be two by the way the casings are being ejected from the rifles. Like two parallel lines." Matt moved on, stopping to examine the ground and brush as he went. Sam Hood followed. Soon they were making their way up a rocky hogback. Matt could tell from the treetops peeking above the rocks ahead that the other side was steep. When he got to the top, he whistled. It was more than steep; it was straight down. The whistle sound flushed a big coyote out from under the rocks below. His muzzle was red.

Matt stood there staring down below, picking the scene apart bit by bit. Like a grid. Then he saw it. The rifle was hanging muzzle down from a fir tree about thirty feet below them. The sling had caught on a tree branch.

"Get on the horn. Tell them we've found Buck."

The warden looked over the side of the cliff.

"I don't see him."

"He's there. Call it in." Matt moved to his left and started climbing down the rocks.

"Jesus." Sam turned away from Buck's carcass and gagged.

They'd managed to chew right into his mid section and start pulling out his intestines. Matt breathed through his mouth as he looked the scene over.

"Look at this," he said to Hood.

"Jesus, Matt, I don't think I can," the warden said, unapologetically.

"Not at Buck. This, on the ground."

The warden moved his head cautiously, trying not to land his eyes on the mangled body. His eyes stopped where Matt pointed to the ground. Letters scratched in the dirt.

"A, P. What the hell is AP?"

"Dunno," Matt moved for a better angle. "Look at the coyote tracks here." Matt pointed. "Maybe it's not AP. Maybe it's AR."

"Like, 'assault rifle?'" Hood ventured.

"Yeah. Maybe."

Matt was puzzled.

"Yeah, what the fuck?"

Matt looked up at the sky and the rugged country around them. He grabbed his phone. He wanted to call Detto. No signal.

Chapter 41

By the time Matt got home, Detto was waiting for him. He felt like he'd been dragged home behind his Jeep, but he managed a weary call to Kate on the way and another to Detto. Detto had gone early to Matt's like he was asked.

When Matt arrived, he gave his friend the run down of the day in the mountains. Then he flipped a shell casing to Detto.

"Son-of-a-<u>bitch</u>!" Vito stared at the shell. "A .223, Kalashnikov extractor marks! What in the name of hell is going on around here? Shit, I thought this was paradise up here. It's the freakin' twilight zone!"

After running through all the angles of Matt's day up in the mountains, the topic turned to Clyde Gash.

"So Gash targets Buck. How do they know he's going to be in the mountains?" Detto was asking.

"You should see it up there. Wilderness. The chances of them finding Buck to kill him are infinitesimal. Didn't follow him, intersected with him."

"Maybe he told them where he was going," Detto suggested.

"Maybe. But it looked more like Buck found the

shooters. Like he stumbled onto them. Not the other way around."

"Well, we'll get Gash and sweat him on this. See what turns up."

"Yeah." Matt was deep in thought. He was thinking about what Kate and Connie had said they saw through the window of Blueberries in Thyme. About how three men thrashed Buck in the alley.

Headlights started in on Matt's driveway, followed by four more sets.

"Here comes the cavalry." Detto watched the Suburbans pulling in.

Chapter 42

Abu bin Seidu had made contact with cells in Burlington, Vermont, and in Hoboken, New Jersey, across from New York City. Assets were in motion; the plan was progressing. Bin Seidu and Khan would make their way to Burlington and then progress unhampered by boat to the target zone of New York. Khan and bin Seidu were at Rashid's remote warehouse talking through the operation.

"Aziz has the boat over in Burlington. Our brothers in New York will have a second boat for the rocket attack."

"When do we move out of here?" Khan was anxious to move forward.

"A few more days. Maybe a week at the most. We do not want gaps in the plan. I believe we will be able to strike on the first target day."

Khan was ill at ease. He wanted to move on, not wait. But he was a soldier not a planner. He understood the significance of striking America on their Veteran's Day, but it couldn't come soon enough for him. And to wait until Pearl Harbor Day was unthinkable. As far as he was concerned, they had the weapons; the sooner they used them the better.

"Kahn, my loyal friend, it is not enough to do the

deed. We must send the message that the time was of our choosing. That we are by the grace of Allah, unstoppable. We will cripple their system and their spirit." bin Seidu seemed to read his friend's mind.

"I will do my part," Khan replied stoically.

Nick and Rami were taking pictures of everything, it seemed. With the extra film Nick's mom had given them, they were empowered to excess. They had taken pictures of nearly everything and everyone in town to the point of annoyance. But now they were hungry and on their way to the warehouse, making their way along a narrow trail in the brush away from the main approach.

Rami knew where his father hid the key to the warehouse, which contained a virtual treasure of candy bars, gum, snack cakes and chips. All to re-supply the family's store. This was not their first raid on the treats. They were judicious, never taking more than one item each so as not to arouse suspicion.

Nick was conflicted. He knew they were stealing and that it was wrong. But there was excitement and empowerment in raiding the warehouse. Besides, Rami's mom Shuri was constantly offering the boys the same items when they went into the store.

But this time they were foiled. When the boys got to the edge of the brush and the little field around the warehouse, they heard voices. After they stopped, they got down and crawled through the brush to see who was there. Rami knew his parents were at the store out by the highway.

After they moved a few yards, they peeked through the tall grass and spotted Rami's uncle and his spooky friend.

"We'll have to come back later," Rami whispered.

"Okay," Nick answered. Then an idea struck him and he grabbed the camera from his pocket. "Let's take their picture and surprise them with it. Everyone likes pictures of themselves."

Kate was having a cup of coffee with Connie Cutter. She was surprised when Connie came to the door. Brutus woofed once then recognized who was there.

"Who's minding the store?" Kate was referring to Connie's organic store.

"Girls are covering. I'll go straight there from here." Connie sounded businesslike and urgent.

When they got settled in at the kitchen table, Connie got right to the point.

"Have you been down at the Kwick Market lately?"

"Yeah, I guess so." Kate wasn't following.

"You see the extended family? Shuri's brother and his goon friend, cousin, whatever?" Connie asked.

"I saw a couple of people pull in the other day. Could have been them. They looked Middle Eastern." Kate felt like a bigot saying it that way.

"Yeah, well, let me tell you, real chauvinist assholes and scary if you ask me. You're not letting Nick spend time around them, are you?"

"Well, to be honest, I haven't given it much thought. I guess I haven't seen what you saw."

"Look, Kate, I don't want to get into your business, but I would keep a close eye on Nick if I were you. These guys look like trouble."

"What kind of trouble?" Kate was a little shocked to be hearing this kind of intensity from her liberal-minded friend.

"I don't know." Connie was starting to feel self-conscious about the alarm in her voice. "Something's not right," she said softly.

"You hear about Buck LaDue?" Kate changed the topic to the really <u>big</u> news.

"They find him?" Connie asked.

"They did. Dead."

"What?" Connie was wide-eyed.

"Murdered!"

"Murdered," Connie repeated softly. Things like that didn't happen in the Kingdom. Connie forgot all about Shuri's strange relatives.

"Did you tell anyone about us seeing Clyde Gash and those men beating on Buck?" Connie asked excitedly.

"I told Matt last night."

"Matt? Why not the sheriff?" Connie was confused.

Chapter 43

"Found the moose."

Matt had climbed into Sam Hood's pickup truck. "Thanks for coming."

"No problem. Thanks to you for everything you did up on the mountain." Hood was referring to Matt's role in finding Buck LaDue's body.

"Find anything else interesting up there?" Matt asked.

"Moose was full of small bore holes. Someone had half butchered it. Magog, I guess. Rest of it was pretty torn up by predators."

Matt nodded his understanding.

Hood continued. "One other thing interesting. Sheriff Drew says they came in on the same ATV tracks that we saw on the VAST trail up there. He said they went all the way to the highway where his team started. Twenty muddy miles of hard going."

"I imagine Gash has ATVs up at his place?"

"He does. But at the risk of pouring cold water on all of this, there are easier ways of getting from Gash's compound out to that VAST trail. In fact, starting from all the way down at the highway makes no sense." The warden shook his head. "It doesn't fit."

"How about Gash not wanting tracks leading to his place?" Matt asked.

"You gotta know the territory up there. There are a half dozen high and dry trails that eventually could connect with the VAST trail. Why would they go through that muddy, swampy hell if they didn't have to? If you know the country, you wouldn't do it. And Clyde and his men know the country."

"So you're saying someone else killed LaDue?"

"I'm saying something's not right here. That's all."

Matt thought for a minute then switched over to the topic of the late night meeting with the federal agents. "We're going to bust Gash later today."

"For murder?" Hood was taken off guard.

"Maybe, maybe not. We've got a guy on the inside. It looks like there is enough to put Gash away for a good while. Conspiracy, gun charges, explosives. And now, maybe murder," Matt said.

"Do you remember what I said about Gash defending that place if he needed to?"

"I do; that's why he's coming to town, so we can bust him here," Matt smiled.

"How'd you manage that?" Hood asked.

"We appealed to his greed. Wendell Gidding receives packages for Gash at the store from time to time so Gash gave him his unlisted phone number. When something comes in, Wendell calls Clyde. He comes for it."

"But he'd know if he had something coming," Hood protested.

"Gidding says packages come in every couple of weeks. Said it has been ten days or so since the last one. The packages are heavy. Wendell thinks it's surplus ammo. He also said Clyde always buys a four-number lotto ticket when he comes in. Always the same four numbers. Never hits it. So we had Wendell tell him he hit three of the four numbers for a hundred bucks. Clyde will be down this afternoon for the package and the hundred bucks."

"Yeah, he'll be here," Hood smiled. Then after thinking, added, "What about the compound? You need that evidence up there and there's still a bunch of loonies with big guns up there. With or without Gash."

"We've got two teams. One will take Gash and whoever he has with him; the other will hit the compound while the leader is gone."

"The place is a fortress," Hood looked worried. "There are fences, dogs, machine guns, explosives and who knows what up there. And you're sending guys that don't know their way around?"

"A couple of guys were up there yesterday doing a recon' and we have aerial photos along with the topographic maps. It's not an ideal set up, but good enough for a go."

"Did they go all the way around the thousand acres? Do they know where the gates are? Where the guards are? Where the dogs are?"

"I wasn't up there with them, but they're good men. They know what they're doing." Matt could see Hood getting worked up.

The warden placed his head on the steering wheel of the truck and was silent for a full minute. Then he whispered, "I'll take them up."

"Jesus, Louie, is there a chuckhole in this goddamn road you <u>haven't</u> hit?"

Clyde Gash was ragging on one of his goons driving the big camo Chevy Blazer into the town of Big Larch Pond. Riding in the back seat were Willie Jones and another goon that everyone just called "Heavy." Jones had never heard the guy's name in the months he had been undercover at the compound.

Clyde had brought a small entourage with him into town. He had a small alarm bell going off in his head. He knew he didn't have a shipment due, but he had once had an ammunition supplier double ship an order to him while charging him once. Maybe that had happened again. Who knows? And the prospect of the hundred dollar lottery payoff was icing on the cake. But, he brought backup just in case.

The big Blazer was nearly alone on the street and they were one block from the store. Suddenly a green Jeep Cherokee ran right out in front of them from a side alley.

Louie slammed on the brakes and Clyde bounced off the inside of the Blazer's windshield.

"Goddamn fuckin' idiot. What's wrong with you?" Clyde was screaming as the driver of the Jeep stepped out and was yelling something about "speeding." It was the big galoot that had dared to eyeball him at Wendell's store. Clyde hit the door handle sputtering, "Speeding? You simple son-of-a-bitch. I'll kick your ass into next...." He didn't get a chance to finish.

As a gigantic white-haired hillbilly landed his feet to get out of the camo Blazer, Vito Debenedetto stuck a Heckler and Koch nine millimeter Bull Pup in his face and shouted.

"Don't move an inch, Gomer!"

At the same moment, a federal agent tapped on the driver's glass and pointed a big .45 pistol at Louie. Before "Heavy" could pull his weapon from under the fat overlapping his belt, Special Agent Dave Whaley, AKA Willie Jones, had a P-32 held to the giant's head.

"It's over, fat ass!" Whaley said.

It was all over within three minutes. Clyde, Louie, and Heavy were handcuffed and being marched off while receiving their rights.

Ray Gash was, by his own figuring, "in charge" at the compound in his uncle's absence. He was ordered to "secure the compound," but as he looked around, things looked "secure" enough. No one ever came around anymore. No one seemed to care what went on up there these days. He knew he should put someone in charge of security before he took off, but he didn't want word getting back to Clyde that he'd gone off poaching. It would be called "hunting" if it had been in season.

Ray hiked a half mile to one of the back gates of the compound, unlocked it and slipped off for a couple hours of blissful stalking in the dense timber.

Sam Hood had taken a wide arc around the compound as he led the federal agents to a back gate. Two were keeping up stride for stride, but the third kept falling back. The warden had asked if he should slow down, but the two agents with him said no. Keep pushing. He kept pushing. Finally he came to a back gate.

"Shit," Hood cursed softly.

The gate was open. Some of the men were out in the woods. Behind them. The two agents with him rushed ahead and crouched near the gate, and one pulled out binoculars. Sam knew they couldn't hear him, but he couldn't resist saying, "No, no, no," under his breath. Sam instinctively got into a crouch where he was standing and ventured a look behind him. What he saw made him go weak.

Ray shot the deer not two hundred yards from the back gate. For thirty minutes, he dressed out the young doe and rigged it to be dragged back to the compound. It was going to be tender, good eating, he reckoned.

As young Gash came up over a small rise dragging his poached prize, he spotted movement up ahead. He dropped the makeshift handle of his tow rope, stood stock-still and strained his eyes. A uniform.

Shit, if it isn't the game warden. Of all the pissy luck!

Clyde had talked about making the warden disappear if he came around anymore. Ray figured this was a chance to gain a fair amount of favor with the "Commander." He crept forward silently and leveled his rifle at the warden's head.

Shit. He's turning around.

Sam Hood was looking at one of Clyde's goons pointing a rifle at him from less than thirty yards. An easy shot. The warden had not unholstered his Glock 40 and probably couldn't have hit the goon if he had. He knew it was a futile effort, but he decided to drop and roll.

The bullet found the mark, going through the head and blowing pink mist out the other side. The body slumped instantly, limbs askew at odd, impossible angles.

Sam lay on the forest floor motionless. The shooter

walked over to him.

"That's why I lag behind," a voice said.

Sam looked up to see the face of the federal agent as he walked on to join his buddies. He got up to see the crumpled body of Ray Gash on the ground. He hadn't heard a shot. He looked back at the agent, confused, until he saw the silencer on his rifle.

Probably used sub-sonic bullets, too.

When he looked back at the body, he could see the side of the head blown away. He thought of his wife and kids. He turned to join the agents, but his rubber legs let go and he went to his knees and bent over, in time to retch on the ground.

"I just don't see how he could have done it," Undercover Agent Dave Whaley was explaining to Sheriff Drew, Matt Striker and Vito Debenedetto as they all sat in Drew's squad car. "I've been in the middle of them the whole time. No one does anything without Clyde, and Clyde hasn't been a hundred yards from the compound except to come into town."

"Well, we have the ballistic information from the scene; maybe we can rule Gash out when we get some data from the compound," Matt was thinking out loud.

"Then what?" Detto asked.

"I don't know what to make of any of this. We respond

to domestic disputes and write a few tickets up here. Not <u>this</u> kind of stuff," Sheriff Drew chimed in.

"I know Gash threatened to kill LaDue, even planned it. I was there. But what you guys are describing wasn't discussed at all. I mean, ambush LaDue in the woods? How does that happen when you don't even know he's <u>in</u> the woods—let alone <u>where</u> in the woods. Hell, they were just going to pop him somewhere easy. They were watching him some, but were a long way from getting a pattern on him." Whaley was emphatic. He didn't believe Clyde killed LaDue, even though he wished it was true. He wanted Clyde Gash and his militia-survivalist asshole buddies put away. Now all they had were the gun charges. How do you prosecute someone on conspiracy charges when they were conspiring to kill someone who got killed by someone else?

"I think conspiracy will still fly." Drew seemed to be reading Whaley's mind.

"Maybe not. Depends on how sharp the D.A. is. But we can make Clyde think it will happen. Maybe sweat him and find something out. There's a rat in his woodpile somewhere," Debenedetto offered.

"Well, now you got him. You'll figure out what to do with him." Matt was distancing himself from the whole thing and was ready to get out of the car. Detto wanted to wring his neck for being so cavalier. Then Sheriff Drew's radio squawked and came to life.

"Sheriff, what's your twenty?" The voice was that of Sergeant Munson.

The sheriff picked up his mike and gave his location.

"You alone?" Munson asked.

Drew told the sergeant who was with him and what their credentials were.

"I'm with an I.C.E. agent named Pryor. He's got some information from the Royal Mounties you all will want to hear. Stay there, we're on our way."

"Roger that, sergeant; we'll watch for you," Drew responded.

"Pryor. That's their guy making the dead drop for you?" Detto was talking to the undercover agent.

"The same," the agent answered.

For the next ten minutes, the four men wondered aloud what <u>this</u> could be about. As if things weren't complicated enough.

Matt got out of the front seat of the cruiser and leaned against the door. He needed some fresh air. Needed to think. He heard a peck, peck, peck on the glass of the cruiser. Detto was trapped in the back seat and wanted Matt to open the door from the outside. Matt smiled at his buddy and turned away. Peck, peck, peck again. Matt ventured a glance. Vito was holding up his middle finger and mouthing, "Fuck you."

Aside from blowing Ray Gash's head off, the assault on the compound was duck soup. No one guarded the front gate, and the two big Suburbans full of federal agents crashed through with no problem.

From the backside, Sam Hood and the three agents worked their way down to the settlement unmolested. The only excitement was when one of the women in the compound started to unleash a pit bull on the agents, but she was dissuaded by a gun in her ear. The mutt stayed on the chain.

The State Police had provided a prisoner bus and it was called up to the compound by radio. As the followers of Clyde Gash were herded to the bus, the agent in charge radioed his counterpart down in Big Larch Pond where Gash had been nabbed.

As Sergeant Munson drove up, followed by a white I.C.E. SUV, Sheriff Drew was opening the back door of his cruiser to let Whaley and Debenedetto out on his side. When Detto cleared the cruiser, he whipped around to look over the top of the car at Matt.

"You are such an ass face!"

Matt smiled.

The sophomoric exchange was cut short by one of the senior ATF agents who walked up to Debenedetto.

"Everything is secure up at the compound. One dead."

"Theirs or ours?" Vito looked shocked.

"Theirs," the agent responded adding, "Guy almost wasted the warden that took the agents up there."

Matt whipped around. "Is he okay?"

"Shaky, but okay."

Matt laid his forehead on the top of the cruiser in relief.

"This is I.C.E. Agent Rick Pryor," Sergeant Munson was walking up to the men with the Immigration Customs Enforcement officer. "Tell 'em what you told me," she urged.

"The Mounties from the Quebec Southern District called us for a meeting yesterday. They pulled a body out of Wallace Pond. The man's throat had been cut. Almost cut his head off they said. Anyway, they find an abandoned van at a cottage. The cottage is traced to the brothers renting it for the fall season. Brothers' names are Ramzi, Middle Eastern, of course. The inside of the van had leather samples strewn about." The I.C.E. agent paused and met everyone's eyes. "But here is where it gets interesting. The inside of the van tested positive for explosives — and radiation."

Both Matt and Vito's eyes narrowed as they looked at each other.

"Anything else?" the sheriff prodded.

"Yeah, they took the one Ramzi brother in. He identified the floater as his brother. When they shook his house down, they found a big crate in the garage and a big pile of leather samples. The leather and the crate tested positive. And when they loaded the leather into the crate, there was a lot of room left over, like something was missing."

"Holy shit!" Detto added a whistle to his comment. "The Royal Mounted Police are talking to Canadian Immigration to track itineraries of anyone coming in as leather salesmen or the like. Trying to run this thing down."

"You see much leather crossing over?" Matt was referring to the Canadian-U.S. border.

"We do," the I.C.E. agent replied.

"Where from?" Matt pressed on.

"Western Canada, South America—and Pakistan."

That got everyone's attention.

Matt stared into space. *Could Buck's dying "AR" have been "Arab," not assault rifle?*

Matt gave Detto a high sign and the two men walked away from the group. Matt flipped his cell phone open and carefully punched in a number and then a numeral code.

"Longbow," said the voice on the other end.

"Longbow, this is Tomahawk. I'm here with Blackjack. We have something to report." Matt went on to tell the voice at the other end what they had just heard from the I.C.E. agent.

"Anything else?" Longbow asked.

"That's all at this point," Matt replied.

"Standby. I'll call back in fifteen."

Matt and Detto walked back over to the group.

"Tell me about this Wallace Pond," Matt said to the group.

"Up off 114 on the border," the I.C.E. agent started. "The pond is more of a lake. About five or six miles long. Half of the lake is on the Canadian side, half on our side. Seasonal camps all around it. A few permanent residences. Pretty rural approach to the lake on the Canadian side. Totally rural on this side."

"They interrogating the Ramzi guy?" Detto asked.

"They are. So far nothing useful," Pryor answered.

"Who's in charge up there?"

The I.C.E. agent gave him a name.

Matt had been deep in thought. "Where's the warden?" he asked the ATF agent who got on his radio.

"On his way down now," he answered.

"We need a command post; seems we got terrorists on the loose." Matt was looking at Sheriff Drew. Drew thought for a minute.

"There's a Grange Hall on the edge of town. South on the highway. I think we could use that."

"I've seen it," Matt responded. "Line it up."

"Will do. Come with me, sergeant," he said to Munson. "Where will you be?"

Matt gave the sheriff his cell phone number. Just then the phone rang. Matt walked away and answered.

"This is Longbow. C.T. in Boston and New York have

been notified that we have a possible tango. New York says they have chatter. We have a team scrambling now, and they will be off the ground in thirty minutes. Where are you setting up?"

Matt gave the description and location of the Grange Hall.

"Roger that. Now, Tomahawk, I have an important question for you," Longbow said.

"Shoot," Matt responded.

"Are you back in?"

Matt hesitated a half beat and started to speak.

"That's enough," Longbow interrupted. "Put Blackjack on."

Matt waved Detto over and handed him the phone. Detto listened gravely, shot a questioning look at Matt, then handed Matt the phone.

"Blackjack is running the operation. You are support. I'll notify the Marshall's office and ATF. You two are reassigned until this is resolved. Copy that?"

Chapter 44

Rami didn't want to go. He and Nick had shot all their film and he didn't see a purpose in it. Besides, these men that he called "Uncle" were stern, severe men and he was afraid. But Nick was fascinated. Following the men around, using his newly acquired skills of camouflage and stillness, was an adventure. The excitement of being in a place and observing wildlife or people undetected was irresistible. He couldn't get enough.

"What are they doing now?" Nick watched as the two men, bin Seidu and Khan, bent to their knees on the ground in front of Rami's family's remote storage building.

"It's the Salat. It is prayer time. I should be doing it too." Rami felt guilty.

"When do you do it, in the afternoon like this?"

"Five times a day. We must face Mecca."

"How do you know where <u>that</u> is?"

"Here, we just face east. In Pakistan we faced west," Rami explained.

As the boys watched the men, the bell in the tower of the Congregational Church in town struck twelve. After clanging twelve times, it began ringing out Amazing Grace. The irony of the moment wasn't lost on the two thirteen-year-olds, and an awkward silence ensued between them.

"Let's go," Nick said finally. "We'll see if Mom will take us over to Mr. Striker's so he can see the pictures. Then we can shoot the rifles maybe."

Vito Debenedetto followed Matt into Striker's house. He was stomping holes in the floor with each step. He had been on his phone from town to Matt's house and getting more steamed by the minute.

"Don't give me that shit, Striker. Why am I running this operation and not you?" Detto accused.

"Look, man, I just don't know if I'm ready...."

"Get over it!"

"Thanks!" Matt was shocked by his buddy. He'd never had this kind of wrath directed at him.

"Thanks, my ass! I just got off the phone and guess what? We got chatter going that's now falling into place. We got a bomb coming in, maybe a dirty nuke, and all this, right here in your pristine, protected backyard might be part of it. And you tell Longbow you're not ready." The "ready" was back in the girl's tone. "I'm serious, Striker, you got to get your shit together. You're the best counterterrorism guy in the country, but you've somehow got it in your pea brain that you can't have a 'real life' too. Somehow, it's one or the other. Look at me and Gigi. Do I get my job done?"

Matt nodded.

"You're goddamn right I do. So what are you, disabled? You can't walk and chew gum? The bad guys are coming out of the woodwork! The country <u>needs</u> you, Striker!" Detto grew quiet. "I need you; I need you, Goddammit."

Matt answered his cell phone. "Kate and the boys are stopping by," Matt explained to Detto after hanging up.

"Now?"

The two men busied themselves for the next few minutes getting their gear collected up and ready to move down to the command post.

"When will the team arrive?" Matt asked Detto.

"In the air now. They'll land at the Guard base in Burlington then chopper over here. The sheriff is marking the field behind the Grange Hall."

"What do you think? Two hours or so?"

Matt was flipping through the snapshots.

"You guys didn't need to get these developed. I could have done it here," Matt said.

"They were too anxious, so I just took them down to the drug store and had them do it," Kate explained.

"What do you think?" Nick asked hopefully.

Matt was sorting quickly through a couple hundred photos at least. There were some very good shots. One or two were outstanding. "I think we'll find some keepers in here."

Vito had spent the time out on the deck with his cell phone plastered to his ear, Kate noticed.

"Is everything okay, Matt? Are we in the way here?" Kate was looking out the window.

"It's fine, Kate, but it does look like I'll be a little tied up for a few days."

"A few <u>days</u>?" Nick was visibly disappointed. A few days was a lifetime waiting for target practice.

"Don't worry, Bud, we'll get our shooting in," Matt said.

"Well, we're going to get out of your way. Come on, boys; the sooner we leave Mr. Striker alone, the sooner he can get his work done."

"I'll walk you down to the car," Matt offered.

When the entourage that had been in Matt's great room moved out the door beneath the deck that Vito was standing on, he moved inside. Still talking on the phone, he sat at the table bench and absently sorted through the pile of photos while he talked. Kate could feel tension in the air at Matt's house. When the boys ran ahead to the car, she turned to Matt.

"What's going on, Cowboy?"

Matt thought for a minute. "We busted Clyde Gash and the kooks up at the compound. One of Clyde's men was shot and killed."

"Did you...." Kate was aghast.

"No. I wasn't even up there."

Detto was talking to Gigi and flipping through the photos.

"I told you, Babe, a couple days. You know how this deal goes."

Vito listened and frowned. "Yes, I know that Saturday is Bella's birthday." He knew it was somewhere close to Saturday anyway.

As he listened, one of the photos caught his eye. He could hear a voice but now was totally distracted. He held the photo up for better light. Gigi's voice was saying something about "listening."

"Sorry, Babe, I gotta go." Vito snapped the phone shut and laid it on the table and went to the window, turning the photo first one way then another. The blood drained from his face.

Matt was still talking to Kate. "Like, maybe Clyde Gash didn't kill Buck LaDue."

"But I told you I saw Clyde and his men pounding on Buck," Kate protested.

"I know, but we have reason to doubt that scenario. I'll tell you more when I know more." Matt wanted to close down this conversation without alarming Kate with other information. Speculative information.

The boys honked the car horn. Kate shot them a stern look. She leaned up and gave Matt a peck.

"I could use a little more of that."

"Get your work done, Cowboy." Kate headed toward the car then stopped and turned back to Matt. She wanted to mention something. Something she didn't want Rami to hear. She walked up close to him.

"I know you don't have time for this," she started.

"Hey, Matt," Vito yelled from up on the deck.

Matt held up his hand to silence Detto. "What?" he asked Kate.

Kate looked over his shoulder to the obviously anxious Vito Debenedetto on the upper porch.

"It's probably nothing. I mean, I feel like some kind of snitch even saying anything. It's not even my story."

"Matt!" Detto yelled again.

"Just a minute!" He shouted back. Then to Kate, "You gotta tell me quick."

"Okay. You know my friend Connie? She saw a couple spooky guys hanging around the convenience store."

Matt looked at the car. "Rami's parents' store?"

"Yes, Shuri and Rashid's store by the highway."

"Spooky how?"

"She didn't say exactly. Probably nothing." She turned again to leave. Matt caught her shoulder.

"Were they Middle Eastern?" he asked quietly.

"I think so."

"Jesus Christ, I'm trying to get your attention on something important and you're waving me off!"

"You were being rude."

"Well, excuse me for offending your delicate sensitivities. Look at <u>that</u>, hotshot." Vito flipped a photo at Matt.

Matt caught the picture and stared at it. Then he took it to the window like Detto had.

"Well?" Detto was impatient.

"Well, what?" The man in the photo was vaguely familiar, but the photo quality was bad. It could have been anyone.

"I think you're holding a picture of Abu bin Seidu, Kemo Sabe."

Matt looked up sharply at his buddy then back at the photo, willing the grainy image to be clearer. "It can't be. He's somewhere up in the Peshawar."

Vito was turned back toward the table frantically sorting through the pile of photos.

"Maybe there's another one," he said.

Matt joined him and rifled through the photos, too.

In the end, there were four photos taken of a pair of Middle Eastern looking men.

When Kate and the boys got home, the boys took off on foot. It was Sunday afternoon, they had school tomorrow, and if they couldn't shoot or take pictures, they would find some excitement somewhere.

"You two stay out of trouble," she called after them. "And call me and let me know where you are."

Nick waved his acknowledgement.

In fifteen minutes, the boys were back in their brush lair near the storage building. But there weren't two men now. Besides the two men Rami addressed as uncle, a third man appeared. And a white Toyota sedan. The whole scene looked different. There was a surreal quiet because of the snow that had begun to fall.

After watching a few minutes, Nick was cold and wet and needed to relieve himself.

"I'll be right back," he whispered to Rami as he slid back in the brush. Rami gave him a worried look. He didn't want to be left alone.

When Omar Aziz pulled into the mouth of the long drive leading to the warehouse, he stopped and let a passenger out. It was a security procedure. Probably not necessary at all. But one couldn't be too careful. He put the Toyota in drive and pulled on down the drive to the Quonset style building.

"Allahu Akbar."

"Allahu Akbar," bin Seidu greeted in his Burlington contact.

Khan stood in the open garage door, an assault rifle propped within inches of his right hand.

"You are alone?" bin Seidu inquired as he looked closely at the car.

Before the visitor could answer, they all jerked their heads toward the field beside them. From the far side two figures came through the brush. Khan grabbed the rifle.

"Let me go! I didn't do anything!" a voice screeched.

Aziz held his hand out.

"Do not shoot. It is Abdullah. He is with me."

The man called Abdullah had a teenage boy by the scruff of his neck marching him across the broad field toward the hut. "Silence!" he hissed as he struck the barrel of a pistol into the cheek of Nick Halliard.

The boy stopped screaming.

"Where is the other one?" bin Seidu asked. The men were speaking Arabic and had encircled Nick.

"There was no other," Abdullah answered. The man had exited Aziz's car and flanked the meeting place looking for security problems. He spotted the boy as he had finished pissing against a tree. He was going to let him go, thinking it was a kid playing in the woods, but the boy was headed directly for the meeting place, so he nabbed him.

When Rami saw Nick being dragged through the clearing by a strange man, he was petrified. Then when he saw the "Uncle" named Khan grab an ugly assault rifle, he panicked. Rami quickly slid back into the brush and went on a dead run through the woods.

"He is always with my nephew!" bin Seidu snapped. "Go find him!"

When Abdullah was a few yards away, Nick took off in a sprint the other way. It was bin Seidu that reacted fastest. The man went after Nick with long fluid strides that closed the distance quickly. Finally, bin Seidu dove, and the man and boy rolled together in a small cloud of white snow. Nick fought to get away, and they rolled around on the ground for a moment. Nick felt a hard object hit his hand during the snowy scuffle and he grabbed hold of it and stuffed it into his pocket. In the end, resisting was fruitless. Soon enough, Nick was being marched back to the building, cars and men. Bin Seidu was shouting at Khan. Something about tape.

In a few minutes, Nick was lying on his side on the floor of the storage building, his hands and legs bound with gray tape and a strip of tape over his mouth. He could hear the men standing together speaking excitedly in Arabic.

"There was no other, but there are tracks in the snow," Abdullah reported.

"Did you follow? Which way?" bin Seidu said.

Finally, Aziz asserted himself. "We did not bring this problem. It was yours before we arrived."

Bin Seidu nodded in reluctant agreement. He turned

away from Abdullah and faced Aziz.

"Are preparations ready?"

"Yes, we can act at any time now."

Just then the men jerked toward the driveway. Rashid al Saeed's big, old, brown Buick was pulling up the drive.

"Shit. It is my worthless brother-in-law. Why is he here?" Surely Rami had not had time to get back to town.

"Allahu Akbar," Rashid said pensively as he slowly got out of his car.

"Why are you here?" bin Seidu asked directly as he walked toward Rashid.

"To get supplies for the store. As always." Rashid was annoyed by the question. It was his store. This was his storage building. It was by his grace that these thugs were using it to stage their plot. Whatever it was.

"And Rami, is he with you?" bin Seidu continued toward the man.

"No." Rashid was confused. "Why are you asking about Rami?"

Satisfied that no alarm about the men's activity had brought Rashid to the remote facility, bin Seidu swiftly brought his right hand up. Rashid instantly recognized the little nine millimeter Sigma pistol that bin Seidu kept near his bed. Then he was dead.

When Rashid's body hit the ground, the snow around his head quickly turned crimson. Khan and Abdullah went to the body to remove it but were waved off by bin Seidu.

"Don't move him. There will be blood in the snow everywhere. Cover him with brush. Hurry, we must leave now. When you're done, load up. Khan will show you. Put the boy in the trunk of Rashid's car."

Khan looked doubtful about taking the boy; bin Seidu could see it in his eyes.

"Mark Murphy will be coming in with the team. He was the lead on the bin Seidu detail. He'll look at these and know. We don't have time to send them to H.Q." Detto was stating the obvious as he and Matt peeled out of the driveway in Matt's Jeep. Snow was flying out from the tires in a wave of cold smoke. Even at high speed, everything was quieter and softer in the snow.

"How sure are you?" Matt asked.

"Maybe seventy percent. You?"

"Fifty percent. But I don't know him like you do." Matt thought to himself a moment. "Probably is him."

Matt flipped his phone open and hit the speed dial for Kate. "Are the boys still with you?" he asked her.

"What about the boys? Is there a problem?"

"Kate, we just need to keep them away from the family members visiting Rami's family until we check out a few things."

"What things? What's going on, Matt?"

"Are they there, Kate?" Matt asked directly.

"No, they're not. They took off about an hour ago, right when we got home. I think they went to play in the woods."

"Can you contact Shuriana and see if they've seen them?"

"I'll do it right now. Please tell me what's going on, Matt."

"It's probably nothing. In the photos the boys took, Vito thought he recognized someone he'd seen on a wanted poster," Matt told the white lie.

Kate took the keys and headed toward the door. Brutus, the big Bernese Mountain dog, went with her. It was okay, his company was somehow reassuring, and maybe he could help find Nick.

She drove down the road near the house, slowly at first, stopping to yell for Nick and Rami, but she soon felt like she was wasting time. She would head to Shuriana's store. Maybe the boys were there, or had been. The all-wheel drive Subaru was agile in the snow, and she used it to full advantage.

When Matt's Jeep burst into town, one of the first things they saw was Sam Hood's green game warden truck parked by Wendell's store.

"Pull over. I've got an idea," Matt commanded.

Detto did as ordered and Matt jumped out as Sam Hood came out of the store with a coffee cup in one hand and a candy bar in the other.

"You go on to the command center. I'll take Hood with me and we'll go check out the convenience store. See what we can find out."

"Okay, the chopper's due in with the team in about twenty to thirty minutes now. Be careful. Let's take them when we're ready."

"No problem. We'll just get the lay of the land," Matt promised. Then he turned to Hood who had an anxious look on his face. "You might want to dump that stuff and fire this rig up as fast as you can," Matt told the warden.

Sam Hood uncharacteristically threw the coffee and candy over his shoulders and jumped into the truck just as Matt got in on the passenger side. "What's the hurry?"

"Drive. I'll tell you as we go. Rashid's convenience store," Matt directed.

"Okay, tell me."

"We think you may be right. Maybe Gash didn't kill LaDue. By the way, I heard you almost got your ass shot up there at the compound."

Sam grew serious.

"If one of the feds hadn't taken out Ray Gash, my family would be making funeral arrangements as we speak."

"I know. I'm sorry you got into this. But if it's a

consolation, you probably saved lives by taking those men up to the back gate."

"Yeah, who knows? So back to the point. Who killed LaDue? At this point I'm guessing it wasn't you."

"We think there's a terrorist incursion. We think they came down the VAST trail from Wallace Pond. Killed a guy up there. Probably ran into LaDue and killed him. Maybe killed the moose, too. Maybe it got in their way."

"So, where are the bad guys now?"

"Don't know. Maybe right here in town."

Chapter 45

Both Sam Hood's truck and Kate's Subaru came bouncing into the Kwick Stop at high speed and slid in the snow to stop. As everyone piled out, Shuriana came out the door with a look of both confusion and fear. Something had happened.

"Have you seen the boys?" Kate shouted across the parking lot toward Rami's mother.

Shuriana was dumbstruck. Her eyes were darting around. Then she saw him, running down the street.

Everyone followed the woman's gaze and spotted Rami al Saeed running and stumbling toward the store.

"Oh, my God, where's Nick?" Kate was looking past the boy up the street.

Matt was first to Rami. He slid to one knee and held the boy up so he didn't collapse.

"They took Nick!" Rami said, gasping for breath.

"Take it easy, son. Who took Nick? Where?"

Rami pointed behind him. "Warehouse." Pause. "Uncle and Kahn, two others."

Khan and Abdullah had everything loaded. One rocket

was in the back seat of the old Buick. Nick was alone in the trunk of the big brown car. Khan and Abdullah got in the Buick. They would block for Omar Aziz and bin Seidu who would go first in the white Toyota. They had the other rocket and the dirty bomb.

The two cars came out of the driveway to the highway, sliding in the snow. The rear-drive Buick sliding more than the Toyota. They turned left, away from Big Larch Pond, and on toward infamy.

"See that cloud of snow up ahead?"

"Yeah, I see it," Matt answered.

"Car, maybe two or even three, 'bout a mile up the road," the warden said.

"Pull in. Let's check it out. Tangos could still be here." It was a judgment call. There was no way to know if the tangos were still at the warehouse or gone. They had to check.

As they pulled in, the truck slowed to a crawl. Sam Hood unlocked the scatter gun attached to his dashboard. Matt unfolded his Kel-Tec carbine, slapped in a 32-round magazine, cocked and locked it. He checked his Glock 19 in his belt. Sam nervously checked his Glock 40 caliber in its holster.

About thirty yards from the clearing where the building stood, they stopped and got out. Communicating through hand signals, they split up left and right indicating they would converge in the clearing. This gave them the cover of the brushy woods to approach the facility.

Both men moved cautiously in an arc and in a few minutes were on the edge of the empty field. After spotting each other and waving, they slowly converged on the building.

"Anything?" Matt asked.

"Lots of footprints in the snow. That's it," the warden returned.

Matt flipped open his phone and hit the speed dial.

"Go, Matt. What you got?" Debenedetto said as he answered the phone.

"Nothing really. Looks like they're long gone." Matt spotted the heap of brush next to the driveway. "Hang on, Detto."

"What is it?"

No answer.

Matt spotted something out of place under the brush and walked to it. The color red with a white snow background.

No! Don't let it be Nick.

Matt pulled the brush away. "Got a body here, next to the driveway," Matt said into the phone.

Sam knelt down and studied the grisly discovery.

"Who?"

"Looks like Rashid, from the convenience store.

Rami's father."

"I'll send the sheriff over. You gonna wait?"

"No, we're going to try catching up. In all this snow, we may still have a chance."

Nick was being jostled back and forth in the trunk of the car. It was nearly dark, but a couple of coin-sized rust holes let in just enough light to see. He struggled in vain against the tape around his wrists. He felt around for a sharp object he could cut the tape on. Nothing. Then he remembered picking up something in his struggle with Rami's uncle. He stretched hard to reach in his coat pocket and pulled out a compact disc case. What could he do with a C.D. case? Then it hit him.

Pressing the open C.D. case down against the floor of the trunk, Nick broke the cover into several pieces. One of them had a nice sharp point.

Kate was coming unglued waiting at the convenience store. The sheriff had arrived and was talking to Rami. Then he came over to Kate to get a description of what Nick was wearing and asked Kate for a photo of the boy. Kate handed the sheriff a recent picture from her wallet. During the hubbub, Connie Cutter had pulled in for gas, then saw her friend.

"What's going on, Kate?"

"They've got Nick!"

"Who? Who has Nick?"

"Those men you were telling me about. The ones here at the store!"

"Those assholes here?" Connie was incredulous. "Why would they want Nick?"

"Come on, I'll tell you on the way." Kate grabbed her friend by the arm and hurried to her car.

Matt's cell phone rang.

"Hey, Matt, it's Detto. Where are you?"

"Running south on the main highway. I think we're getting close." Matt was a little breathless. The truck with Hood at the wheel was running over seventy miles an hour through unplowed snow. No one in their right mind would go half that speed. Hood had it under control, making small adjustments when the truck started to slide. The warden looked determined.

"Okay, we'll try to get something coming from the other side. The sheriff can call the State Police. By the way, the team is here; we're getting set up."

"Sounds good. I'll let you know what we need here when I know."

"A couple of other things, Matt. Mark Murphy came in with the team. Looked at the photos. He's ninety percent.

I think we can assume it's bin Seidu."

"What else?"

Pause.

"Detto, you there?"

"Yeah, the other thing is that Kate is behind you."

Matt jerked around in the truck to look out the back. All he could see was a cloud of white in the wake of the big truck tires.

"What?"

"I mean the sheriff called and said she took off in her car headed your way about five minutes ago."

"Got it. There's no way she's keeping up with our speed."

"You're looking for Rashid's car. It's an older brown Buick."

"That's what the warden here thought, too."

"The tag is Alpha, Zebra, Frank, one, nine, four."

Matt repeated the numbers back. "Got it."

Matt turned to Sam Hood when he got off the phone. "You hear that?"

The warden kept his eyes locked on the road ahead. "Yeah. Hey, look up there. See that rise in the road about a mile up there?"

Matt could barely make out the hill through the snow. "Yeah, I see it."

"Watch it for a minute.... There."

Matt watched as a car in a white cloud went up over

the rise, followed closely by a darker colored car. "I see it."

"Not it," the warden corrected. "Them. It's two cars running together. One light colored, maybe white. The other looks like Rashid's Buick."

"Can you catch them?" Matt asked as he did a calculation in his mind. *How many tangos? Two? Four? Six? Probably not more than six.*

"We'll be up on them in the next ten minutes."

Nick had his hands free. He pulled the tape off his legs and tried to pull the strip off his mouth. It hurt. A lot. He imagined it like a band-aid. He grabbed with both hands at the corner of the tape he had picked loose and jerked quickly.

Nick's head shot up and hit the underside of the trunk lid. His eyes filled with tears and something warm was running from his lips into his mouth and down his chin. Blood. He tried to wipe it away with his sleeve but when the wool jacket touched his lips, he jerked back in pain.

A few weeks before, Nick had been watching television when he saw the news about a little girl who had been abducted, put in the trunk of a car, and the girl found a way to get the trunk open from the inside. Nick started fumbling around frantically at the latch area of the trunk lid.

"Okay, Matt, we're sending a team up behind you and we're calling the guard chopper back. Tell Hood to monitor the sheriff's frequency on the radio. You'll be able to stay in touch with the back up. Sergeant Munson is bringing them."

"Roger that. The car out front is white or maybe light color. Sedan. Maybe a Nissan or Toyota. We don't know which car has the boy, <u>if</u> they have him."

"Take it easy, girlfriend. You're not going to do Nick much good if you kill yourself," Connie told Kate.

The Subaru was good in the snow, but they were following in the tracks of a truck with a much wider wheelbase. Kate couldn't keep both the left and right tires in the tracks at once. Consequently, one tire would run in the track while the other busted through deeper and deeper snow. The effect was that the car would lurch to one side then the other. Kate was both scared and frustrated. She started to cry.

"I shouldn't have brought you!"

"Hey, it wasn't <u>my</u> idea. You grabbed me, lady."

"No, I mean you should have stayed so that if something happened to me," she cried harder, "you could take care of...."

"Don't even go there. Straighten up and drive this car!" Connie commanded. "Nick <u>needs</u> you, Kate. You! Just slow up a little!"

The road undulated up and down now. At one moment Matt and Sam could see the two cars in front of them, and the next moment they would drop out of sight, reappearing as they came up the next rise in the road. They were close now.

"How do you want to do this?" Hood asked as he drove.

"I don't know. If we tap and spin the first one, the other gets away. Maybe we should... Watch it!"

Matt and Sam instinctively ducked as they saw the muzzle flash of a gun coming from a man hanging out the passenger side window of the old Buick. The shots went astray and Sam held his speed.

Nick fiddled with the trunk latch in the dim light of the rust holes. Finally, he found a square opening of about a half inch. He tried pushing his finger tight to the square hole and turning, but his cold fingers just slipped over the surface. Finally, he grabbed his tried-and-true tool, the broken CD box lid. Nick jammed the point of broken plastic into the square hole and twisted as hard as he could. The plastic shattered. The trunk popped open and sprang up high.

Matt looked ahead as the trunk of the old Buick came open and a boy's head popped up. *Nick!* He could see blood on the boy, but he could also see that he was sharp and alert. They made eye contact and Matt waved him to duck down.

Another burst of fire came from the Buick. This time the side-view mirror on the warden's truck exploded in metal and glass.

Matt rolled down his window.

"You can't shoot with that boy up there," Hood protested.

"Don't worry, I'm just going to give them something to think about."

He waited until the road curved slightly to the right, showing part of the right side of the Buick, and squeezed off two quick rounds from the Kel-Tec sub 2000. Both shots hit forward on the right front fender, well away from the boy. The shooter in the Buick ducked back into the car.

Abdullah was struggling with the big rear-wheel drive Buick. He had nearly lost control several times.

"They are shooting back, even when they can see the boy in the back!" Khan said to Abdullah.

"Maybe they are willing to sacrifice the boy."

"I will try again." Khan went for the window. Meanwhile, Abdullah pressed more firmly on the gas.

Khan leaned out the window and fired a burst from the modified AK-47. He saw sparks fly on the truck and it was slowing down. He smiled and started back in the window. Suddenly, centrifugal force was holding him hanging out the window. The car went up over a mound in the road and started spinning badly.

"What's wrong?" Matt asked urgently.

Sam was struggling to hold the truck. It started lurching from side to side and he took his foot off the gas.

"I think they hit our front tire," Hood said as he wrestled to hold the truck straight.

Matt looked out ahead. The car had disappeared over a rise. He knew they must be pulling away from them now.

The wounded truck was now down to thirty-five miles an hour and was still a handful to control.

As they came up over the rise, Matt and Sam yelled at the same time.

Suddenly, the windshield of the warden's truck exploded into thousands of bits of glass. Bullets were thunking the truck everywhere. Matt ducked toward the right side doorpost; Sam did the same on his side. Suddenly, there was a sickening crash.

When the Buick finally stopped spinning, Khan was

out of the car in an instant and had the assault rifle lying across the top of the car pointed back toward the rise in the road. Abdullah looked up just in time to see the top of the truck coming up over the rise and scrambled for the passenger door that was hanging open. He needed to get out before they were broadsided.

Nick was dizzy from the spin-out but was able to raise his head just in time to see the truck coming for the side of the car. He ducked. A violent jerk. Then nothing.

Matt felt something inexplicably cold on his face. He moved his lips. Snow. He was tasting snow. He shook his head to clear the cobwebs and looked up just in time to see a man several yards past the wrecked Buick. The man was trying to stand up. When he did get to his feet, he picked up a rifle and started toward Matt. Matt felt around him in the snow frantically for the Sub 2000 carbine. He didn't see it.

Pow. Pow.

Sam Hood's right arm hung uselessly at his side. His right shoulder had hit the steering wheel of the truck when it impacted the side of the Buick that was sideways on the road. As he lay in the ditch on the roadside, he could see under both the Buick and the truck which were melted together. A face. He could see a face looking at him under the car. Then a gun. *Oh, shit.*

Warden Sam Hood rolled painfully in the ditch and fumbled with his left hand for the Glock 40 on the right side of his belt. In his left hand it felt about as familiar as a rock. Two shots and the snow kicked up around him.

Sam held the gun above him and started pulling the trigger, then his head inched up carefully and he could see where to concentrate the fire. He kept squeezing off rounds.

Matt could see the warden on the other side of the truck. When the warden raised his gun, it triggered something in Matt's fuzzy brain and he reached for his own handgun. He looked back up and saw the barrel of the rifle coming up over the Buick. Matt fired two shots from the Glock under the Buick, toward the man's feet. He heard a grunt and the barrel of the gun disappeared from sight.

Matt looked for the man under the Buick, but the tires blocked his view. He saw a muzzle flash from under the car and he dove for the side of the truck.

"Sam!" Matt shouted.

"Right here," the warden answered to Matt's relief.

"How many?"

"I think we're down to one. He has a rifle."

Matt felt up onto the floor of the truck. Moving his hand frantically, he finally gripped the barrel of the little Sub 2000. He pulled it down and started laying down a stream of fire under the Buick. He stopped shooting. Nothing.

"He's running." Sam had caught a glimpse of the man under the Buick. He had gotten up, fumbled with the back door of the car and had turned heading down the road away from them, leaving a trail of blood in the snow.

"Stop!" bin Seidu commanded.

Aziz stopped the white Toyota.

"Something is happening." Bin Seidu was looking out the back glass of the car. "Back up."

Aziz put the car in reverse and backed up slowly. As they came to a rise in the road, bin Seidu couldn't believe what was unfolding in the road two hundred yards behind them. The two men got out with their weapons.

Gunfire rattled. Men were lying in the road, cars wrecked.

"We must go on!" Aziz insisted as he stood beside bin Seidu in the road.

"Wait!" Bin Seidu watched as one of the men got up, opened the back of the Buick, pulled out the Surface-to-Air missile and started for them, hobbling down the road.

"It's Khan. Cover him, he has the rocket."

Matt jumped up to finish off the man running away, but

was astounded by what he saw. There were muzzle flashes as the man stopped, turned and fired one-handed with his rifle. And now there were two more shooters down the road another hundred yards past the fleeing, wounded man. Bullets started thunking everything. The car, the truck, the brush and trees, along the road. Matt took off running out in the open away from the car and truck. He had to draw their fire away from where the boy lay in the trunk of the car.

All of the fire followed him. From a small swale in the roadside, Matt popped up and fired at the man struggling away and then at the other two shooters down the road. The nine millimeter rounds were virtually ineffective at this distance. A lucky shot could kill the closer man, but it would take a miracle to hit the far shooters, one of which had a rifle like the man they had flushed from the car.

Matt ducked away and then sprang up firing. Then again. The man was getting away, but moving slower it seemed.

Sam Hood knew that Matt had run away to draw fire. At the distance the perpetrators were at now, Sam knew his pistol and shotgun were useless. The warden, still in the ditch, was hidden from the shooters by the crushed vehicles. He had an idea and started struggling to his truck. The Winchester hunting rifle that had been in the rack by the back glass had popped out and was hanging from one of the hooks by the rifle sling.

Hood leaned against the truck, unbuckled the swivel on the rifle, grabbed the stock and pulled. The rifle came to him but then stopped as the end of the sling became entangled with the hook. Sam reached up higher, found the upper sling swivel and fumbled with it until it also came loose. The rifle slid out onto the ground.

The warden never carried a rifle in the truck with a shell in the chamber. The rifle was bolt action, and the bolt was on the right side.

Sam laid flat and looked under the car. The man was now way down the road. More than a hundred yards. He had to hurry. He sat up and laid the rifle butt first on the ground and held the barrel pointing up with his knees. Then he reached over to the bolt with his left hand. It was awkward but he was able to jack up a live round.

Matt fired until his clip was empty, then pulled it out and slammed another 32-round clip into the little carbine. If he used all these he had thirteen more rounds in the Glock pistol. The Glock magazine fit in the Kel-Tec carbine. That's why he carried the combination of weapons. He poured more fire down the road.

Khan was cursing to himself. He had been hit. Repeatedly. His left foot was burning and bleeding badly. His right hip was grazed and felt like a hot poker on his leg. Worst of all, a round had hit him in the gut. Entrance wound. No exit. Not much energy in the round.

Still, his insides ached, and in spite of his adrenaline rush, he had slowed to a shuffle that gained ground by the inch. He wasn't going to make it. He was out in the open, the man shooting was doing damage, even with an insufficient weapon for the distance. He knew he would be hit again.

Suddenly, Khan threw down his rifle. He started struggling with the case on the missile until he had it free.

The shooting stopped. Matt chanced a good long look. He knew full well what he was looking at, but he couldn't believe it. A Surface-to-Air missile.

Striker screamed. "Incoming! Sam! Incoming!"

Then he started his sprint.

Sam Hood had the trusty Winchester laid out across the hood of the old Buick. He had taken his left hand and lifted his right arm out so that it too laid on the car. He had almost passed out from the pain. Then, gripping the forestock of the rifle with his right hand, he bent over the scope of the rifle.

He couldn't make sense of what he saw. The terrorist was holding what looked like some kind of big bazooka. It was pointed right at them. He tried to get the cross hairs on the man as quickly as he could.

Khan was looking for the trigger of the missile with his finger. He could hear bin Seidu yelling in the background. "No!" But it wasn't going to stop him. He finally found the trigger with his finger. Just as he was squeezing it, he felt a heavy slap on the chest. Allahu Akbar!

Matt dove into the open car trunk and landed heavily on Nick. Then he heard the whoosh. He tried to cover the squirming boy. "Stay still, Nick!"

There was a thud and then the car shook violently.

When Sam Hood fired the shot that went through Karim Raziq Khan's heart, the recoil of the hunting rifle slammed his broken shoulder. He screamed and then blacked out.

The fiery missile lurched out of its tube in a wobble motion. A man that's dead before he hits the ground does not make a steady platform for a launch.

As it accelerated, the missile seemed to straighten out a bit but still pitched up and down. When the rocket reached the Buick, the warhead was pitched up above the car. The missile hit on its side at the top of the car then shot up into the sky. As it went up through a grove of huge maple trees, the nose finally hit something solid.

When Kate Halliard saw it, her legs and arms went weak and she started gasping as if she'd been held under water to her absolute limit then broken through the surface in a fit of panic.

The fireball was enormous. Like an erupting sun shrouded with smoky black lace, it momentarily eclipsed the countryside of pure white. Plumes of jet black smoke danced on top of the fire and rose hundreds of feet in the air. Kate's senses were overwhelmed with massive shapes of black and orange on the white canvas of the snow-covered world. She had no reference point to immediately understand something so otherworldly.

She willed herself to close the distance to the inferno of hell.

The explosion rocked the two smashed cars. Matt covered Nick as fiery limbs and shards of trunk rained down on the scene.

Sam Hood, his hair singed from the fire-trail of the rocket, rolled in the pure cold snow for relief.

Burning embers sizzled as they settled in the snow and served as the only sound to signal to the survivors that the world was still here awaiting their return.

"Matt!" the warden yelled as he rose up, holding a snowball to the side of his head.

"We're okay." Matt yelled from the trunk of the car. Then to Nick, "How you doing there, Sport?"

Nick's bloody head bobbed up as Matt rolled off him.

"I think I'm okay. My ear kinda hurts." During the spin-out and subsequent crash, Nick's head had hit the same trunk latch that he'd jimmied open, resulting in a cut to the top of his ear. Blood ran down the side of his face and neck into his shirt. The combination of that and the blood from his previously taped lips made for a dramatic scene that Matt was grateful only he could see.

"Let's get you cleaned up." He lifted the boy from the trunk of the car and held him facing away from the two dead terrorists. Matt started gently washing Nick's face and ear with fresh snow. Then he made a ball of snow and held it to Nick's ear to curb the bleeding.

"How's that feel?"

"Cold, but better."

"Just hold it there." Matt guided Nick's hand up to the snowball. Matt stood straight to survey the scene of destruction.

"How you doing, Sam? You look hurt."

"I'm all right. Got a little burn on the side of my head."

He could still smell burnt hair. "And I think my shoulder is dislocated."

"Hold your arm close to your body until we rig up a sling."

"What happened to the other two?"

"Gone." Matt looked toward the now empty space up the road where the two men had jumped out of their white Toyota. "Gone," he repeated. His mind was reeling, contemplating the consequences.

"What happened?" Nick asked, snapping Matt's attention back to the boy. "Why did Rami's uncle and the others take me?"

Chapter 46

"We need to get off the main highway." Abu bin Seidu was stating the obvious to Omar Aziz.

The snow had stopped and visibility was now good. Both men knew an air search would commence immediately. Aziz pulled the wheel and turned onto a country road. The Toyota slid until the front-wheel drive pulled it straight and they drove on the undulating road away from the state highway.

Passing several quiet farms, bin Seidu finally saw one of interest. The farmhouse was an archetypical New England two-story. White, lapstrake siding, pristine and simple. Across the road stood a great, white barn with a silo at one end. It looked like the other barns they had passed. Except this one had a tractor-trailer truck next to it. The big white cab sat before a long shiny, stainless steel tank. Bin Seidu had seen milk collection trucks before. And this one had the engine running. The flap on the top of the exhaust stack was fluttering up and down as black diesel smoke blew through it into the frigid air.

This was the one.

"If you want twenty dollars per hundred weight, you gotta go organic, Burt," Tony Maza was exasperated. The dairy industry was under pressure from oversupply coming from "super-farms" and a decreased demand for product in a marketplace driven by health warnings de jour and fad diets. Raw milk was down to eleven dollars per hundred weight and family farmers struggled to hold their heads above water.

"By Jesus, how am I gonna do <u>that</u>, Tony? "I'd have to go back to the bank. Hell, everything here is up for collateral as it is!" Burt Gunthier complained to the milk truck driver.

"I told you, Burt, Homer Medford up at Westmore is buying his grain from Canada. Organic grain. And we're picking him up at twenty per hundred!" Tony was frustrated. These family-run farms had few good options. They were all mortgaged to the hilt. The price of milk was way down with little hope of rebound. Some farmers had taken the herd buyouts offered by the state in exchange for tight regulations on how they could ultimately dispose of their own land. And it was the land value that provided any hope of a decent retirement. If they couldn't subdivide it or sell to a developer, the value was far less. Not enough to go to Florida on. But some of the milk producers had gone "organic," thus keeping the wolves at bay for a few more years. *But most are hardheads*, Tony thought. Like Burt Gunthier. They were just in denial about it all!

"But what's Homer payin' for that grain? I heard it was wicked expensive!" Burt protested.

"Good Christ, Burt, I know it's expensive, but he's gettin' twenty dollars. Put a pencil to it. You're a smart man!" *Actually you're dumber than a stump, you stubborn old woodchuck,* Tony thought to himself. He threw up his hands in defeat and turned toward the door. He took two steps and stopped cold in his tracks.

When the Subaru rolled to a stop in the midst of the chaos and carnage, both women were shocked silent. Burning shards of wood, wrecked vehicles, their fluids leaking onto the ground, human bodies prone on the ground, their crimson blood standing in stark contrast to the snow-covered countryside.

Then Kate spotted Nick and struggled to throw open the door. "Nick!" Kate ran toward her son who was still being attended to by Matt. She slid to a stop and dropped to one knee and grabbed Nick by the shoulders, took a quick look at his bloody lips and the wound on the side of his head, then she hugged him tight.

"I'm okay, really!"

Kate turned Nick toward her car and yelled to Connie, who was looking at Sam's burnt hair. "Connie, get my medical kit off the backseat of the car!"

"I really think he's…." Matt didn't get the "okay" out

of his mouth when Kate turned to him with a vicious look and stabbed a finger at him. She didn't say a word. She didn't have to.

Matt's shoulders slumped as he held a palm up and shook his head up and down. That was it. The wall was back up.

"Matt!" Sam yelled. "Just got off the radio. Posse is almost here."

Sergeant Munson's squad car rolled up behind the Subaru. Besides Sally Munson, three figures jumped out. All dressed in S.W.A.T. style black, two brandishing AR-15 rifles, one with a bull pup machine gun like Vito Debenedetto's.

Kate and Connie looked at the members of the National Joint Anti-terrorism Task Force in shock. Then they both shot accusing looks at Matt, as if to say "Can this scene possibly get worse?" Matt cringed but approached the men and they all quickly went into action.

In a few minutes, the wrecked vehicles were pushed out of the way and the sergeant's car was speeding away carrying Matt, Sally and two task force members. One A.T.F. guy stayed with Sam Hood. Matt had suggested that Sergeant Munson stay, but she was having none of it. There was no time to argue and it was her car.

Matt sat up front with Munson driving. He grabbed her radio microphone and got Detto on the other end and went to work.

He tried not to think of Kate and the look on her face.

Omar Aziz pulled in next to the barn, all tell-tale sound muffled by fresh snow. They pulled around back and the two men got out with their weapons. When they walked in the milk parlor door, one man was walking right at them just ten feet away.

Abu bin Seidu raised his AK rifle with one hand and easily shot the man between the eyes.

Aziz ran over to the farmer, who was glued to the ground with shock, and shot him twice with the pistol.

Bin Seidu looked back outside the door to see if anyone was alerted. He studied the calm, serene scene for several moments. No sounds, no movement, no alarm.

"Hide them," he said to Aziz.

"Here." Aziz looked over into a little stall.

They grabbed the two men and pushed them over the rail then picked up straw off the floor and covered them up.

"Should we cover the car?" Aziz asked when they went back for their remaining missile and the nuclear suitcase.

Bin Seidu smiled as he looked around. "No, with the snow it blends in perfectly. God is great."

In moments, they and their deadly payload were in the big truck and they were pulling out onto the road.

"Where is the disc now?" Vito Debenedetto asked.

"With Sam Hood and the agent we left behind," Matt reported.

"Okay, we have a convoy on the way now. Wreckers, EMT units, the sheriff. Everything we need to clean things up. What happened to Kate and the other chick?"

"I have no idea. Maybe they started back already."

Detto could smell a problem. "We're going to want to talk to the boy."

When Kate was certain that Nick was reasonably intact, she turned her professional attention toward the warden.

"Let me see it." She pulled the snow-filled hand away from the side of his head. "First degree. No blisters yet. Keep the ice on it." Her tone was clinical. Matter of fact. Detached.

Kate turned toward the two bodies now pulled off the side of the highway leaving a grotesque trail of pink across the snowy road. She took a step, but Sam Hood grabbed her arm tight with his good hand.

"They're dead, Kate. You can't do anything for them." Then looking the woman in the eye, he added softly, "And Nick would be dead too, if it hadn't been for Matt Striker."

"Nick wouldn't have been in this position if it hadn't been for Matt."

Chapter 47

"**O**kay, ladies and gentlemen!" Debenedetto shouted over the din of activity in the Grange Hall.

Everyone grew silent and turned their attention away from the topographic map, road maps, photos, telephones, computers, coffee and most of all, away from each other. The hall had been transformed in total. What just a few hours previously had been a quiet, silent meeting hall was now the throbbing heart of an anti-terror dragnet. Agencies of every color were represented: the State Police, National Guard, the sheriff, ATF, DOE, Defense department, Federal Marshals, ICE, NSA. Lines were open with the FBI and CIA. Vito Debenedetto was in command.

"We have two tangos and we've lost them." Vito looked around the room glaring as if their missing status of the terrorists was the fault of each person in the room. "And we <u>will</u> find them."

"I want regional ATTF in Boston and New York alerted." He looked at individuals in the room as he barked his orders. "I want the Mounties contacted. Maybe they have more intel. Contact police and sheriffs in every major town in Vermont, New Hampshire and Massachusetts. Get us satellite images of this area over the past three hours. I want more birds in the air." He looked at the State Police Commander.

"I can get two more helicopters in the air and one fixed wing."

"Okay, do it. What about the Guard?" He looked at a Lt. Colonel.

"We have two more that can go up. We still looking for a white Subaru?"

"Until we know better."

"White Subaru on a snowy day," the Lt. Colonel muttered.

"Hey, you buy the ticket, you take the ride!" Vito admonished.

"We need stolen car reports for the past three hours." He turned to the group.

"Our people can handle that," Sheriff Drew assured. "What else?"

"Anything weird. I don't know what that means yet, but we'll know when it happens." Vito then turned to a guy on a computer. "And I want the code on that C.D. cracked yesterday!" he barked.

The guy on the computer was unfazed except to raise a hand to signal that he had heard. He kept punching the keys.

Debenedetto turned to Sam Hood, whose right arm was in a blue sling. His burnt hair gave him the look of the haircut from hell.

"How about you study those topo maps and tell us where they might have dived off into the brush?"

It was dark when the milk truck pulled into the rest area high on a knob overlooking Burlington, Vermont. Aziz had called ahead and a white Chevy van was waiting for them. Aside from a couple of truckers, the rest area was deserted at the late hour.

Aziz approached the van carefully, wary of a trap. He pecked on the passenger side window while standing behind it. The window came down.

"Allahu Akbar."

"Allahu Akbar."

Aziz waved to bin Seidu. In a few minutes, they had transferred their arsenal to the van and had pulled out. The milk truck sat, engine idling, parking lights on blending in with the other trucks that held their sleeping drivers.

Detto had a blank tablet and pencil and started scratching on it. "Okay, here's where ICE finds a dead guy who turned out to be a Pakistani named Ramzi. He was from Sherbrooke, here. Here is where LaDue gets it. This is the town, Rashid's store, here is the warehouse and the highway runs like this. He scratched on the paper, then spun it around toward Matt, then spun it back and added,

"I almost forgot, here is Clyde Gash's compound." Then he spun it to Matt again. "What do you see?"

Matt studied the paper for a minute, then held it up to a regional map that was on the wall behind them.

"Okay, let's say they come into Canada on some ship. Maybe Montreal, Quebec City or somewhere in between. They make a connection in Sherbrooke, just above the border. How was the guy Ramzi killed?" Matt interrupted himself.

"Throat was cut."

"Okay, so maybe they don't have firearms yet. They come across this lake, Wallace Pond, probably at night and make a contact over here on the Vermont side," Matt was pointing to a spot on the map.

"Then they start down this VAST trail coming south to Big Larch Pond."

"Why not the highway? Why bother with the wilderness?" Detto asked.

"The ICE guy says they patrol the hell out of these highways coming down from the border. I imagine everyone in town here is aware of that." Matt paused a moment. "Including Rashid." He turned to Vito. "Do we know if he has a computer? If he does, we need to get it."

Detto jumped up and went across the room to the sheriff, then returned.

"They're going for it now."

"Warrant?"

"He's got a judge in his pocket. No problem. Okay, what else?"

Matt looked at the map again.

"So Rashid meets them here." He poked the map again. "He's got equipment for them, and they come down the VAST trail."

"So you're saying Rashid was in this up to his eyeballs."

"Absolutely." Matt paused a beat. "And maybe Shuriana too. We have to find out." It was obviously paining Matt to say this.

"Okay, go on."

"So along the way, they run into Buck LaDue. Accidentally. They don't want the alarm blown, so they take him out."

"But, what's LaDue doing out there?" Detto said.

"Poaching. The warden says LaDue was one of the worst. It's a few weeks before deer season, maybe he's out scouting. But he's got his rifle in case he sees something exciting."

"And he runs into them out in the middle of the freakin' wilderness?" Debenedetto was unconvinced.

"It's not as crazy as it sounds. There's this big VAST trail, the tangos are on it with an ATV. Wildlife like to travel the trails, too." Then to prove the point, Matt added, "The moose was right on the trail. Buck is a hunter, he knows this, so he drops down to the trail to look around."

"I don't know," Detto said.

Matt went on unabated.

"Maybe he hears them. Maybe hears the ATV. Decides to check it out, walks into a bee hive."

"Okay, then what?" Detto pressed on.

"They come on down. Hole up with Rashid, make contact with other cells and here we are."

"Yeah, here we are. Where the fuck are they?"

Matt looked back at the map.

"Boston or New York. I'm betting on New York."

"Why New York?" Detto agreed but was prodding Matt to continue.

"Because these guys are like a dog with a bone. They want to hit us in the economic gut and simultaneously take advantage of the population density to up the carnage." Matt stopped and thought again quietly. "Have you called Gigi?"

"No, but I'm giving it some thought."

"Don't think too long. Send her and the kids on vacation."

"They're in school," Detto said, referring to his kids.

"So take them out of school," Matt said gravely.

Detto changed the subject. "How they gonna get there?"

Just then, the guy who had been on the computer rushed over to the two men and interrupted.

"We networked into the code busters at Langley and at NSA. It was an encryption that was on the system...."The computer guy was in turn interrupted by the sheriff.

"Sorry, fellas, but I thought you'd want to know, we got two dead people over west of Burke. A farmer and a milk delivery man. We got a white Toyota -- and the milk truck is missing."

Matt and Vito jumped up and started to wade into the room. Vito turned back to the computer guy who had an anxious, confused look on his face.

"Gimme the bottom line," Detto said.

"Bottom line, we're still translating, but we know they were talking to a cell in New York and one in Burlington, Vermont."

"Good work," Detto slapped the geek on the shoulder. "Get us more. Go!"

Within minutes the mission was redirected. The search was on for the milk truck.

There was no new information until early the next morning, except that Sergeant Munson returned to the command center with a forensic artist. They had debriefed Rami and had a sketch of another man. No one recognized it so they faxed it to NSA for their analysis.

The shoddy short north end of Burlington was as close to a cultural melting pot as the otherwise homogenous community had. Big, wood frame houses dating back to the early twentieth century and earlier stood on narrow lots. The rugged crabgrass lawns were coated in a purifying dusting of snow. Compared to the squall in the Northeast Kingdom, the snow hadn't amounted to much. No plows, no salt, no snow shovels.

Several old Victorian-style homes had long ago been subdivided to provide low income rentals. The top floor of one of those once grand structures was where Aziz called home.

"We must push the schedule up," Abu bin Seidu stated then adding, "We must stay one step ahead. If we do that, and with Allah's will, we will complete our jihad."

"But now there is one missile." Aziz wondered if the plot could still work.

"It is not a problem, we will adjust," bin Seidu stated flatly.

"But we must leave now. This morning, before they realize what is happening. Omar, I must use your computer."

"It is here, my brother." Aziz pointed to a closet of the bedroom.

Bin Seidu got up and moved toward the closet, fumbling in his jacket pockets as he went. Suddenly he stopped and the search of his pockets became frantic.

"What is it, my brother?" Aziz looked worried.

"Where is the disc?" bin Seidu sputtered, as if anyone would understand what he was talking about.

The disc he was looking for had his past encrypted messages and responses on it, as well as the encryption program itself. He knew he could make his next contact, but it would be in the open. No encryption. The blood drained from his face.

"Look in the van!" he commanded. But he knew it could as well be in the milk truck or the Toyota.

With all the noise in the command center, Matt nearly missed the call on his cell phone.

"What the hell's going on, Striker?" came Kate's angry voice. "Why was Shuri arrested? It's not enough that she just lost her husband? She didn't kill her husband; she was at the store. You know it was those other men. Connie was right, they <u>are</u> assholes. Murdering assholes. Go after them. Leave Shuri alone! What about Rami? He's frantic!"

"Whoa. First of all, I doubt that Shuri was arrested. She probably was taken in for questioning."

"Yeah, against her will. What's next, you going to put a tail on Rami?"

"Goddamnit, Kate, shut up and listen to me!" Matt's words shocked Kate quiet. "I'm not running this investigation, but if I was, I'd do it the same way. They need to talk to Shuri to understand what's going on. These guys aren't common criminals. Common criminals don't run around with rockets! These are terrorists! And we have to stop them before things get worse."

"I understand. The world has gone crazy and the crap

from the crazy world is spilling into the Kingdom. This isn't New York or L.A., for God's sake, it's the Northeast Kingdom!"

The big Carver thirty-two was sitting in the flat water at the Burlington municipal boat docks. The twin V-8s were purring and the two water-level exhausts were making a low powerful blub, blub, blub noise. The tanks were full with two hundred gallons of gasoline.

Omar Aziz and Abu bin Seidu were joined by another Burlington cell member named Karim. Karim had been on Lake Champlain on several boats he had chartered and had even run a test down through the thirteen locks of the Champlain Canal into the upper reaches of the Hudson River, above Albany, New York. He knew the drill.

"Everything is ready," Aziz reported to a solemn Abu bin Seidu.

Bin Seidu was nervous. He was unable to use his encryption to contact the cell in New York. The disc was lost. He prayed that it stayed lost.

But, he made his contact nonetheless, and he prayed his simple self-fashioned encryption would be fully understood at the other end. *Allah be with me.*

"Yes, we will go now!"

With that, Karim slid two levers back to put both engines in reverse. When the boat was clear of the docks, he deftly slid one engine up into forward and the big boat turned on a dime. Once headed for the broad lake, he smoothly brought the RPMs up to plane the boat off.

The only activity they noticed on the lake was a small vessel coming out from the Burlington base of the United States Coast Guard. Karim could clearly see three armed men on board.

"Look over there!" Karim shouted over the roar of the V-8s.

"Who are they?" bin Seidu asked.

"Coast Guard."

At that moment, the Coast Guard vessel switched on a blue flashing light and increased its speed substantially.

Aziz, bin Seidu and Karim held their breath and fingered the weapons they held out of sight. The Coast Guard boat continued coming and was now even with them about a hundred yards to the starboard side. Suddenly it turned sharply north and increased speed yet again.

The big white Carver carrying the terrorists turned south and increased its speed.

The milk truck had been found near Burlington. Agents were combing it and the police chief of Burlington was being contacted. The DOE guys tested Rashid's warehouse for radiation. It was positive. So was the Toyota and, as expected, the milk truck.

"What's the set-up in Burlington?" Detto was asking the state police commander.

"There is no ATTF per se, however...."

The computer guy interrupted the two men.

"This makes no sense. They have more intel off the CD now. But it sounds like they're going by boat. How the hell do you get from Vermont to New York by boat?"

The state police commander straightened up with excitement.

"I'll tell you how." He started moving through the crowded room toward the maps on the wall.

Detto followed and whistled loudly. When Matt Striker looked up toward the familiar noise, Detto waved him over.

"Listen up."

"Here is Lake Champlain." The commander was pointing at the big map. "Up here you can go out the Richelieu River out to the St. Lawrence Seaway--"

"You're not suggesting they're going that way, are you?" Detto didn't get the commander's point.

"No. I'm trying to give you the lay of the situation," he continued.

"Sometimes, in fact, regularly, boats come down the Richelieu into Lake Champlain, then go the full one hundred and twenty miles down the lake," his finger traced the way on the map, "to this little town of Whitehall, New York."

"Then what?"

"Then," the commander pointed at a tiny thin blue line on the map, "they start going through these locks. Thirteen of them. And it dumps you out where?" He answered his own question. "Right here on the Hudson River just north of Albany, and then it's smooth sailing all the way down to New York City."

"No shit?" Detto was astonished. He'd lived in New York all his life. He never knew about this northern waterway.

"Yeah, no kidding. Traffic is fairly light except maybe in July. There just aren't that many people who know about it."

"I'll be damned," Matt stared at the map, his mind clicking.

"Let's get with Burlington. See what they know about a boat going out of there. There couldn't be that many this time of year. They might be on their way." Matt could feel adrenalin starting to pump.

"Hey!" Detto yelled across the room. "Get that police chief in Burlington on the phone." As he walked across the room, one of the DOE guys snapped a cell phone shut and spoke to Debenedetto as he passed.

"The milk truck was dirty. The bomb had been there all right."

Detto nodded his understanding and went on to the phone.

"Hello, Chief, this is Major Vito Debenedetto. I'm a federal officer at a command center over in the Northeast Kingdom. Are you familiar with what we're doing?" Before the chief could answer, he added, "I'm sorry, what's your name, Chief?"

"Mike St. Clair."

"Okay, Mike, call me Detto. So do you know about us?"

"A little," the chief began. "The state police are over here at our shop, and I know some of their people. Some DOE guys and maybe some other guys have been over here looking at a truck up at the rest area on Interstate 89."

"Yeah, that's us." Detto had a sudden thought. "Sorry to skip all over the place, but do you guys have a lot of boat docks on the lake over there?"

"About a hundred and twenty of them."

"Okay, hang on," Detto said.

Then Debenedetto yelled across the room to the DOE guy as he covered the phone.

"You still got a team in Burlington?"

The guy shook his head affirmatively.

"Keep them there!" Detto ordered.

"Chief?"

"I'm here."

"Okay, here's the deal. Tangos, several--"

"Tangos?" the chief asked.

"Sorry, Mike, terrorists, Middle Eastern, small group probably. Ring any bells?"

"Not to me. Let me check with my guys."

"Okay. We have good reason to believe there is a cell in Burlington. Also, if we send a couple DOE guys in, can someone in your office show them to the boat docks?"

"Sure, send them, and I'll ask around on the other end and call you back."

"We're in a time crunch here, Mike."

"Got it." The chief hung up.

Detto looked at Matt who was standing beside him listening to one side of the conversation. "Pull the Delta guys together. We gotta get going quick," Detto said with quiet urgency.

Detto stood up and walked off, looking for the state police commander, saw him and got eye contact and waved him over.

"Who in this room knows the most about that waterway?"

The cop looked around the room then back at Debenedetto.

"I guess that would be me. I keep a boat for fishing over on Shelbourne Bay. I've been through the locks a half dozen times."

"Okay, see that guy over there?" Detto pointed at Striker.

"Yeah, the big guy?

"Go with him. I'll be right over."

Debenedetto stepped away and hit his speed dial.

"Longbow, this is Blackjack."

"Talk to me," came the reply.

Vito Debenedetto explained what was going on to his direct supervisor at the secret counterterrorism unit in Maryland.

"Okay. Be advised that Homeland Security is on their way to take over command of your location."

"Roger that. In the meantime, Tomahawk and a few of the other guys and myself are going operational to stop these tangos. I'll put the sheriff up here in charge until Homeland shows up."

"You're putting a county sheriff in charge?"

"Trust me, boss, he's sharp and he knows what's going on here. His name is Dick Drew. I can't wait here for Homeland. We need to move out now."

"Okay. Your ass if it doesn't work out."

Matt was going over a proposed plan with the others when Detto and the sheriff joined them.

"So we take them, here in the canal if we can. They probably have to move slow...." Matt looked at the state police commander who reinforced Matt's speculation.

"Twelve mile an hour speed limit on the canal. Very narrow."

"Okay, so, Detto, hope you don't mind that we got started," Matt said defensively.

"Time is of the essence. Keep going," Detto urged.

"We can chopper over to Glens Falls, New York. Be

there…" Matt looked at his watch, "…well before dark. Maybe fly over the canal to help us pick a spot."

"I've got some ideas on that," the state cop chimed in.

"Okay, great. We can check with the lock operators and see if we can get a location of the boat. Do we know what they have yet?" Matt asked Detto.

"No. But maybe in a few minutes." Detto was thinking about Burlington's Chief St. Clair.

"Good," Matt continued. "So we assume that en route we get the boat i.d.'d, locate it, and board it in the dark. Where are we on the moon?" Matt said to no one in particular.

"Quarter moon tonight," one of the Delta guys piped up.

"Okay, not bad; maybe we'll get some cloud cover too. We can ask the chopper pilot. He'll know."

Ten minutes later, black bags of gear were being loaded into the National Guard helicopter in the field next to the Grange Hall. Vito Debenedetto rushed out to the team.

"It's a thirty-two foot Carver. White. Looks like this." He showed Matt a grainy faxed image that had been taken off the manufacturer's website.

Chapter 48

Halil Hadid didn't know what to think. His face was flush and hot, his hands clammy with sweat. He sat staring at the e-mail. No encryption. Just a message saying that "the celebration has been advanced by eleven days." It was signed with the correct code name. *How could this be? Was it a trap?*

Hadid looked at his calendar. *Tomorrow. The day these godless infidels called Halloween? Not Veteran's Day? Could this be true? Could they be ready tomorrow?*

Actually, everything was pretty much ready. Halil Hadid was anal about preparation and details. His cell members had gone over and over the plan. The Zodiacs were ready. The express cruiser was ready. He would have to scramble the men.

But is it a trap? He stared at the screen. *How could they be sure? There would have to be extra precautions.* He started calling his people.

Karim had not been through the Champlain Canal this late in the day, nor at this time of year. They had twelve locks down and one to go until they reached the unobstructed waters of the Upper Hudson River. He hit the horn as he approached the thirteenth lock and listened to his marine radio channel 16.

Nothing happened.

"What is wrong?" Abu bin Seidu hissed with a touch of panic.

"I don't know," Karim was instantly nervous.

Aziz started handling the AK rifle.

Karim hit the horn again. Then they saw a man come out of the hut next to the lock. The man turned and fiddled with the door. It looked like he was locking it.

Bin Seidu grew more tense.

"What is wrong with the lock?" Karim was now out on the bow waving and yelling to the man.

The man pointed to his watch. "Closed for the day," he shouted. "Seven o'clock tomorrow morning!"

Karim stood bewildered. He looked at his watch. Three minutes past five p.m. He walked back around to report to Aziz and bin Seidu. Sweat formed on his upper lip.

"So by the time the DOE guys get to the chief's office in Burlington, the chief has it figured out." Detto was explaining to Matt how they now knew what kind of boat the terrorists had acquired. "He said the boating community in Burlington was pretty tight-knit. He makes a few calls and figures out that a guy named Aziz bought a time-share interest in a thirty-two Carver -- for the month of October, which gives him early November for free. They lay the boat up after that. The guy the chief talked to was all excited because no one was interested in buying the month of October before this. Season's pretty much over."

"So how do you know this ties in to bin Seidu?" Matt asked.

"I'm getting to that," Detto said. "Anyway, we got the i.d. crisscrossed. First, the DOE guys go down to the now-empty boat slip and it tests positive for radiation. Must have set it down on the dock. Then, we get a response from NSA on the sketch that the boy, Rami, helped with. They send us a list of seventeen tangos in the system that pretty much match the sketch. One of the names on the list is a character named Omar Aziz. Heard of him?"

"Nope."

"Me neither. Anyway, I think we got 'em."

"What else?"

"Nothing. Except this little tidbit. New York ATTF says they got chatter going on a guy they're keeping tabs on. Making lots of phone calls all of a sudden. He's talking code; they're trying to figure it out. That guy's name is Halil Hadid."

"Wasn't he an un-indicted co-conspirator on the 1993 bombing?" Matt asked.

"The same."

"Pakistani?"

"Right again."

One of the other Delta team members moved back from the pilot's cockpit to where Debenedetto and Striker were talking on the floor of the helicopter.

"Excuse me, gentlemen, the locals have talked to several of the lock operators on the canal. They've gotten through twelve locks for sure. We don't know if they got through the last one."

"Why not?" Detto demanded.

"Can't find the guy who operates lock thirteen. Closed up shop. Didn't go straight home. Maybe went to eat or something." The man shrugged his shoulders.

"What do you mean he 'closed up shop?'" Matt asked.

"Yeah, I didn't get that either, so I asked the state cop. He says they close the locks at 1700 this time of year."

"Close? Like a store closes?" Detto was amused.

"Hey, it's what the man says." The team member was a little defensive.

Matt and Detto looked at each other and smiled.

Detto turned back to the subordinate.

"Get on the horn. Push them to find that guy from lock thirteen." Detto then turned to Matt. "Maybe we got lucky here. Got them trapped between the locks."

"Yeah, maybe." Matt was worried. The terrorists were moving faster than he had hoped.

"Detto, we gotta split up the team," Matt said urgently.

The team member who told them about the locks came back.

"We have a situation. Locals have already checked the guy's home, where he eats, where he drinks, where his girlfriends live, nothing! So they go over to lock thirteen and start running the tags on cars parked in the area. His car is still there. They can't find him. They're going to get dogs and divers."

"Shit." Matt looked at Detto.

"Okay, Kemo Sabe, how about this? We drop off Butch and some of the guys, coordinate with the locals, set a trap at lock thirteen, in case they're still there. Get a guy to operate the lock, let 'em in, close it, lock everything in place and walk away. We set up a perimeter around it and hold them there in the lock. What do you think?"

"Sounds great. But I don't think they're going to be there," Matt said flatly.

"Me neither."

Matt turned to the messenger.

"Find out what that boat is capable of. Top end. And what the fuel capacity is along with fuel consumption at the high end of its speed." Detto handed the man the manufacturer information.

"You got it."

"Okay, we'll leave Butch and a couple guys here," Detto pointed. "The Vermont state cop, too. He'll be smoother with the locals maybe."

"Good. Then let's get airborne and go way down in front of these guys."

"Sir, can we speak with you? We have a sick man on the boat," bin Seidu spoke with urgency. "I think he may need a doctor!" Seidu was out on the bow of the boat with Karim. He spoke softly to Karim.

"Go back to the controls. Ease the boat up to the dock."

"What's wrong? Do we need to call an emergency squad?" the lock operator looked concerned and headed down toward the oncoming boat.

"Oh, no. Maybe it was just bad food. He keeps throwing up. Even if there was a drug store, we could get him something for relief. We don't know the area."

The boat was now three feet from the dock and bin Seidu threw a line at the lock operator, which he caught automatically. Then while the man wrapped the line around a cleat, bin Seidu jumped off the boat, walked up behind the man and put a gun on his ribs.

"We got enough fuel in this bird to get us down to the city?" Matt asked the pilot as they took off.

"No problem. It's only a hundred and sixty miles," the pilot responded. Matt patted him on the shoulder and went back to the team on board the chopper.

Detto had two pairs of night vision binoculars out of the black bags they had taken with them. He handed one to Matt, the other to one of the other team members.

"We'll watch on the way down. Maybe get lucky. I got to get on the phone and talk to my people down in the city."

"Your people?" Matt mumbled.

"I heard that!"

Chapter 49

The big Carver had its throttles pushed wide open and the engine roar was deafening. Bin Seidu wondered if the motors would hold up for the five-hour run down to New York at this punishing speed. He looked at his watch. They were early. Too early.

Suddenly, the boat turned violently, and he and Aziz were thrown to the floor of the boat's bridge. Bin Seidu looked up in time to see a massive wall of steel passing within a few feet of the boat.

Karim was familiar with running lights on boats. But these lights were something different. It looked almost like a Christmas tree sticking up from the river. *Is it sitting in place or moving*, he wondered as the distance closed. Suddenly it dawned on him. He had read about these. He turned the wheel sharply and just missed the huge empty barges that were being pushed upriver by a tugboat. He was thrown to one side.

When he regained his balance, Karim pulled the throttles back. "I am sorry! I did not know."

Aziz and bin Seidu were shaken by the close call. They crawled back up to their seats. Then bin Seidu saw a device with a screen on it mounted to the dash of the boat. He turned a knob on the device. Above them, the arm of the radar started turning, the screen went from black to gray to green. They could see the shape of the shoreline. Had it been on they would have seen the barge coming. Bin Seidu shot a look to kill at Karim.

"I am sorry," he repeated lamely as he looked down in shame.

"Yes." Bin Seidu let the word hang in the air for several moments. Then he ordered, "Run slower. When we see a closed marina, we will tie up for a while. We want to arrive during the morning rush hour as planned."

Aziz took bin Seidu aside. "If he makes another mistake, I will shoot him myself and throw him over."

"Nothing?" Detto approached Matt who was looking down with the night vision equipment.

"Looks like some commercial traffic down there. Probably run at night to avoid daytime amateurs," Matt speculated. "Lots of marinas with boats, but we can't take the time to check every boat from here." Matt was frustrated.

"It would have been a stroke of luck to catch them out in the open tonight," Detto said.

"Yeah, well it would be a little luck we could use right now."

Detto was referring to the New York preparations. "We

got a couple unit guys picking up a Blackhawk at Sikorsky in Connecticut. They're going to help us out. Good news is that they happened to be up there to pick up the bird. Bad news is it's not armed."

"Not armed?" Matt questioned.

Detto waved him off.

"Doesn't matter. We can't just blow the boat up anyway."

Matt figured as much. "So what are you thinking?"

"Belt and suspenders," Detto replied. "We have a fast boat meeting us at the heliport on the East River. You and I are going to board that boat and take these assholes out. No big boom."

"And if we don't?"

"Coast Guard has a patrol boat with a rapid fire cannon. They think they can put the fire at the water line and six or eight hits will sink 'em.

"With any luck, no big boom. No luck, we're screwed."

Matt thought for a few moments. "Diversion while we board the boat?" he asked.

"That's what the Blackhawk is for. We also have a couple ATTF choppers standing by with snipers if needed."

"Okay, let's go ahead and put them up with the Blackhawk. They can help i.d. the boat as it approaches," Matt advised.

Chapter 50

Halil Hadid and his two cohorts had used every trick of evasion that they knew. They doubled back on themselves, went in and out of subway entrances, switched taxis; finally they switched over to a waiting car in an obscure corner of Central Park. They headed for their boat.

The Harlem River commanded about as much glamour as the name would imply. It was more of a stinking tidal ditch that ran from the infamous Hell's Gate of the East River eight miles to the Hudson River between the George Washington Bridge to the south and the Tappanzee Bridge to the north. Bracketed by the FDR Freeway and Interstate 87, the narrow slough was infamous for finicky drawbridges that left boats stranded and the occasional floating body, left in the water to be discovered by the rowing team from Columbia University during a morning workout.

But, to a swift boat with five feet or less of clearance, there were no obstructions.

Hadid and company arrived at a dumpy, ragtag marina at the junction of the Harlem and Hudson rivers two hours before daybreak. They fired up their aged, twenty-six foot Sea Ray and headed up the Hudson, towing two swift rubber boats lashed side by side.

The Carver was underway, running from one G.P.S. waypoint to the next, radar now on, making good time.

Bin Seidu looked to the eastern sky. *Was it the first light of the coming dawn, or was it the glow from the city?* His pulse quickened.

"I think I see the bridge they call Tappanzee," Aziz said as he strained to see through the binoculars. He handed the glasses to bin Seidu who in turn took a look downriver. He lowered the binoculars and looked at the map spread out on his lap.

"It must be the bridge." *Allahu Akbar.*

The chopper came down on the pad along the East River.

"Come on," Detto motioned and headed for the dock. Matt and one of the other team members started to follow him until Matt stopped.

Striker was looking around the docks. One passenger ferry, one ridiculous, big, red, offshore race boat and that was it.

"Detto!" Matt shouted.

Debenedetto turned.

"Where the hell is our boat?" Matt asked.

"Right here!" Detto pointed at the race boat.

Matt followed his buddy up to where the boat was tied to the dock. It was thirty-five or thirty-six feet long. Sleek and narrow, the boat was fire engine red with huge gold leaf lettering on the side trimmed in black. The huge letters spelled "Pumper Thumper."

Matt shook his head.

A man emerged from a little cabin door and stepped up into the cockpit.

"Gentlemen, meet Sean McKinney of the F.D.N.Y."

The men all introduced themselves.

"This F.D.N.Y. standard issue?" Matt joked.

"No freakin' way," McKinney said as he tossed goggles to each man.

"What are these for?" Matt asked.

"You'll see."

In a few minutes, he got the picture. There was a deafening roar as three high performance V-8s pushed the red rocket up past ninety miles an hour.

Dear God, don't let a bug hit my face at this speed.

He was almost used to the speed when the awesome boat hit the wake of the Staten Island Ferry as they rounded Battery Park headed for the Hudson River. The boat shockingly shot out of the water completely airborne, the bow fifteen feet above the stern, and the stern three feet above the river surface.

Matt held a grab bar, bracing for the slam of re-entry,

but the boat touched the water as softly as a glider coming back to earth.

Some hearty souls had been in line, camped out, for the night. Now that dawn approached, lines of people were pouring through the narrow crosstown streets toward the Jacob Javits Convention Center, hard on the Hudson River just below the entrance to the Lincoln Tunnel. They made their way from Times Square, the Port Authority, Penn Station and the toney townhouses along Central Park. Tour buses lined the streets, belching passengers that had been picked up from central locations, mostly motorcycle dealerships, from Long Island, Southern Connecticut and New Jersey.

Bikers, biker wannabees, and the curious converged on the convention center by the thousands. The world motorcycle show was in town, and it would attract sixty thousand or more people anxious to see next year's models from Harley Davidson, Honda, BMW and all the others.

Sexy bikes, sexy babes and all the custom bike-builders that mug it up on television with their rude, crude jibs, jabs and jive.

It wasn't a show. It was a happening. And if anyone waiting to get in saw the big old speedboat go by, they gave it no attention. Their definition of cool had two wheels.

Weapons at the ready, bin Seidu, Aziz and Karim pulled up next to the boat tied to a support under the Tappanzee Bridge just a few miles north of Manhattan.

"Drop the anchor," bin Seidu ordered Karim.

A man emerged from the cabin of the smaller Sea Ray.

"Allahu Akbar," Halil Hadid greeted his comrades with audible relief. It wasn't a trap after all. They could slip the safeties back off on their weapons.

"Allahu Akbar," the three terrorists on the big Carver returned the greeting as two other Middle Eastern men emerged from the little cabin of the Sea Ray.

"I will get the two boats ready." Hadid started to untie the two rubber boats tied to the stern.

"We have made adjustments to the plan," bin Seidu announced. Everyone stopped and turned toward him to hear more. "We will not deliver our package with the big boat. Aziz and I will take it with your smaller boat." Bin Seidu rightly figured that half the law enforcement world was looking for the Carver by now.

Abu bin Seidu continued to hand out assignments, and the men all took their places. The two rubber swift boats pushed off and were underway in the light of early dawn. One went up the river with one man aboard. He would live for another day. Halil Hadid and one of his men were off and away on the other rubber boat, their deadly rocket lying on the floor. They would run full speed cutting through the Harlem River. Since their clearance height was well under five feet, there would be no obstructions at all. And the low profile made it difficult for anyone to chase them.

Aziz and bin Seidu moved themselves and their package over to the light beige Sea Ray.

Karim stood on the bridge of the Carver feeling awkward, self-conscious and afraid. He had not been given orders. He watched the unfolding, his mind reeling with the possibilities. Finally, many minutes after the rubber boats had pushed off, bin Seidu spoke to him.

"Karim, you will stay here with the boat."

Karim looked around. Traffic was picking up on the bridge above, commercial vessels were appearing in the distance on the river and it was nearly full light. *Was he to stay here and be arrested — or worse?*

"And then what?" Karim allowed irritation to taint his voice.

"And then nothing." Bin Seidu raised his pistol and shot the man in the head.

"Today we deliver ourselves to Allah," bin Seidu said to Aziz. "Push off."

Chapter 51

Dunkin Davis had been on the force for twenty-five years. His father had been on the force. Retired with a gold watch and drank himself to death within eighteen months of leaving the department. Dunkin's younger brother, Benny, was on the force down in Lower Manhattan. He had stood there and watched the people jumping from the twin towers and then the towers themselves collapsing down on themselves. He had been covered in gray dust. It was a hell of a day.

Dunkin had mellowed out over the years. He had gone from head-thumper down in Brooklyn to neighborhood good guy up in Queens where he lived. He had a morning routine. After he checked in at the precinct for the daily roster duties and activity updates, he drove over to a little park in North Queens that was across from Rikers Island and adjacent to LaGuardia Airport. He would open the brown bag that his wife Eve packed for him, pull out a package of Ho Ho's or Ding Dongs (he never knew from one day to the next what he would get), take the top off his beat up old stainless Thermos jug and take ten or fifteen minutes to himself.

It was everything. The rich smell of coffee that filled the

cruiser, the chocolate surprise from Eve and the serenity of looking out over the water and watching the passenger ferry laden with working stiffs plow past, headed for the madness of Manhattan.

He had it made now. A few more years and full retirement and, unlike his dad, he and Eve had plans. Warmer climates and good fishing. They would grow old together.

On the mornings that he was able to go to the park, he would emerge from the cruiser and give a big wave to a guy up in the guard tower at Rikers Island Prison straight across the water. Kindred souls. Someday he had to find out who that guy was.

The unwritten law on the water was that when you passed a boat nearby you waved. And someone in the other boat would wave back. It was etiquette borne out of camaraderie.

"Fuck you, asshole," Sean McKinney's voice had come over the radio for all to hear. He had just passed a ratty old Sea Ray north of the George Washington Bridge, and the dumb fucker didn't return his wave. The guys in the boat looked right at him.

Matt turned and looked closely at the old boat and its passengers. McKinney was going so fast he couldn't focus too well on the occupants, but something in the back of his mind clicked a little. The radio crackled.

"We got the Carver," the voice came from one of the helicopters that was in support of the operation.

"Where?" Detto's voice dominated the radio.

"Under the Tappanzee Bridge," came the return.

"What's it doing?" Detto was straining to see ahead. The Tappanzee Bridge was in sight, but they were too far away to see the details, even in the bright blue of the full morning light.

"Just sitting there. Or more accurately, it swings out under the bridge to the north then swings back under and pops out on the south. It must be anchored there."

Matt was trying to shake cobwebs from his brain. *Are they going to blow the Tappanzee Bridge? Not that it won't cause chaos and destruction, but the high value targets are downstream around Manhattan.*

"Can you give it a quick pass and have a look?" Matt asked the pilot.

"Roger that," came the response.

Matt tapped McKinney on the shoulder.

"Slow down," Matt ordered.

"What are you doing?" Detto protested.

As the roar of the engines subsided, Matt pushed the microphone of his radio up away from his mouth.

"Something's wrong. I just feel it."

Detto was annoyed but had had enough experience with Striker's intuition not to dismiss it out of hand.

"Like what?" Detto didn't get an answer. The radio crackled again.

"We got a body. Laying on the bridge of the Carver. His brains are all over the bridge of the boat."

"Anyone else?" Matt asked the pilot.

"Looks pretty quiet to me. No movement anywhere."

"Turn around!" Matt yelled to McKinney.

"What the fuck?" Detto said.

"They switched boats! It's the smaller beige boat that didn't wave to McKinney!"

"The Sea Ray?" McKinney asked.

"Whatever. I don't know one from another," Matt said.

Detto took over the radio. "Ladies and gentlemen, we have reason to believe that our tangos have a new ride. Stand by." Then to McKinney Detto asked, "What is it?"

"Sea Ray, beige, older, twenty-five to twenty-eight feet," McKinney spoke into the radio.

"Okay, folks, we are turning and in pursuit. The vessel was last seen at the G.W. Bridge headed south.

"Shall we take it out?" the chief of the Coast Guard cutter asked.

"If it closes on the city before we get to it, affirmative. But give us a chance to get on board that boat first." Then to Sean McKinney Detto added, "Pour the coal on, Sean. Let's see what this tub will do."

Sean rammed the three throttles down to their limit.

Matt couldn't believe that the boat had more speed

than they had experienced.

"Blackhawk One, this is Team Leader; raise up and spot that tango and give us a coordinate on it."

The big boat roared, and McKinney took one hand and shoved a heavily-laminated chart to Debenedetto.

"I've got him about dead even with the top of Central Park. My GPS says he's doing about twenty knots," the Blackhawk pilot reported.

Detto started to bring the chart up to look at it. As he did, the wind caught it so hard it shot back and hit Matt in the face. Detto held on, and he pulled it down into the cockpit of the boat out of the wind. The two men knelt down to a hunch over the map.

"Nice move, dipshit," Matt said with his microphone covered.

"But I didn't let go, did I?" was Detto's reply.

In a few seconds, the pair popped back up.

"What's our speed, Slick?" Detto asked McKinney.

"Hundred and twenty."

"And if the other boat's going twenty knots, that's what, about twenty-three miles an hour, right?"

"That's right," McKinney said again.

Detto was back on the radio. "Okay, people. This is Team Leader. We're going to overtake this joker just north of the Lincoln Tunnel entrance. We will board the boat and take control. Blackhawk One, are you clear on what we need from you?"

"Roger that, Team Leader. We will be on time and on target."

"Team Leader, this is Coast Guard Cutter forty-four. If you are unable to control the vessel--"

Detto didn't let the commander finish. "Sink it."

"If you are still on board?" the chief asked.

"Sink it. Do you read?"

"Roger that."

When Officer Dunkin Davis got out of his cruiser, the guard in the tower at Rikers was already waving. In fact, he was waving both arms high and jumping up and down. Then he was pointing dramatically down toward the water.

What the hell? The officer followed the signal with his eyes. *Some kind of little boat.* Davis scrambled to his cruiser for a small pair of field glasses in the glove box.

"Holy shit," the officer said to no one.

Out on the water, two men were approaching LaGuardia Airport from the east. One of the men was hoisting a big long tube up to his shoulder.

Dunkin ran back to the cruiser. "Control, this is unit fifty-seven," he said urgently.

"Go ahead, fifty-seven," came a lackadaisical voice.

"We got a guy with a missile. We got a guy who's gonna shoot down a plane!"

"What's your twenty?" the voice came back, infinitely

more alive.

"Wards Island Park, North Queens. The guys are in a small rubber boat with an outboard. They're going east between the park and Rikers. They're not eight hundred yards from the end of the runway!" Davis was getting frantic. "Call Rikers! Call Rikers. They have high-powered rifles. Tell them to shoot, for God's sake!"

The guard at the tower was frantic. He was sure he was looking down at a man with a rocket. The man was starting to stand up. For the third time he spoke into his radio.

"I'm telling you, this nut job is going to shoot down a plane!" he spoke to his commander at the prison.

Pop. Pop. Pop.

The guard heard the distant sound of gunfire. He saw the cop on the other side running along the shore of the park shooting at the small boat. And he could see the shotgun pellets falling to the water, short of the mark. Then the cop threw his shotgun down and drew his pistol and started shooting wildly.

"Towers three and four. We've been called by ATTF; they want us to take out that boat if we can. Do you read that?"

"I got it," the agitated guard at tower three said.

"What boat?" the guy at tower four responded.

The guard raised his Remington 30.06 semi-automatic

rifle and trained it on the target.

Halil Hadid and his fellow jihadists were within range, expecting to see an airliner rise coming at them at any moment.

Pop. Pop. Pop.

Hadid turned to see a lone policeman shooting toward them from the shore. But nothing was happening. Yes, it was. The bullets were hitting the water between them and the cop. They were out of range.

But then there were splashes in the water around them. Not close, but it got his attention and he panicked.

If they could not hit a plane in the air, they would hit one on the ground. If they could spot one on a runway taxi, it would still have a heat signature for the rocket to lock in on. He stood in the boat for a better look, spotted something and shouldered the missile.

US Air Flight 6464 was a shuttle flight that ran to and from Boston all day. It was full of primarily businessmen and was on a taxi getting ready for take off. Then the pilot got a strange order. Stop where he was and shut the engine down immediately. <u>That</u> was strange.

Hadid caught sight of a plane on taxi. At first he didn't see it. It was camouflaged by other planes and buildings as it rolled in front of a General Aviation hangar.

He quickly acquired the target, and as he squeezed the trigger, he could see that the jet was stopping.

The missile flew.

The rubber boat received a hail of gunfire. Both terrorists were hit, and the rubber boat hissed as air escaped through the bullet holes. The guards kept firing.

Behind US Air 6464, a mechanic had fired the engines on a Lear jet and started moving it in the direction opposite the airliner. The missile locked onto the heat of the Lear because the airliner was now shut down.

The mechanic moved the little jet on the tarmac around the side of the hangar.

The missile lost the heat mark of the Lear as the plane went around the corner, and the rocket flew straight into an open hangar door.

By the grace of God the only one that had been in the hangar at this early hour was the mechanic that now moved away in the Lear jet. But there were five other planes in the hangar, most of them holding fuel to their capacity.

US Air Flight 6464 shuddered from the concussion of the blast. A ball of orange flame momentarily engulfed the Lear jet outside the hangar. The impact lifted the tail of the little jet and slid it sideways.

The NYPD helicopter that was assigned to Vito Debenedetto's operation was already banking away when Detto heard the pilot on the radio.

"They've hit LaGuardia!" The pilot was looking at a ball of fire, the likes of which he had never seen. Black smoke was curling out from the flames, engulfing everything to the point that he couldn't even make out the flight control tower anymore.

"We can turn and run up the East River," the Coast Guard chief was saying into the radio.

Detto was momentarily frozen in place. *What the hell?*

Matt jumped in on the radio.

"Hold your positions! Hold your positions! It's a decoy. Do you read? A decoy!"

It made no sense. The masses were in Manhattan, not at Laguardia, and the Sea Ray was headed for Manhattan.

Detto responded instantly.

"Blackhawk One, your mission has not changed. <u>Do you read</u>?"

"Roger that," the pilot returned.

"Coast Guard forty-four, stay on <u>us</u>. <u>Do you read</u>?"

The chief's voice came back. "Roger that, Team Leader. But I gotta tell you, all hell has broken loose at LaGuardia!"

"Stick with us!" Matt blurted into the radio.

Chapter 52

Abu bin Seidu had seen the big speedboats in the Persian Gulf and in the Mediterranean Sea. The toys of the decadent rich. Including the oil sheiks.

Now the big red one that had passed by them at high speed was coming down river behind them. *The infidels will always be dependent on the oil. Always. It is their weakest point and they will pay dearly.* He turned back toward the business at hand.

Death to the infidels.

The men in the speedboat were closing on the terrorists fast. But even so, they could not help but look to the east and see the black, billowing smoke against the bright, clear cobalt blue sky that was so rare in New York. And the parallel between this crisp blue sky and the one in September of 2001 was not lost on a single one of them.

"Blackhawk One, prepare to move in," Detto said confidently into his microphone.

It was a simple enough plan, not unlike what the terrorists themselves were executing. Create a diversion — then attack.

"Okay, Kemo Sabe, let's get ready," Detto said to Matt.

Matt handed the Heckler & Koch bull pup to the other team member.

"When we get ready to jump, if one of those guys turns a weapon toward this boat, take them out."

"Will do," the man responded.

"Sean, stay out wide to the west. Make them think we're passing them, then dive under them and cross close to their stern, I mean really close," Detto instructed his friend from FDNY.

"Let's all hope they get locked onto the Blackhawk," Matt said.

"They'll have to have nerves of steel not to," Detto predicted.

Sean McKinney had eased the speedboat across the channel of the river toward the New Jersey side. He pulled the throttles back to eighty miles an hour. He didn't want to shoot past the target.

The people outside the Javits Center grew restless and fidgety. Rumors were flying. A plane had been shot down. No, the terminal had been blown up. Terrorists had bombed JFK and Newark airports. Each rumor advanced with typical New York "I got the real scoop" conviction.

Some people were looking up at the bright blue sky, the way deer learn to look up when hunters use tree stands year after year. The threat had come from the sky before. Better look up. Stay alert. Be ready.

But no one looked out at the brown water of the Hudson River.

Aziz could see the smoke now from LaGuardia. He tapped bin Seidu and pointed. Abu bin Seidu smiled.

"It is happening again," he said as they looked east. "It is our destiny. Today is the greatest moment of jihad! Allahu Akbar." Abu bin Seidu felt a rush of warmth and satisfaction.

A loud gasp from Aziz caused bin Seidu to look away from the beautiful sight.

"No. No," bin Seidu said resolutely as they saw the helicopter gunship coming directly at them, right down on the surface of the water.

Aziz watched the gunship close in. Suddenly it flared off to the east and headed toward the tall buildings of Manhattan.

"My brother!" Aziz shouted, "it is going. Going toward the--," Aziz felt the boat shudder.

Matt and Vito stood on the big, upholstered engine cover of the speedboat. They were elevated to the same height as the stern of the Sea Ray. If they got close, the jump would be simple.

"Okay, here comes the chopper," Detto said.

Matt crouched so that he could spring up. He would be first, then Detto.

As the big red boat crossed the wake of the terrorists' boat, McKinney pulled back on the throttles to give the men time to leap.

When bin Seidu heard Aziz, he stopped scrambling to open the case containing the dirty nuke and looked up from the small cabin to the cockpit.

What he saw shocked him.

A man was flying through the air coming over the stern of the boat. He had a gun. Bin Seidu grabbed his pistol from the seat in the cabin and fired three shots through the cabin door.

When the bullet hit Vito Debenedetto in the chest, he fell back onto the engine cover of the speedboat then slid to the floor of the cockpit. The big red boat then continued on away from the Sea Ray. But not before Detto shot Aziz, who was at the helm, with a burst from the bull pup. But now, Matt was alone with the terrorists.

Aziz slumped over the helm on the starboard side. His body weight pushed the throttle forward and held the steering wheel in place.

Matt was trying to make himself small on the port side of the cockpit as teak and fiberglass splintered around him. The man in the cabin was still shooting.

"God damn!" Detto rolled on the floor of the speedboat. His team member with the bull pup was trying to pull him to his feet.

"Just a minute, Goddamnit!" Detto shouted. The bullet that had slammed into his armored vest had knocked him on his back, and the pain was overwhelming. He got to his knees then got one foot on the floor.

"What's wrong?" the Coast Guard chief was shouting into his microphone.

"Aziz!" bin Seidu shouted, confused. No one answered, but the boat was still going. Then he saw a hand coming around in front of the cockpit door. The hand had a gun.

Pop. Pop.

Matt tried to make himself as flat as a pancake on the cockpit floor. Then he raised his hand and fired two shots into the little cabin.

Nothing.

Had he hit the terrorist or was he lying in wait? His radio crackled.

"Matt!"

"I'm here."

"You're headed for the docks, Matt. You're going to have to jump off," Detto shouted.

Matt raised his head to the gunnel of the boat. Sure enough, the boat was running in a wide arc that would eventually lead to the docks on the Manhattan side of the river. He tried to get his bearings. The old aircraft carrier *Intrepid* stood at its permanent dock to the east. He couldn't see past the ship.

Matt started for the helm, but two more quick shots had him diving once again to the port side. He would have to think quickly. He knew the Coast Guard gunship would have to start firing soon if he didn't succeed.

Striker reached up and grabbed the stainless steel rail that went around the gunnels of the old boat. Unlike some boats, the gunnels were very narrow, only a couple inches, but he thought he could make it around the side of the boat.

Matt gingerly eased along the gunnel, then carefully bent down to peek through the side cabin window.

Nothing! Shit!

He jerked his head back toward the cockpit half expecting to look down the barrel of the gun that would blow him off the side of the boat.

Nothing!

He looked back in the cabin. No one there. Then he caught movement out the corner of his eye.

Bin Seidu hustled forward to the v-berth in the bow of the boat and fumbled with the hatch that led out to the deck of the boat. He wanted the bomb to be outside. Unobstructed when it went off.

Eight pounds of C-4 were wrapped around cesium 137 and americium 241, deadly nuclear material. When it went off, thousands would die in the first thirty minutes, perhaps hundreds of thousands in the coming months. Besides the horrendous loss of life, the economic losses would be staggering. Buildings, cars and possessions would be contaminated and have to be abandoned. The cleanup would take decades. Manhattan would be a nuclear wasteland.

When he lifted his head up through the hatch that he had pushed the bomb up through, he couldn't believe his luck. Or rather the will of Allah.

He wouldn't have to set the bomb off out in the river; they were heading straight for the docks. Straight for Manhattan. It wouldn't be the financial district, but a radioactive swath would cut Manhattan in half. The deaths would still be in the tens of thousands. Allah willing, maybe more.

"What's the order, Team Leader? We're running out of room here," the Coast Guard chief was looking at the old military ship *Intrepid* and the party boats at their moorings that would soon be the background into which they would have to fire. He didn't like it.

"Hold!" Detto shouted. Then saying, "Matt, you have to do it now!"

Matt had made his way around to the forward part of the cabin. Up over the cabin roof he could see bin Seidu crouched over a suitcase device laying on the deck.

"Seidu!" Matt shouted. He wanted the man to be distracted enough to look up long enough to be shot. To have his hand off the bomb's trigger for an instant. It worked. Bin Seidu looked right at him.

When the Sea Ray hit the big rolling wake of a barge that had passed on the river, Matt hadn't seen it coming. The driverless boat pitched wildly, and Matt's feet slipped off the narrow gunnel. He fell straight down.

Bin Seidu scrambled on his hands and knees when the boat rocked wildly. The dirty bomb slid away from him. He jerked his head back toward the shooter. The man was gone.

No, he wasn't. Bin Seidu saw a hand grasping the bow rail.

Matt's ankles were skimming across the surface of the water, twisting his body. It took every ounce of strength to hold on to the rail.

Vito Debenedetto was forced to do the hardest thing

he had ever done. Matt had disappeared, but he could clearly see the terrorist on the bow of the Sea Ray.

"Fire now!" he said into his microphone and then stood to watch the horror unfold. His stomach and his knees went weak. He was forced to hold the side of the big red boat to observe the death he had just ordered for his best friend.

Bin Seidu could not resist. Instead of sliding over to the bomb, he was driven to first pry the hand loose from the rail...

"Fire at will," the Coast Guard chief commanded his crew.

Bin Seidu lifted his fist to slam the hand on the rail when another hand came up from the side of the boat.

Matt's grip was loosening. His brain screamed *Hold!* But the flesh of his hand was faltering in its resolve.

Then the miracle happened. Just for an instant, he saw the terrorist's face emerge above him over the side of the boat.

And in that instant, Matt pulled his other hand up and fired his pistol once before he dropped into the dark muck of the brown water.

The Coast Guard gunner had sweat pouring from his hands and brow in spite of the cool air. He had never been ordered to fire into such a tight spot, where collateral damage was so clearly imminent. But he exhaled deeply to steady his hands, looked through the gun site and commenced to fire.

The small cannon fire landed on the side of the boat, blowing fiberglass through the air. Then, as the firing moved astern, a round hit the fuel tank, and just as the bow of the boat started to crumble into the dock, the stern of the boat erupted in a fireball.

The cannon fire finally took the attention of the people in line for the motorcycle show away from the sky and out toward the Hudson River. People were screaming and diving to the sidewalk or running madly.

When the boat hit the dock bow first, the dirty bomb was loose on its deck and still traveling at twenty knots. The impact launched the case up in the air. It flew through the air towards the thousands at the Javits Center. Then it hit the concrete deck of the big dock and slid. And kept sliding.

Finally, it came to rest.

Detto moaned audibly at the sight in front of him. The fireball subsided, and splintered pieces of the Sea Ray were visible through the smoke, some floating, some smashed and entangled in the pilings that held the dock up. Nothing moved. He was headed for the side of the boat to puke, when the shouting stopped him.

McKinney and the man with the bull pup were jumping up and down screaming. "Yes!"

What the hell? Detto looked up to see a head pop to the surface of the water twenty yards offshore from the wrecked boat.

It was Matt Striker.

Detto slumped to the floor of the boat and gasped air in sweet relief.

Epilogue

Matt stood on his upper deck drinking in the magic of the winter scene. The meadow was a blanket of white; the trees, bushes and tall grasses on the border of the woods were sugar frosted, hoary and gray where the sun had not yet reached them, bejeweled and sparkling where it had.

Across the tops of the trees he could see a dark spot racing across the grizzled, snowy ice of Big Larch Pond. Snowmobiler. Headed for one of the spurs that led to the labyrinth of VAST trails now in full use for their intended purpose.

The traveler would meet comrades at some predetermined junction of trails, and then a caravan of sleds would glide through the backwoods of the Kingdom. Maybe they would go up and cross the border into Canada and drop back down into the states through Maine, work their way back to the Kingdom through New Hampshire. They might swing through Dixville Notch and pay homage to the little precinct where the American democratic process of choice begins on dark November mornings.

Matt's coffee mug steamed in the crisp morning air. A young doe walked out onto the brushy point where Matt and Nick had practiced their stealth. She looked toward the house, strained her neck, flicked her ears and stamped a foot on the ground as if to voice indignation at the being on the deck of the house. *Stop intruding on my world*, the petulant youngster seemed to say.

The deer lost its nerve and bounded silently back into the woods. Matt held his coffee cup high in salute.

The crunching and squeaking of tires on the dry snow caused Matt to turn his head back to his own kind. He had hoped that the vehicle coming up the drive would be another, but this one made him smile nonetheless.

"Come on up, Sam, I'll pour you a cup of joe!" Matt yelled down from the deck.

"Good morning for it. Wicked cold," the warden replied.

Sam Hood made his way up to the cabin along the snow-blown path that Matt had made through the deep snow. He stopped for a moment and looked up at the plume of smoke wafting straight up in the windless, bright blue sky. *Stove is stoked up, cabin will be warm.*

"Looks like you're all packed and ready to go," the warden said as he reached the upper level of the cabin.

"Yeah, not much to it. Don't have much room at the other end."

Matt was referring to the little apartment that he

rented down in the countryside of Virginia near D.C. It was a loft apartment over the garage of an older couple who had once raised horses on their upper Shenandoah farm. The little dwelling served as home during the rare times that he had a few days between contract assignments.

"By the way, I heard you took Nick out on Youth Day."

The day before hunting season began was a day for kids under the age of fifteen to go out and hunt under the supervision of an adult.

"Yeah. I felt awkward about that, Matt," the warden confessed.

"No need, Sam. I'm glad you could do it. I was hoping someone would take the boy."

"Heard anything from her?" Sam was referring to Kate Halliard. The warden was conflicted. The whole thing was none of his business, but knowing the players as he did made the unraveling painful to accept.

"I talked to her a few weeks back." Matt went quiet remembering the conversation.

"I just don't see why they would deport her," Kate had said to Matt. She had been agitated by the treatment of Shuriana after the terror attack. "She had nothing to do with any of it!"

"Maybe, maybe not."

"Oh come on, Matt."

"I've seen stranger things."

"Yeah, I believe you, but this isn't one of them." Kate could be like a dog with a bone.

"So, you trust her with Nick?" It was a low blow and Matt regretted it immediately.

The meaning wasn't lost on Kate. She responded with restrained anger. "*Yes*, I do. More than I trust him with you."

Matt shook his head, disgusted with himself for provoking her. "I'll make a call. But you gotta understand, Kate, they may not listen to a thing I say. No promises."

"Thank you, Matt." Kate's tone was soft and familiar. "You <u>are</u> a good man." She hung up.

"Wanted me to put in a word for Shuriana and the boy, Rami," Matt continued talking with Sam Hood. "Hey, how's the shoulder?"

"A lot better," Sam said as he worked his elbow around in a circle to demonstrate his mobility.

A silence grew between the men.

"I'll keep an eye on the place for you," Sam offered.

"I was hoping you would." Matt walked over to the trestle table, picked up a key and tossed it to the warden.

Sam fingered the key for a moment. "Look, Matt, I'm sorry about how all this...."

"No need to put that on <u>your</u> shoulders, Sam." Matt smiled broadly at the warden as he held out his upturned hand. "Kate and I both have our baggage. It was complicated from the beginning. And I don't regret a day that I was up here and look forward to coming back."

"Good luck to you, Matt. Let me know if you need anything."

The men shook hands and Matt slapped Sam on the shoulder.

"You keep working with that Glock. I may not be around to help with your sorry shooting come qualification time."

When the warden's truck started out the driveway, Matt flipped his phone open.

"Longbow," the man said simply.

"This is Tomahawk," Matt said. "I'm back in."

THE END

Acknowledgements

There is little question that the many contacts, presenters and agents I met at Thrillerfest in New York and the Harriette Austin Writers Conference in Georgia helped shape my approach to the craft in both small and large ways.

However, there are a few people who had important tactical contributions to this work.

First is three-time best selling author David Compton. David not only edited the manuscript, he contributed many suggestions and, as important, challenged uninspired prose. I appreciate his professional expertise tremendously.

In addition, I am deeply appreciative of those who read rough work from beginning to end and, in some cases, line edited each page. June Kimbell, Dale Veach and Dick Drew, thank you so much!

A very, very special thanks to "C3"---Cathy Carson Castle, who not only line edited this work, but helped me overcome my irrational fear of the comma. If there are mistakes in the work they, undoubtedly, are due to the few times that I ignored her advice.

Most of all, I thank my wife, Beth, for the hard work she brought strategically, tactically and inspirationally. You're a rock and I love you for it.